The Price of Revenge

The Bad Boys of Wall Street

Ember Leigh

CONTENTS

CHAPTER ONE

AXEL

A gorgeous fury.
That's what New York City had; what drew me in.
It was the "starving hysterical naked" madness of Ginsberg, but it was more than that. Way more.
NYC throbbed with a pulse—one that you could see, feel, taste, and fuck.
It was the fury of ambition. The need to not just rise but explode.
That's what brought me to this fascinating shithole. *Shithole* being laced with love, of course. The way fraternity members love their house; that distant, codependent, beer-stained love. The type of love that would absolutely ditch you in a heartbeat if something better came up; except what could be better than being a billionaire in New York City?
My brothers and I might have been Kentuckians by birth, but we were New Yorkers by creed.
Ambition brought us, the gorgeous fury snagged us, and the sprawling, unchecked future made us stay. That and a little unfinished business.
We came to explode.
And I was a motherfuckin' firework, baby.

"Axel. Earth to Axel." The annoyed intonation of my brother Trace's voice jostled me from my reverie. I'd been staring out the floor-to-ceiling windows overlooking Manhattan. Looking out at the mess of Manhattan always got me thinking about where we'd started in this gorgeous, furious city.

"What?" I tuned into the conversation. A bit too late for my brothers' tastes. They both rolled their eyes in unison. Sure, I should have been listening. But this damn cityscape was so damn *sexy*.

"I said Francis is coming so we can discuss the list of new properties he scouted for us." Trace's big leather chair creaked a little as he leaned back in it, arching a brow at me condescendingly. He was older and taller than Damian and me, but he really showed his older-brother superiority through his unflinching use of judgmental eyebrows.

"That's great," I said, steepling my fingers as I turned my attention back to the world beyond the window. It was a gray day, early summer. The clouds were so thick and low I could practically touch them from this floor of the building. I could imagine the humid bite of the outside air, even though here in the conference room, it was a perfectly conditioned sixty-seven degrees.

"Why do you look like you're passing a kidney stone?" Damian asked me. I was the youngest in our family board room, but not by much. Damian and I were the same age for roughly one month, which meant we'd been in the same grade all through school.

"I can barely hear either of you over Trace's eyebrows." I winced as Trace rolled his lips inward, trying not to laugh. "Calm your brows, bro."

"You are such a fucking twatnugget," Trace said, launching his pen in my direction. Our pens were custom-made and heavy enough to double as a weapon should the need arise, so I dodged it as best I could from my chair.

"That's a new one," I said. Some people exercised their brains with sudoku or crossword puzzles or that incomprehensibly annoying new game, Wordle. My brothers and I chose to keep our cerebellums active by inventing new insults for each other. "I give it an eight out of ten."

We might have moved millions of dollars an hour but we were still brothers to our cores.

"Eight out of ten? The scale is rigged. Listen, can we get back to this property?" Trace motioned to a fresh-faced young man on the other side of the glass wall of our conference room. The guy popped in, a big smile on his face, eager to please. And he should be, because we paid really fucking well at Fairchild Enterprises.

We had no other option but to play the game our way. To the wealthy, elite assholes of Wall Street and Manhattan in general, we would always be the hillbillies. It didn't matter if I flew to my house in the Hamptons in my helicopter. To them, being self-made meant we were new money, which only resonated as an insult on their side of the aisle. Because my older brother Trace made our first half-million by squeezing Wall Street—a financial move that some of these dickheads looked down on—they thought we were dumb money on top of that. And because we refused to dress, look, or act the part of the snide holier-than-thou jerkfaces they wanted us to be, we were also considered ugly money.

New. Dumb. Ugly.

I'd cry about it if I didn't have so many zeroes at the end of my bank balance.

But this wasn't an empire for empire's sake—no, we wanted a community to go along with it. One designed strictly for the so-called new, dumb and ugly. We weren't those Monopoly fuckers who freebased dollar bills and set fire to the competition. We actually had morals, thankyouverymuch. *Rigid* morals, at that, though we were inclined to embrace slight hedonism.

Because nobody said you had to be celibate as one of the good guys. Even though, to most of the elite circles here, we were unequivocally, hands down *the bad boys.*

"Can you pick up that pen and bring us a fresh round of espresso?" Trace asked the new hire, Kyle.

Kyle nodded effusively. "Of course. Of course. Anything you want." He picked up Trace's pen, returned it to him with a strange sort of bow, and then hurried out of the conference room.

"He gets five stars for the bow," Damian murmured. "Does he have Asian heritage?"

"No. I think he just gets flustered around us." I reached for my own Fairchild pen-weapon. "Which is understandable."

Damien and Trace snorted. We shared mischievous grins before returning to the papers in front of us.

"So now that Francis is almost here, and we haven't reviewed his findings—let's continue." Trace started with the eyebrows again, but I didn't give him shit about it for now. More would come. It always did.

Damian rustled through the papers, that line forming between his eyes when he was deep in thought. That happened a lot, because he was always thinking about extremely complicated things. As a natural-born mathematician and college-bred hacker, he was reliably thinking of some extremely relevant detail.

"I don't like the look on *your* face now," I told him.

"Look at the properties," Damian said. "You'll see."

I scanned the sheets in front of me. I was predisposed to disappointment. I'd been searching for almost a year for the perfect building to add to our portfolio, but nothing had been just right. This wasn't a throwaway project—this was the heart and soul of our empire. The big business we'd acquired last year, Strata, expanded our interests from simply wealth management to tech, as well. Now we wanted to formalize our charity endeavors. Give them a home and room to soar.

Everything we did was so that we could give back. And this building would serve as the hub for that work from here on out.

Of the papers in front of me, only one looked remotely attractive. I picked it up, scanning the stats. Okay, maybe I was wrong. This place looked perfect.

"Wait. Where is this?" I flipped through pages, trying to orient myself. "And when did it go on the market. Are we calling them already?"

"We will if you say so," Damian said.

We needed something big, something totally ours, and something that could contain transitional housing, schooling, social events, and our charity headquarters with room to grow. This fifteen-story building had it all. Including a holdover community garden from previous tenants.

"Hey, everyone," Francis tittered as he came into the conference room, iPad in one hand and dramatically sweeping his other back over the finger waves in his dark, gelled hair. As our collective executive assistant, he wrangled the three of us like the stray cats we were. If anybody wanted to get to us, they had to get past Francis first, and he wore his company-provided Gucci suits like armor.

The new hire bolted in behind him, a small tray with three dainty espresso cups jostling as he came inside. "Here's the espressos you wanted. Sirs." Kyle sent us an unsteady smile.

Damian waved him off. "You don't have to call us *sir*. You're fine."

Kyle nodded, his face careening between crestfallen and euphoric as he set a cup by each one of us. Then he stumbled toward the door, looking at us over his shoulder. Francis eyed him through the glass wall as Kyle scurried away down the hall.

"How is Kyle working out?" Francis asked as he set his things down at an empty chair.

"Very eager," Trace said diplomatically.

"Do we need to talk to HR?" Francis settled into his seat with a grimace, arranging his suit coat delicately. The man cherished his Gucci collection, possibly even more than he did his current boyfriend.

"He's fine," Damian said. "I met him and his parents at a tech convention a few years back and wanted to help him out."

Francis had a strange, pursed smile as he swiped through screens on his iPad. I could tell what he was thinking, so I said it out loud.

"Yes, another charity case, Francis."

"Hey, I didn't say anything," Francis laughed, crossed his legs under the glass table. He'd worked with us for a few years now, so he was one of the few people on Wall Street who really knew us. Our story. Our painful history. And why our future was so important. "Now what did you guys think of my buildings?"

"This one." I pushed the paper his way. He glanced at it and nodded.

"Okay. Let's pull up the owner info." He tapped efficiently at his screen while I steepled my fingers and looked out over the city. Trace slurped noisily at his espresso. He'd become an espresso snob when we regularly had more than fifty thousand dollars in our bank accounts.

"Oh." Francis narrowed his eyes at the screen and then looked up at me. Almost guiltily, which was concerning.

"What?"

He blinked a few times. "You're not going to like this."

"Like *what*?" Damian asked.

Francis set his iPad down. "The building is owned by Margulis Realty."

The name thudded into the conversation in exactly the way you'd expect a huge pile of shit to land. I reached for the expensive pen-weapon, flicking my thumb back and forth over the tip.

We came to New York City to explode, but fireworks singe when you get too close. Quite a few Wall Street insiders didn't just dislike me and my brothers, they hated us. Once upon a time, the twattiest nugget of them all tried to pull the rug out from under me.

He believed he owned Manhattan, and I was trespassing.

Because, well, he sort of did own Manhattan. Allan Margulis, the owner of Margulis Realty.

He didn't count on how bright and brilliant my bang would be. Allan was textbook pissed when I asked his daughter to marry me. Madder still when she accepted. And went reality TV-variety apeshit when I refused to back down and started planning my future with her.

His fury stained everything. Including my relationship with the one and only woman I've ever loved. That's a scar for another time. The type of shit I would only talk about if I got drunk and sad enough. But that man no longer shut doors on me.

And I'd be damned if he kept me from this building.

"We can keep looking," Trace offered, looking at me hopefully.

"Let's fast-track an offer," I told Francis before looking to my brothers. "Right? It looks good to you guys?"

"It looks perfect," Damian said, "but—"

"He's not gonna sell to us, Axel," Trace said in a low voice.

"That's for his board of directors to decide, isn't it?" I asked. "And I'll make sure they vote to sell. Francis, offer a full million higher than the asking price."

Francis barely blinked at this as he recorded our notes. I didn't even need to know the price. I just needed the building.

"And schedule my meeting with them under the name Spencer Wattford," I added quickly.

"Jesus, Axel," Damian said, dragging his hands down his face.

"Do you think it's worth going there just to get kicked out of the building?" Trace asked.

"They won't kick me out," I promised him, though really, I had no idea.

Because if there was one company I'd avoided like the fucking plague, it was Margulis Realty. What went down between me and the Margulis family eight years ago is the sort of thing I strove to not think about. But the truth was that even when I didn't think about it, it pushed me higher. Hotter. Brighter.

So yes. I was deeply interested in purchasing this dream building even though it was being sold by the man who told me that I was a joke. The same man who convinced his daughter, the ex-love of my life, to see me as a joke as well.

Allan Margulis and his miserable tribe of money-hungry, dollar bill-freebasing, sacks of turds.

My ex-fiancée, Cora, included.

If there was one person I'd be happy to never look in the face again, it was my ex. Because apparently our love had not been so impervious and ever-lasting, though she spent three years of our lives convincing me of the opposite. But some things must be endured as the price of revenge.

This building purchase was only the first stop on the revenge train; I'd been laying the tracks for the past eight years. I'd always wanted to take down Allan Margulis, the final exclamation point on my life. Somehow, I'd make it happen. While I still didn't have my plan in place, this building would be the doorway. I could *feel* it.

"I'll see when I can get you on their schedule," Francis said, swiping so furiously on his screen that one gelled strand of his dark hair came unglued. Then he pulled out his cell phone, tapping out the phone number. "Any chance we could get some bodycam footage for if they *do* kick you out, though?"

I hefted with a humorless laugh. "I'm sure Allan would love to personally kick me out of his building. But I bet he won't."

Francis was on the phone with Margulis Realty, his sugary-sweet customer service voice something better fit for Hollywood.

"How can you be so sure?" Trace asked.

"Because I know his kryptonite. It's public drama." I flashed my brother an evil grin. "That man knows how far I'll drag him into the tabloids if he tries any shit."

My brothers and I discussed the details of the building while Francis wrapped up his call. He set the phone down, looking victorious.

"Spencer Wattford will be meeting the Margulis board. *Today*."

"Today?" I laughed incredulously. "Fuck yeah."

"I bumped one of your afternoon appointments to make it work," Francis said. "But it sounds like they're motivated to sell."

"An extra million can be pretty convincing," Trace conceded.

Damian didn't look convinced. His arms were crossed, and he shook his head. "We do want this building. Don't pull any shit that will get in the way of that."

Ah. My brother knew me too well.

"I'll behave perfectly," I assured him. To Francis I said, "When does Zero get back from the dog walker?"

Damian groaned again. "Axel. I swear to God."

"I don't have time to listen to your complaining," I said with a smile. On the inside, I was so jazzed I could hardly contain myself. But some trepidation came along with the excitement. Okay, a serious amount of trepidation.

I hadn't been within ten feet of these assholes in eight years.

Which was why I needed Zero.

I grew up in the foster system with my brother Damian. I knew what it meant to be shuffled from one house to the next, all your shit stuffed unceremoniously into a trash bag.

You started to feel like trash yourself.

That's why, when I adopted my dog, I went to the dog pound.

Zero was part Rottweiler, part something else nobody was sure of, and my most faithful companion. Zero was stocky with a dark, glossy coat. He knew what it felt like to be loved, lose that love, and then bounce between all the wrong households. He also knew what it felt like to finally find a forever home, like the one Damian and I had been lucky enough to find.

Zero and I got shit done. Zero was also the number of fucks we collectively gave about what outsiders thought of our business practices. And he was coming with me to Margulis Realty.

One of the best parts about my plan to meet with Allan Margulis—that intolerable, soulless, dead-eyed billionaire who was probably born half-robot—was that he hated dogs.

But when I showed up offering him twenty million dollars in cash, he couldn't say shit about my dog.

God, I loved being me.

"Axel, you can't take Zero," Trace rapped his knuckles against my doorframe as I got Zero leashed up later that afternoon.

"The fuck I can't." I stood, smoothing down the front of my button-up. I wore a light gray business suit. Perfect black tie. Alligator shoes. I could be in fucking *Vogue*. I'd tell Anna Wintour to make sure to give Zero his own suit, too, for the photo shoot.

"Dude, we want him to say yes. Not chase you out of the board room."

"He wants money, and that's what we've got. He'll deal with Zero because he *has* to." I sent Zero a mischievous grin. He was in this with me. He sent me a lopsided dog grin, his tongue hanging out. His dark brown coat positively gleamed. I tutted for Zero to follow me as I headed toward the doorway. "Besides, the board has to vote in the best interests of the company. And the best interests of their company is to make a cool million extra, whether or not a dog is present."

Trace grimaced as he stepped aside. "I hate when you're right."

"I love when you doubt me." I clapped his shoulder as Zero and I breezed by. "Just lets me stroke my own ego."

"Maybe that's why I do it," Trace called after me. "Being a good big brother and all."

I waved to our employees as I left. Everybody knew Zero. Everybody loved him. Zero snorfled as some admin employees cooed on his way out. Once we hit the elevator, my cool grin faltered. In the back of the company car—a luxuriously tricked-out Cadillac Escalade in two-tone black with black wheels to match—I finally let my shoulders sag.

"We got this, Zero," I told him as he panted next to me. But the truth was, I didn't know.

A battalion of assistants scanned guests lists in advance of functions, galas, and more, to help us avoid the Margulis family. On the rare occasion I found myself even remotely near a Margulis, I left before I could chance seeing Cora.

You'd think that nearly a whole damn decade later this would be easier.

But it wasn't. Which only proved to that whispering little gremlin in the back of my mind that Cora and I really were some sort of twisted soul mates or something.

Not that I'd ever give her the time of day. This meeting could only be awkward, since I presumed both Allan *and* Cora would be in attendance. Soul mates or not, Cora made a choice eight years ago. And then she'd made several other worse choices since. There was no room for change, compassion, or forgiveness in our current, crystalized realities.

Fuck 'em all.

My driver delivered me to the front doors of the Margulis Realty building. I grinned up at the sleek tower and scratched Zero behind the ears. The last time I'd been inside, I'd been in my last year of grad school with barely a thousand dollars to my name.

And now look at me.

"I'll let you know when I'm done," I told Harry, the driver. "But be close by in case I need to make a quick getaway."

Harry nodded, smirking through the rearview mirror. "I'll be here, boss."

I exited the Escalade, Zero hopping out alongside me. Zero waited obediently by my side, off-leash as he'd been trained. I tapped the window to let Harry know we were good. Curious glances flitted our way as New Yorkers streamed by on the sidewalk. I tutted for Zero to follow me and I strutted into Allan's building as if I owned it. Security immediately closed in, blocking off the hushed, marble lobby.

"You can't bring that dog in here," a buff guard who looked like a retired MMA fighter told me.

I checked my watch, pushing my sunglasses up on my head. "I have a three o'clock with Allan Margulis."

"Name?"

"Spencer Wattford. Call him yourself and see." I sent them cool grins as they checked a kiosk. After a moment, they waved me through.

"Come on, Zero," I said, loud enough for passers-by to hear. "It's time for you to meet big bad Allan Margulis."

I immediately heard Damian's voice in my head—*Jesus, Axel, you want to tank the deal or what?* What could I say? My brothers played it safer than I did. But I had some fucking bones to pick.

I whistled to myself as I headed to the elevators, masking my anxiety. I passed the plant display near the elevator lobby. Eight years ago, I had stowed my shitty leather jacket behind some ferns right there before I went to inform Allan I planned to marry his daughter. I'd needed to use an alias—Spencer Wattford—to get onto his schedule. So really, today was also a trip down memory lane.

For all parties involved.

Zero and I were the only ones in the elevator as we soared up to the thirtieth floor. He sniffed the inside of the elevator car curiously and stayed close to my side as we walked into the reception area of the Margulis executive office suite. As the doe-eyed receptionist looked up at me, several evil thoughts crossed my mind: I should fuck her to prove something to Cora, though what that would prove, I wasn't sure; I should get the entire administrative staff enrolled in Fairchild Wealth Management, to nag further at Allan; I should fuck the entire administrative staff to prove something else, though I wasn't sure what, and Jesus, that would be a lot of fucking.

"Can I help you?" she asked.

"I'm positive you can." I offered her a winning smile, which she immediately returned. Sometimes, I felt like Leonardo DiCaprio as Frank Abagnale in *Catch Me If You Can,* but with more tattoos and a fuckton more money. Except I wasn't conning anyone anymore. My checks didn't bounce. I had faked it until I fucking *made* it. "Spencer Wattford here for a meeting with the board."

"Okay, let me find your appointment." Her attention turned to the computer. She tapped the keyboard a few times and then nodded. "Yes. They're already waiting for you. Let me tell them you're here."

"Excellent." I looked down at Zero, finally deciding on which one of my evil ideas seemed best. "Would you be able to pass me the information for your HR department as well? I've been talking to Mr. Margulis about the upcoming switch for the employees' financial planning, and I'll need to organize a few details with your benefits coordinator."

"Oh, sure. Of course." The receptionist searched in a drawer, and then handed me a business card. Bingo. I knew where to launch my insidious side-plan, and now my dick was in no danger of falling off. "If you'll follow me, I'll show you to the conference room."

I brightened my smile at the same time my insides churned. Zero and I followed the receptionist down a carpeted hallway and around a corner. She pulled open a dark wood door, gesturing for Zero and me to enter.

I thanked her and steeled myself. And then I cast my sights on the Margulis board room.

Inside, everyone I'd ever had a problem with had conveniently gathered around the same glass-topped table. The sunlight from the gray early summer afternoon filtered in, casting muted patterns on the walls.

But the most beautiful part about the crowd in front of me was the scowl that formed on Allan Margulis's face. I loved watching Spencer Wattford's true identity sink in for the second time in his life. And his expression when he noticed Zero at my side made the whole thing even better.

And the worst part?

Cora Margulis sat directly in front of me.

I couldn't look at her, only allowed myself the quickest impressions. Glossy brown hair pulled into a sleek ponytail. Lips the shade of a mulberry wine. Gold wedding ring glinting on her finger.

Eli Rossberg, her husband, at her side.

CHAPTER TWO

CORA

The Princess of Manhattan.

That's what the tabloids called me. The rag mags. The publications posing as news.

And really, could I blame them? That's what my parents created me to be. They raised me like a rag doll with a porcelain head. Fit to toss around as needed. Always picture perfect on command.

No emotion. No reaction. And always at the ready.

Thank God I'd been practicing the subtle art of turning my emotions off with the flip of a switch for my entire life. Because I needed that porcelain control when Axel Fairchild walked into the boardroom of Margulis Realty.

"Good god, Allan Margulis! What a joy to see you again!" Axel strutted into the board room with every ounce of earned swagger. At just over six feet tall, Axel was a broad-shouldered badass. He always had been. A gorgeous, dark-furred dog trotted along beside him, ears at attention.

Electricity zipped through the air. Every inch of me wanted to crumple at the sight of him. To crawl to him on my knees, to beg for one last touch from him. To do anything to make up for all the years we'd lost, for my actions that had robbed us of a chance to be together.

From the outside, my position on the board was just one more piece of the perfect puzzle I'd been assembling my entire life. Next quarter, I'd become CEO. I was mere steps away from accomplishing every last item on my professional to-do list. And at age thirty-one, no less.

And while the tabloids loved to comment on the picture-perfect princess life—with exceptional attention paid to my business-casual wardrobe—they had no idea what the reality was.

I wasn't a princess.

I was a prisoner.

And this board room was my cage.

My wardens—sorry, fellow board members—were stretched out along the edge of the table. It wasn't just my father, but also my husband Eli, as well as two others, Robert and Frank, who were outside majority shareholders like Eli. But based on the way Axel focused on Allan, you'd think no one else existed.

My father let out a low chuckle, tapping the end of his pen against the side of the table. "Mr. Fairchild. What an unwelcome *surprise.*"

"No, no. Call me Mr. Wattford." Axel flashed a devilish grin. He hadn't looked my way yet, and every inch of me was anxious to make eye contact.

Axel had grown up in nearly every way possible. It had been eight years since I told him we were over for good. Eight years since I'd last heard that cocky, rough-silk voice that acted as both balm and sandpaper, depending on who it was directed at.

Eight years since my heart had last felt full.

Axel loomed larger now. It wasn't just the expensive, tailored gray suit or the neatly trimmed dark blond hair that suggested daily maintenance. He'd bulked up. Muscles filled out the suit, suggesting an altogether new terrain underneath. New tattoos crept from the sleeves of his suit coat and past the collar of his button-up, licking up the sides of his neck.

Axel was a new man. A self-made man.

He was exactly the man I'd hoped he would become if I removed myself from his life.

Eli turned to me, his brows drawn together. One strand of his blond hair had slipped from his immaculate updo, the same swept back, high class Hamptonite style he'd adopted about five years back and hadn't budged from.

"Am I missing something?" Eli asked, his eyes sliding back toward Axel. "Why is this hillbilly in our board room?"

"May I sit? I'd love to chat business." Axel gestured at the row of empty chairs facing our side of the table. "I've got an offer I think the board will be keen to accept."

"Absolutely, Mr. Wattford," Frank said, gesturing to the seat across the table from him.

"Call him Mr. Fairchild," my father said, practically in a growl of his own. "And send that dog outside."

"Oh, gosh. Sorry, Mr. Margulis." Axel rolled out a leather chair and settled in, expelling a satisfied sigh. "He's my emotional support animal."

Eli hefted with a laugh. "Figures a guy like you would need some extra support in this line of work."

Axel's gaze didn't waver from my father. And now his game was clear. He *was* ignoring this end of the table. My heart rate increased, helplessness taking over.

I hadn't expected to be face-to-face with him like this. Not today, not ever again. Not after what I'd done to him.

But now that he was *so close*, all the dormant truths and unspoken sentiments were clamoring to escape. Things I was forbidden to admit. Truths that were kept back so that our current reality could continue.

After so many years protecting these truths behind the bars of my heart, I couldn't remember whose reality would come crashing down if they were revealed: mine or his.

"I came to learn more about this property and make an offer." Axel slid a piece of paper toward Allan and Frank. "It's exactly what my organization has been searching for."

My father sniffed, eyes on the paper, a corner of his lip curled up. "We're entertaining multiple offers on this property right now."

"We're prepared to offer you a full million over the asking price," Axel went on, unfazed. His hand dropped to his dog's head, starting a lazy stroke between his ears. "Zero and I, that is."

"Is Zero your dog, Mr. Fairchild?" Robert asked with a little smirk.

"I consider him more like a brother," Axel said.

Eli's smirk turned lethal. "Because you're just a pack of dogs over there at Fairchild Wealth, aren't you?"

Axel looked down at Zero. "Did you hear something, boy? Sounded like an insufferable little whining noise." Axel tutted, squinting as he looked around the room, pretending like he was searching for something. "Must have been a mosquito."

"Jesus Christ," Eli muttered. "Listen, *Wheel Axle,* if you're going to treat me like, that you can get the fuck out of my board room right now."

"Gentlemen," I snapped, looking between Eli and Axel. "Please, let's hear more about the offer. I think it would behoove us to know as much as possible." I sent a small smile to Axel, but his eyes were on Zero. Eli sent me a prickly glare.

Axel cleared his throat, settling back into the chair with a curious little smile. He focused in on my father. "If you'd prefer cash, I can arrange for that by tomorrow. And if you're strapped, I can make a down payment today. You tell me how much. A couple hundred G's, at your office door by..." He checked his watch. "Five p.m. That'll give you a nice little cushion until the rest transfers tomorrow."

"There's no need to send such a payment," Frank said. "In fact, board protocol requires that there be no acts of bribery—"

"Oh, no, there's no bribery," Axel said. "I just wasn't sure of your financial solvency. Maybe Margulis Enterprises needs some liquidity. I'm prepared to assist if that's the case."

"There's no need to concern yourself with our financial solvency," my father said, enunciating each word with a particular breed of disdain. "Make your offer and leave."

"One point five million over asking price. And as an added bonus, I'll use my real name the next time I come to your office building," Axel said with a finger gun toward my father.

If my father weren't so utterly disgusted right now, I would have laughed. Because beneath how horrifying and anxiety-inducing this situation was, it was also hilarious. Even I could admit that, between the heart palpitations.

Axel Fairchild had a way of pushing buttons, but in a charming way. Depending on who you were, of course.

"Can we get that in writing?" Frank asked, peering over the frame of his bifocals.

"My assistant will send it over. The offer will be contingent on viewing the building and the usual inspections, of course." Axel's grin widened to maniacal grade. I'd seen every version of his smile. I was uniquely qualified to comment on the ins and outs of this man, even after so many years apart. We'd spent three blissful years together, from junior year of college almost through grad school. He'd asked me to marry him. I'd said yes.

And then the tsunami of tears and devastation arrived.

"That should be easy enough to arrange. Someone will reach out to you to schedule a showing. And I think that concludes our meeting,"

Robert said, looking over at my father for confirmation. "The board appreciates your offer."

"Zero and I appreciate your wonderful hospitality," Axel said, coming to his feet. Zero rose as well, grumbling slightly at the disturbance. "Let me just reiterate what a joy it is to see you again, Allan. Absolutely wonderful. You were always so kind and supportive to me."

The sarcasm was so thick everyone in the room nearly choked on it. I pressed two fingers to my temple, fighting not to react. But dammit, Axel made it hard. Eli rolled his eyes, letting out a disbelieving laugh. Frank lifted a brow, turning to look at Allan.

"Did you know that?" Axel pointed at Frank and Robert. "This man is a selfless gem. An absolute paragon of generosity."

"Get out," Allan spat.

"Your meeting with the board has concluded, dummy," Eli added. "Go on now. Skedaddle." He flicked his hand dismissively toward the door.

But this time, Axel's gaze swept our way, raking over Eli and me with such force it took my breath away. His gaze doubled as a fist to the cheek, and I deserved it.

Because after Axel had asked me to marry him, I'd married Eli instead.

"Don't get me started on *this* guy," Axel went on, his voice full of *ostentatious douchebag.* "This fucking peach right here." He tutted and cocked his head, and Zero followed him to the door. "I'll be eagerly awaiting your response."

Axel strutted out of the board room exactly as he'd come: cool, collected, Zero alongside. Once the door shut behind him, Eli let out an exasperated sigh.

"I thought we were safe from that piece of shit entering our world."

My father only scowled at the table. I knew why, though. It wasn't just because Axel had shown up.

It was because Axel had him in a corner.

"I take it there's some shared history we're unaware of?" Frank asked.

"You could say that," I said with a small laugh, smoothing the top of my skirt. I still wasn't even sure Axel had seen me. Maybe it was for the better, if he hadn't. I fingered the simple diamond-studded pendant I wore around my neck, but my wedding ring glinted in the sunlight, catching my attention. He probably hadn't seen the necklace, and almost certainly had no idea of its significance. And maybe he hadn't seen the wedding ring, either.

I was forbidden from removing the ring. As the foremost Prisoner of Wall Street, I was legally obligated to uphold the best version of our family brand at all times.

Even in the midst of an ongoing and contentious separation from the man at my side.

My family had a brand manager, like most of the wealthiest families did. It was completely normal in our circle to run a family like a finely tuned corporation. And that difference had always been a wedge between Axel and me. He'd never been able to understand. Or maybe he just didn't want to.

"But honestly, it's all water under the bridge," I went on, fixing my gaze on my father. "What concerns us right now is the sale of this building. He made a good offer."

"An incredible offer," Robert conceded. "History or not. I think we're obligated to accept."

Axel had gotten it right. No avalanche of annoying traits or painful history would affect an offer so high above the asking price. Axel knew that. We all knew that.

The board would have to accept.

"We should wait for more offers," Eli said. "If that pissant can offer one point five over asking, then a better offer will be coming in soon."

"I agree," my father said. "It may be a hotter property than we realized. Besides, who knows what he plans to do with the building. I'd much rather preserve the integrity of our brand than sell too quickly to someone like him."

Someone like him. It had always come down to that with my father.

Axel was *someone like him* because he wasn't *someone like us.* My father had never let Axel forget that. Axel could never be in the inner circle of elites on Wall Street. Because Axel had grown up poor. Because he'd been raised in Kentucky. Because he didn't play the game the way my father and his peers preferred.

Because, because, because. My father had a laundry list of reasons for despising Axel. And clearly, Axel's own success had not forced my father to budge on any of them. It didn't matter that Axel could compete on the same level. He and his brothers were intrinsically missing something that the inside circle demanded.

"If no better offer comes in," Robert said, "we'll have to vote to accept the Fairchild offer."

"We can cross that bridge when we come to it," my father said.

"What if we talk him up in price?" I asked suddenly. I didn't want Axel's offer to be off the table so quickly. Besides, I wanted to know more about what Axel intended to use the building for. I'd had my eye on this building, as well, but my intended uses didn't align with my father's vision, so he would never just hand it over to me. And I couldn't beat Axel's bid to buy it outright—I had other uses for my personal funds. "We can arrange an additional meeting. Probe his plans for the building. And maybe squeeze an extra one or two million out of him based on what we hear."

"Do you really want *his* money though?" Eli asked with a sneer.

"The board does not discriminate as long as the fiduciary interests of the shareholders are prioritized," Robert said.

"Agreed," Frank added. My father was stewing over this.

"Let me get more information then. If we *have* to accept his offer, let's make it to our benefit and not his," I said, the words tumbling out of me before I could even think. "Besides, this will help us drag our feet and allow time for another offer to come in," I added.

Really, before Axel showed up, I hadn't cared who owned it. But now that he'd shown an interest, I wanted it to be Axel. I knew the work his side projects did. The charity he'd founded and oversaw. The man moved mountains for the less fortunate. Because he himself had been the least fortunate.

I respected the hell out of him. It didn't matter that he wouldn't look me in the eye.

It only confirmed what I suspected—I'd forsaken any chance for a reconciliation with him. Axel Fairchild held a grudge like it was the last piece of beachfront property in Los Angeles. There was no way in hell he thought about me or even remotely cared for me. Even though Axel still owned every last piece of my heart.

And maybe that made me uniquely positioned to negotiate this deal.

My heart still wanted glimpses of Axel, the man I'd turned down, the only man I'd ever loved. If I couldn't have him, I still wanted to be near him. One more time.

Even if it was to discuss numbers and the intended use of the building on Tenth Avenue.

"You really think you can talk him *up* in price?" My father's voice betrayed every ounce of doubt.

"Of course. The man upped the offer on his own in our ten minutes of conversation. Why wouldn't he respond to more pressure for a higher price tag? That will be easy once he sees the building."

My father's scowl deepened. Eli heaved an irritated sigh.

"As long as you *promise* this is in the interest of shareholders," Eli said, pinning me with a suspicious look. "The Fairchild brothers deal dirty. You don't want to get caught up in something sticky."

"I assure you, there's nothing more clear-cut than this property sale," I said. It was a Herculean effort most days to school the annoyance out of my voice when Eli and I interacted. It had been that way for the past three years at least. Our marriage had been a slowly unraveling ball of yarn, the messy ball of knots you find in estate sales. I don't think our marriage had ever been a lovely, well-maintained work of art. It had only ever been disjointed, a struggle. I couldn't even remember the last time we'd shared a bed. Things had gotten so bad recently, I'd started staying at our Central Park condo.

The big D-word was on the horizon, but I wasn't sure how to broach it yet. Eli still thought we had a future together. He never understood that I'd been groping for an escape hatch since the day we said *I do.*

"That's what everyone says right before they get caught in a web of scandal," Eli said with a knowing smirk.

"I promise whatever web you get caught in won't be because of this," I said.

"I agree with Eli," my father blurted. "Any business with those brothers is risky. I don't want them even breathing near us."

"See?" Eli smirked my way. "They're a liability. Best to be avoided."

"I agree with Cora," Robert said, tipping his head in my direction. "He's shown willingness to up the offer. I say we fleece him for whatever he's willing to spend and offload the building ASAP."

"Agree with Robert," Frank said. "Cora, are you willing to enter into these negotiations?"

I fingered the diamond pendant again, feeling the first glimmer of excitement inside me for God knew how long. I'd been wearing this necklace like a talisman ever since I'd broken up with Axel, though I wasn't sure if it offered protection from my reality or if it was more of a homing beacon, calling Axel back to me despite what I'd done to him.

The pendant had been created using the diamonds from the engagement ring he'd given me. I never had the heart to give it back to him, and giving it away didn't seem right either.

So it became something new, created from the love I'd shared with Axel. They were the only diamonds that meant something to me. Certainly much more than the rock on my finger.

"If that's what's needed," I said, schooling the excitement out of my voice. I was approaching the pinnacle of my career—about to become the CEO of Margulis Realty—but hell if it generated any enthusiasm. Millions of ascending businesswomen would give their ovaries to be in my position. Millions more businessmen would gouge their investments to be able to claim this title.

And me? I was about fucking done with it.

But I didn't know where to turn. How to leave. Or what to even hope for.

I'd been imprisoned for so long by the expectations of my family, I could barely remember what it felt like to truly choose something for myself.

All I knew was that I had a sanctioned meeting with Axel Fairchild on the horizon.

That alone felt like a small win.

Something that would keep the Princess of Manhattan going for another quarter until I had everything they'd always wanted for me.

CHAPTER THREE

AXEL

Sandpaper comes in multiple grits. I learned this when I worked for a contractor in high school to help make my adoptive parents' mortgage when money was tight.

There's medium grit for small surface flaws. Coarse grits for big imperfections.

And then there's cataclysmic grit, which was the current state of my mouth after the binge drinking shitshow of the night before.

I grunted, shifting on the soft surface that I could only assume was my bed. I didn't have much memory of how my night had ended. I'd called an emergency party in the penthouse, invited a fuckton of friends and single girls to come over, and let the alcohol work its magic.

Truthfully, I was afraid to open my eyes and answer to the hangover that was no doubt lurking nearby. The overall grit of my mouth did not bode well for mental clarity today.

"Mmmm. Axel." A soft feminine voice at my side jolted me. I decided to risk it and cracked one eye. Mirabella was beside me. And shit, I still had my suit pants on from yesterday. At least my shoes had come off at some point. My white button-up hung open, revealing the latest ink I'd added to my chest, swirling letters that spelled *JORDAN*.

It was a tribute to one of my sisters. Both were long gone. The only visible reminders I had of them were their names inked on my body. Kaylee's name stretched down the length of my right forearm. Their memories informed every fucking thing that I did with my heart and my hands.

My lips parted to say something to Mirabella, but my voice withered in the parched landscape of my mouth. I groped blindly for the bottle of water I kept on my nightstand. Just twisting to reach it from where I lay on my more-enormous-than-king bed was a struggle. All my internal organs seemed to protest. A wave of nausea arrived. Fuck this hangover.

"Are you awake, boo-baby?" she purred, pawing at the waist of my pants. She was one of those lanky runway models with naturally puffy lips, exotically beautiful, and always down to fuck. The touch of her made the nausea worse. I chugged water like I'd been living in the desert for a year. Water dribbled down my chin. I tossed the empty bottle on the floor.

I collapsed back onto my bed, pushing her hands away. "Too hungover."

"Oh, come on. You *promised* we'd get freaky in the morning," she whispered into my ear. We'd been hooking up for almost a year, but it was always on my schedule. The whole arrangement was strictly sex. She knew it. I knew it. We were both fine with it.

Sex was the way I took my mind off things. That and drinking excessively. Usually I didn't have too much on my mind.

But yesterday threw a curveball into my status quo.

"Not today," I grunted, my eyes drifting shut. Yes, I was too hungover. But the thought of being inside Mirabella was unappealing for other reasons, which I couldn't articulate.

But part of me suspected—no, *knew*—that it had everything to do with seeing Cora.

I'd done everything right. I'd gone in there with enough swagger to capsize a boat. I'd been professional yet snarky as fuck. I didn't even look at Cora or her disgusting husband.

So why did my insides feel like they were about to explode?

The last time I'd felt like this was after the trip to California to beg Cora for an explanation, to give us a chance like she'd promised. Begging did no good; she'd ended it, even though we were supposed to get married. Clearly, I needed to call my fucking therapist again, because just the shadow of a glimpse of her perfect face had reduced me to jelly. And that was unacceptable. Hell, it sounded insane.

"Come on, Axel." Mirabella tugged at the fly of my pants. She'd find nothing interesting there. I couldn't get a hard-on now if my life depended on it. *Though if Cora showed up...*

No. Those thoughts needed to stop. My cock would never participate in anything Cora Margulis had to offer. Even if my cock *wanted* to, my extremely complicated moral code would not allow it.

"Mirabella, that's enough." My voice was a hoarse croak. I draped my arm across my eyes. "Just go."

"Axellll," she whined.

"You heard me."

She huffed. The bed moved slightly as she got up. Even that motion invited more nausea. I listened as she collected her things, grumbling.

"You gotta be kidding me. What's the point of spending all this money on this dress if I can't even get fucked?"

"Go," I repeated, with more force and less hoarse.

"I'm going," she snapped, her Brooklyn accent stronger than ever. "Hopefully your dick will work next time."

Comebacks filled my head, but I didn't have the energy to deliver them. My bedroom door opened and shut, and I drifted back into the semi-dreamscape of my hangover. The world beyond my bed seemed impossible to navigate. But I needed to get upright. Get some food in me. At the very least some damn electrolytes.

I heaved myself to sitting, regretting the brilliant idea to host last night's party. It had been fun for the first ten shots. After that, things turned hazy. Someone had called the helicopter for a drunk air tour of Manhattan. My pilot may have received a lap dance. After that, it was anybody's guess.

I stumbled the eternal distance between my bed and the door. I flung my door open. The scent of bacon and eggs drifted toward me, and my stomach rumbled. So there was hope. I began the long walk from my wing of bedrooms toward the common area of the kitchen and dining area.

"Ahhh, there he is!" Trace's voice boomed through our enormous kitchen, and I squinted, shielding my eyes against the excessive amount of sunlight that filled our fifty-third floor penthouse. Technically, our penthouse occupied floors fifty through fifty-three, and our kitchen was somewhere in the middle.

"Do you have to scream?" I asked.

"Look at you. The walk of shame." Damian clapped me on the back as I shuffled past them. Our private chef was just putting on a new round of bacon as I scooped up the last piece from the platter on the marble-topped island.

"It's not a walk of shame if it's your own house," I pointed out, crunching into the bacon. Yes, that felt tolerable. Pig fat, good. "Thanks, Butch." Butch was our chef. He lifted his spatula and nodded. We had a habit of hiring outsiders, and Butch was no exception. He was a down-south guy like ourselves, an unwitting NYC transplant who just didn't quite fit in with the normal bourgeoisie.

"You need a Gatorade or what?" Trace asked.

I grunted. He nodded and disappeared to hunt one down.

"There's not a day that goes by I don't thank God we have our own separate floors in this place," Damian told me with a wistful look on his face. "I don't even want to know what you got into after y'all got back from that helicopter tour."

"I actually do want to know," I told him. "Since I don't remember shit."

Trace returned with a blue Gatorade a moment later. "Do you really? Some things are better left forgotten."

I snorted and twisted the cap, tipping the electric blue drink into my mouth. Between that and the bacon, clarity was returning.

"But last night was a one-off, right?" Damian asked, something serious in his moss green eyes. "I don't want you to start the hard partying shit again."

"When have I partied hard in recent memory?" I asked him. "I have my fun in the Hamptons house anyway. I don't get why you're worried."

My brothers shared a glance, which sparked my irritation.

"Well?" I prompted. "I haven't thrown a rager in the penthouse in over a year. Prove me wrong."

"It's not that," Trace said. "It's..."

I sipped at the Gatorade while my brothers beat around the bush. When nobody added anything, I snapped, "What?"

"Cora," Damian blurted.

Their meaning smacked into me. I guess the motivation for my post-Margulis party wasn't as opaque as I imagined. Maybe I was the only one being fooled at this point.

"Right." I rubbed at the back of my neck. "It was a one-off. Promise."

"You sure you want to go through with the offer?" Trace asked.

"Dude, it's fine. It's gonna be worth it. I wouldn't have volunteered to go into the Margulis orbit if I didn't think it would be worth it."

But even as I spoke, my stomach bottomed out. Ten minutes around Cora with zero eye contact had given me this hangover. What would an actual conversation with her provoke?

"One of us can go in your place," Damian said. "I mean it."

"It's just a few meetings, and then the building will be ours," I reassured them. "How hard could that be? Besides, you know my salty ass needs to see this through with Allan."

My brothers shared another glance. But my rationale had seeped into them. They believed me. Butch came over to the island with a freshly stocked platter of bacon. I grunted, digging in.

"You know you make the best bacon of anyone out there?" I told him as I crunched into a hot slice.

"It's bacon, Axel," Butch said. "You can't fuck it up."

"Somebody could," Trace said, grabbing for some before checking his watch. "All right. Time to head down to the office." Yeah, we were *those* guys—the ones who owned the penthouse in the same building where they worked. It just made sense, since we shared the penthouse. Our apartment was big enough for five families and gave us a chance to convene for breakfasts and, on occasion, dinner. And we each kept our own escape pads for when we'd had too much brotherly love. Mine was in the Hamptons. We each had residences back in Louisville, too. We had plenty of personal space—the penthouse was our brother space.

"Are you coming in today?" Damian asked as he scanned me from head to toe. "You're looking rough."

"Uhhh, I might take a personal day." I chugged the rest of my Gatorade then let out a satisfied sigh. "Yeah, gonna take a personal day."

"Let us know if you get any updates on the building," Trace said, adjusting the cuffs of his button-up before grabbing his briefcase off an island stool.

I gave them a thumbs up, and they headed toward the private elevator that took them straight to our office suite.

When it was just Butch and me in the kitchen, I said, "You really should have come on the helicopter ride."

"You didn't invite me," he teased.

"I'll invite you next time," I promised. "Maybe we can have a picnic up there."

We chatted for a little longer while I finished up breakfast at the kitchen island. We had a cozy breakfast nook that I loved to use on lazy mornings, but anything farther than right in front of me was too fucking far away with this hangover. After a glass of orange juice, I was ready to crawl back into bed. Confronting reality with this hangover was hard, and I still couldn't shake the emotional recoil my brothers had hinted at.

After Cora had broken up with me, I'd fucked the majority of Lower Manhattan and drank the contents of its bars, simply as a way to not think about losing the love of my life. I didn't think I'd do that again, not by a long shot. But I saw what they were getting at.

I turned the volume on my phone up as I head back to my bedroom. After a hot shower and slouching into sweats and nothing else, I was ready for my personal day. Every ping and beep that signaled a call or email made me sit up and check it out.

Lunch came and went—a chicken and quinoa power bowl Butch knew I loved. Though you'd never guess it from looking at him, he was a gourmet chef who'd kicked around Paris and Amsterdam. Nobody cooked a better filet mignon than this man. After lunch, I planned on returning to my restful hangover state in my bedroom, but motivation kicked in. I headed to our personal gym and spent the rest of the afternoon on weights and listening for any ding from my phone.

The hours spun away, but nothing came from Margulis Realty. I was getting fucking irritated. I'd expected a call by noon. How hard was it to set up a showing for a motivated buyer? They were a realty company, for God's sake.

Just before the close of business, the call came. I was mid-sit-up, and I dragged my forearm across my face before I answered.

"Hello, I'm calling for Axel Fairchild." The voice on the other end of the line sounded faint. Maybe scared. Most likely a low-level assistant.

"Speaking."

"Hi, I'm Tabitha with Margulis Realty. I wanted to set something up with you for the showing of 225 Tenth Avenue."

"Great. What's the earliest available?" My abs trembled from the position I held on the ab bench. My six pack would thank me tomorrow.

She tutted. "I have a slot for Friday."

I paused, swiping the call to speaker phone so I could look at my calendar. Friday was tomorrow. Maybe they *were* motivated to sell. "Tomorrow sounds great."

"Ah, no. I'm—I'm so sorry. *Next* Friday."

My gumption deserted me, and I collapsed back onto the bench with a *whuff*. "Excuse me?"

"Yes. Next Friday we can set up a viewing."

"That's a week away," I spat.

"Yes, sir."

"No." I stared at the calendar in my phone as though it would show the Margulis schedule. "It needs to be sooner." I didn't like how much time they were taking. I had a hunch that Allan didn't want to sell to me, which made it that much more important to close this deal. Anybody else could waltz in there and scoop up this building. I wouldn't let that happen. This building would be *mine*.

"Mr. Fairchild, I'm not really sure—"

"Listen, how much money do I need to shove up Allan Margulis's asshole in order to see this building sooner?" I spat. "Excuse me—shove into his *bank account.* My apologies for the mistake. Now please, speak to Allan or Cora or, Heaven forbid, *Eli* in order to get me a viewing with a bit more enthusiasm." I paused. *"Please."*

The assistant stammered for a moment and then asked me to hold. I smiled to myself through the banal hold music. When she returned a moment later, she sounded unnaturally cheery.

"Would tomorrow work?"

"Wonderfully. Send the date and time to my email, please. Thanks for your help."

I hung up and tossed my phone onto the foam floor near the ab bench. Accomplishment thrummed through me, but it was lined with something else. A sour taste in the back of my throat.

I knew what that was. I knew that feeling all too well. I lobbed a sigh, moving from the ab bench so I could retrieve my phone. I swiped through screens until I came to my investment apps. Today's business required some important transactions.

I purchased a swath of shares in a company I'd been watching that worked on providing the best educational start to kids in underserved populations throughout the country. Then I hopped over to my donations app, where I divvied up a hundred thousand dollars between STEM-focused non-profits and transitional housing efforts for orphans and foster kids in the eastern US. I picked a different region of the country to focus on each week.

And then I topped it all off by donating fifty thousand to the World Hunger Foundation.

Wall Street might have its rules, but I lived by a different set.

And my rules dictated that good would prevail. Nastiness and scumbaggery would not. This was the other side of the coin I now held. With immense wealth at my disposal, I had the power to balance the scales if I chose.

And my choice? I'd bring Allan Margulis down for his despicable attitude. If he'd stomped on me and steamrolled his own daughter, then there were untold legions of others who'd suffered a similar fate under the thumb of this limp-dicked turd monger. The side effects of seeing Cora again were worth it, if it meant that I could somehow pull off the bigger idea that had rumbled to life behind the building.

Find a way to burn Margulis Realty to the ground.

CHAPTER FOUR

CORA

My family owns property. It's what we do.

One of my most vivid memories from childhood was when my father had acquired a resort in the Caymen Islands. We'd gone to visit it, sun hats and brand-new bathing suits at the ready. During our initial tour, I was fascinated by the gently waving palm trees and the stucco buildings. Everything seemed perfect. Like an impregnable paradise that nothing, not even God, could disrupt.

But nothing is safe in this world, including a palm tree paradise. Our native liaison taught us the warning signs of a hurricane. He said the way his family knew to prepare for bad weather was by whether the matriarchs of the family had issues with headaches or arthritis. My father had laughed in my mother's direction: *Be sure to warn us if you get a headache.*

For years I'd associated headaches with an upcoming storm—whether meteorological or personal. And though I knew now *why* the pain preceded a hurricane, the arrival of a headache could still stop me in my tracks.

Like today. The day after seeing Axel for the first time in years, I had the mother of all headaches.

Which meant the brewing storm would rip up all the palm trees.

I winced as my head pulsed. I'd been counting the seconds until my appointment to meet Axel for the building tour. Of course I was the designated representative to show it—I'd have it no other way. But that didn't mean I wasn't also completely disintegrating inside. I didn't know what to expect. I just knew that I had to be there.

A soft knock at my office door stirred me from my thoughts.

"Who is it?"

"It's me, beautiful." Eli's voice on the other side of my office door prompted a frown. I hated the way he still put up the front. But I wasn't fully ready to stop it, either. The rest of the world still saw us as happily married. Behind the scenes, I'd opened my own secret bank account and started fumbling my way through setting myself up for life post-divorce, even though I couldn't imagine it yet.

Fake it till you make it, Cora.

"Come in."

The door swung open, and Eli sauntered in. He closed the door gently behind him before allowing his cool smile to fade.

"You're going to show the building in an hour, right?" he asked, cocking his head.

"I am."

"Ah." He clucked his tongue, pausing just in front of my desk and raked his gaze over me. "Kind of seemed like maybe you were going on a date, given that ridiculous shade of lipstick."

I blinked, schooling my reaction. It was always a tight rope with him, and I was the most skilled circus performer, just trying to stay aloft in the Eli Show.

"I've worn this shade plenty of times to work before," I said, turning back to my computer. "And I'd prefer you not insult my fashion choices."

"Fashion choices, huh." The lack of amusement in his voice spoke louder than anything. "Well, I'll be joining you today. You'll have to at least act like you like me."

But I don't. I focused on my computer screen, feigning intense interest in my inbox even though I couldn't read the words in front of me. "I don't know what you're talking about. We're always in sync when we're out."

Our arrangement was hardly uncommon. Business marriages were still all the rage in elite circles. Preservation of fortunes and ongoing business alliances—that's what drove most marital pairings these days. Liking your husband was not even in the top five things to consider. Nothing else had ever entered the equation on an interpersonal level.

Truth was, most couples in our circle were one missed Valium away from total anarchy.

But I couldn't care less what he thought about *us* in public now. Really, I wanted to know why the fuck he planned to come along.

Maybe he could sense the question swelling inside me, because he said, "Well, someone needs to make sure you do what you said you'd do with the Fairchild sleazes."

"You don't think I'll make good on my promise to get them to up their offer?"

"I don't trust a damn thing when those brothers are involved."

I didn't have the energy to get into this. "Fine."

"I've already called the car." He swiped through his phone, looking bored. "So maybe you can work on getting ready."

"I *am* ready."

He dragged his gaze over to me, blatantly looked me up and down again, and then said, "Oh."

I ignored the burning in my chest as I shut down my computer and tried to focus on the task at hand. Eli constantly weaponized my physical appearance, and though I thought my frustration with it would dissolve over the years, it had only grown unchecked and unburdened, like cancer cells. Meeting with Axel face-to-face was going to be hard enough. Now I'd have Eli there, breathing down my neck, analyzing every interaction, judging my every word. If I'd been looking for a perfect way to ruin my day, this is what I would have chosen.

"Let's go." I grabbed my purse from my desk drawer and twitched the drape of my silk blouse into place as I rose. Eli fell into step beside me as we walked toward the elevator. He nodded and waved to assistants as we went, acting like a prince. He kept his hand pressed to the small of my back until we were inside the elevator with the doors shut, when I stepped away from him. Eli buried his attention in his phone. We didn't speak, and I was thankful for it. Between this headache and the upcoming hurricane, I needed every chance I could get to sneak some breathing room.

Our car waited at the curb outside, the sleek, black sedan our chariot through midday traffic. We were less than a half mile away, but no amount of money could make traffic move faster—and the building in question didn't have a helipad. Eli and I settled wordlessly into the backseat. Each of us was absorbed in our own worlds, two completely disparate halves trying to prove to the outside world we were a whole.

This was the norm, and it had never felt right. Eli had been hand-picked by my parents, and I'd gone along with it, because it was the only path forward. I'd figured I'd get used to it. To him. After all, didn't everyone else in our circle get used to it after long enough? But six years into our marriage, there was no getting used to it. Not even close. Eli's monitoring of my activities and outward presentation rivaled my father's. I only needed one overbearing father in this lifetime.

And if I had my way, I'd be removing one overbearing husband from that list soon.

But could I go through with it? On the one hand, even contemplating the idea made me feel foolish. Wrong, even, when I supposedly had what everybody else would ever dream of. The wealthy, successful husband. Name recognition. Powerful family members. Allies and partners across the globe. Enough money to buy whatever I wanted, whenever I wanted.

But those trapping weren't what mattered. This much, I knew for certain.

There was a gaping hole in my heart that Axel had left behind, and no amount of wealth or business success could distract me from its ache.

The uptown trip passed quickly as I buried myself in my thoughts. When we pulled up to the fifteen-story brick building, my muscles tensed. *Here goes nothing.*

Eli and I went to the big double doors at the front. He had the key and worked on opening it up as I watched for Axel. The big doors creaked open. The building had been unused for roughly six months, so there was no telling what we might find inside.

A two-toned black Escalade pulled up to the curb. The tinted windows didn't allow us to see inside, but I knew from the way my forearms prickled that it had to be Axel. A moment later, the back door opened.

"Oh good, the clown is here," Eli muttered as he came to my side.

Shiny black dress shoes touched the sidewalk. Broad shoulders stretched beneath a navy-blue suit.

Dark brown hair...but wait. That didn't make sense. Axel had dirty blond hair. As he turned, I realized I was looking at Trace.

I rolled my lips inward, fighting the urge to shout my greeting. Damian stepped out next. *Shit.* I hadn't counted on all the brothers being here. This made things worse. Now I had to face down the extended family of my hard decision eight years ago. Axel pushed open the front passenger door and joined his brothers. The last thread of my composure was stretched nearly to snapping. I absent-mindedly fingered the diamond pendant around my neck.

"Guess the *clowns* are here," Eli corrected.

The three of them were all dressed to perfection—tailored suits in varying shades of blue, shiny shoes, the trendiest sunglasses. They conferred briefly amongst themselves, the tight melons of Axel's ass snagging my attention as he leaned in to say something to Damian.

They turned toward us, Trace leading the way. Axel slid to the back, his face neutral, hands stuffed in his pockets.

"Hello there!" I clapped my hands together, smiling brightly. For the first time, it wasn't forced. I was genuinely glad to see them. I'd never stopped rooting for them or wanting the best for these three. "Trace, Damian, Axel. So glad we could all make this last-minute meeting work."

"This building looks great so far," Trace said, tipping his head back to look up at the façade. "We're just glad Axel could get in to make the offer before someone else scooped it up."

"We best move quickly," Eli said. "There are offers flying in for this property."

"That's why you originally wanted us to wait over a week to see this place then, right?" Axel asked. "Because time is so much of the essence."

Electricity snapped through the air. Shots had been fired and we were *seconds* into the showing.

"Let's go inside," I blurted. "I can't wait for you to see this place. And I'd love to know a little bit more about what you plan to use it for. This building has a unique footprint, so the fact that it aligns with your plans is intriguing."

I led our group into the building. Eli stayed close to my side, his hand on the small of my back as we walked into the cavernous foyer. Our footsteps echoed eerily through the abandoned reception hall.

There were still remnants of the previous tenants—a planter with a fake palm tree, an empty reception desk, signs pointing toward the elevators.

"We want our charity headquarters to be here," Damian said. Trace and Axel had started a slow trek to examine different parts of the foyer. "It will be a bit of a mixed-use scenario. Offices, but also social functions. It was the ballroom that snagged our attention."

"Sounds so noble," Eli commented.

I fought the urge to roll my eyes. I kept my hands clasped in front of me as I smiled at Damian. "I've been following the work that your charity does."

"Oh, have you?" Damian said.

"Yes, have you?" Eli echoed.

"These sorts of things interest me," I said.

"That's great to hear." Damian offered a strained smile, his eyes darting between me and Eli.

Eli wrapped an arm around me, pressing a small kiss to my cheek. "Let's keep moving."

"Sure. We can take a look at each floor. And we'll definitely stop by the ballroom." I started toward the elevators. "The electricity is on, so we can use the elevators."

Axel and Trace meandered toward us. Trace's easy grin was the counterbalance to Axel's distant scowl. Like during the meeting yesterday, Axel was careful to not look my way. It grated on me more than I could express.

Our group headed for the elevators. Trace and I fell into an easy back-and-forth about the details of the building as we boarded the big elevator—the previous tenants, when it was constructed, the original building price when my father bought it in the eighties. That sparked a lengthy comparison of prices in Manhattan, then vs. now, a conversation I was grateful to engage in as the elevator crept toward the top floor. Anything to distract me from the tension simmering beneath the surface here. Axel remained stony and silent while Eli hovered mere inches from me, taking any chance he could to touch the small of my back or lean in closer.

We checked out the offices on the second floor first, then did a quick walk-through of each floor thereafter. For some bizarre reason, the entire fifth floor was decorated in gaudy gold and mauve tones, complete with clay busts littering the area, like a former emperor of Ancient Rome had somehow time traveled to utilize—and then vacate—the floor. Trace and Damian did most of the talking. Axel stayed in the far reaches of whatever room we visited while Eli watched Axel like a hawk.

"No helipad?" Axel finally asked as he peered out a door that led to a rooftop patio.

"Not equipped at the moment," I said. "But a conversion might be possible. I'm not clear on the dimensions and structure of the roof spaces. But we can find out."

"Is it really appropriate for charity cases to have access to helicopters?" Eli asked, loud enough for Axel to hear.

Axel's blue gaze whipped over to Eli. "Did anybody ask you for your opinion?"

"The board sure will," Eli shot back.

Damian executed a one-eighty to join Axel on the other side of the room. Smoke practically curled from Axel's ears, but Damian leaned in to whisper something to him. Trace sent a forced grin toward Eli.

"We travel primarily by helicopter around the city," Trace explained, though he didn't need to.

"Oh. How many helicopters do you have?" Eli asked, not missing a beat.

"Two at the moment."

"That's great. Keep up the hard work, boys, and you might get lucky enough to have a fleet someday." Eli's smile flickered across his face, the falsest semblance of good-naturedness I'd seen from him yet. "But all kids start with toy trains, right?"

I gritted my teeth. Shooting Eli a stern look. He completely ignored me.

"On to the ballroom," I suggested, clapping my hands. "Gentlemen, please follow me." I led our rapidly disintegrating group back to the elevators. *Let this end well. Please let this end well.* The words were on repeat in my head like a mantra. If nothing else, I did not want to see this afternoon end in curse words or deeper animosity. This wasn't the time or place to address the past—but it certainly wasn't the time or place to make the future worse.

Everyone coalesced at the elevator doors again and we boarded silently, the tension so thick it choked as we went up to the top floor.

This was the most awkward and uncomfortable property showing of my life.

"So," I said breezily, holding up a hand to showcase the beautiful if slightly neglected pillars that lined the hallway. "Here's the best part about this place. Not every building in the neighborhood has a ballroom, that's for sure."

"This could hold some serious functions," Trace mused, shoving his hands into his pockets as we entered the main ballroom. The ceiling vaulted away from us, shimmering gold and textured. The wood floor was scuffed, but not irreparable. It was a dusty gem. One that made even my jaw drop. Seeing this building up close and personal had just reawakened my own ideas for a space like this. I'd even convert one of the floors into an Eli-proof residence that no bribing guards or copying keys could allow him to enter.

"There is no fifteenth floor," I said once silence had settled again. "This floor takes up the space of two levels due to the vaulted ceiling."

"Are you sure it's not three?" Trace asked with a laugh, his head tipped back to admire the ceiling.

"She said two," Eli snipped.

Trace looked back at Eli but kept his mouth shut.

"He's fine," I said quietly to Eli, my smile straining at my cheeks. This was a balancing act I never wanted to replicate, acting like my marriage to Eli wasn't doomed, while confronting the only man I'd ever loved and his two amazing brothers.

The Fairchild crew was quiet as they scoped out the ballroom, occasionally pausing to point out something or confer with each other. I drifted along the large windows overlooking Manhattan, allowing myself to get lost in the cityscape beyond.

"Are the taxes current?" Axel asked suddenly, heading our way with a fire in his eye. I was so affected by the intensity pouring out of him that I forgot how to speak. No words came to my lips. Not even a croak.

"That's a pretty ridiculous question," Eli filled in for me.

"Of course they're current," I finally blurted, glancing at Eli. "But we can provide the city records if you'd like to see."

"That's unnecessary," Eli told me. "He can take our word for it."

"I'd like to see every bit of documentation available," Axel said, his gaze focused on Eli. "Unless that's too ridiculous for you."

"It's embarrassing—for *you*," Eli spat. "Needling the nation's most respected realtor over presumed back taxes?"

"I didn't presume shit." Axel's voice had a growl at the edges. My heartrate picked up.

"Clearly."

"Do you always have an issue with prospective buyers asking basic questions?" Axel asked. "Or is that a benefit reserved solely for us?"

Eli's laugh couldn't have been more bitter. "Trust me. Our usual prospective buyers have a bit more class."

"More class?" Axel challenged.

"Eli," I hissed.

"Class would be *knowing* that a company such as yours does not sell buildings that are in arrears for property taxes," Eli said to me, as though this clarified everything.

"Please," I said in the lowest, most threatening tone I could muster, "just be quiet."

Eli was unfazed as he looked back at Axel. "That sort of attitude could really get in the way of getting what you want."

"I'll give you a million dollars *extra* if he doesn't say another word," Axel said, his jaw flexing as he stared at Eli. Then his gaze cut over to me. "Deal?"

The stormy blue swirl of his eyes finally made contact with me, and I was not prepared. My insides seized. I was certain my heart stopped beating for a full five seconds. All the unspoken and tamped-down emotions of the last eight years came rushing back through me, a walloping force that turned my throat into a clamp.

I drew a deep breath, hoping no one would notice the sheen of tears in my eyes. I turned to Eli. "Can we have a word?"

I brushed past him, heading for the hallway near the elevator. Once we were both hidden from the Fairchilds' view, I spun on him. "Okay, what the fuck are you trying to pull here?"

"Keeping things in line." The satisfied air floating around him was so thick I thought I'd choke.

"By ruining the deal?" I asked. "Do I need to remind you that a fifteen percent gain on asking price would be beneficial to the company?"

"How do you even know they've got it?" Eli retorted.

"How do we know *anyone* has it until the deal advances?" I asked. "I don't understand why you insisted on coming if all you planned to do was get in the way."

Eli leaned in, the corners of his mouth dipping downward. "I came to make sure you do what you promised."

"And I'd be able to do it if you weren't hellbent on getting in the way."

He hefted with a laugh, peering over my shoulder to look at the ballroom. "Am I getting in the way? I thought your goal was to talk them up. And which one of us actually did that?"

"You can't be serious. You almost cost us the deal."

That snide laugh again. Sometimes, the ring on my finger burned so badly I wanted to chuck it into a landfill.

"The board wanted a higher price. Which one of us got it? Come on. Be honest with yourself. You were so busy being fucking *compliant* with your little lover boys you forgot how to work the crowd."

His words stung like a slap, and I straightened my back, forcing myself into a fierce neutrality. I would not scream. I would not react. I would not pursue this conversation for even a millisecond longer.

Eli's phone buzzed, and he answered it without hesitation. He strutted away—it sounded like a business partner had called—and I cleared my throat, pressing two fingers to the center of my forehead. Something throbbed deep inside of me. Probably the cancer that I'd given myself just by staying married to Eli.

Which reminded me of the real priority here.

Get Eli the fuck out of my life.

Eli chatted for a few moments and then pocketed his phone. "It's your lucky day. I'm needed at the office."

A loving wife would ask why. Instead, I said, "Good."

He sent me a steely glare and spun on his heel to jab the elevator button. Over his shoulder, he said, "Tell the esteemed Sleazechilds that it was so *lovely* to see them again."

I watched him board the elevator, counting the seconds until the doors closed and I didn't have to look at his smug face anymore.

Is this what all marriages become?

As soon as he was gone, I squeezed my eyes shut. A shudder of emotion ran through me. Thank God he was gone. *Thank God. Thank God. Thank God.* I took a moment to relish the newfound peace his absence allowed me. When I turned, the brothers had drawn nearer.

Axel lifted a brow as he inspected the arched doorway. "Living the dream, huh?"

I opened my mouth to respond, and a laugh escaped. I had no words. I was the woman who had it all and hated every bit of it.

"I'm sorry about that," I said, gesturing toward the elevator in an attempt to save face. "There's been a lot of interest in this building. Contentious interest, you might say."

"I can see that," Trace said, offering a quick smile. He looked at his brothers. We were all gathered now. Mere feet away from each other. For the first time in what felt like a lifetime. "But no worries. You know we're motivated to buy."

"Yes, as does the board. I promise they will react favorably to the offer." I paused, grasping for something else to talk about. Now that Guardian Eli was gone, I felt like I had free rein to say...something. Anything. Even the slightest nod to the past. "I will do whatever I can to make sure this building ends up with you three."

"That's sweet of you," Damian said.

"I am a huge fan of the work you've been doing," I went on, feeling my cheeks heat up. This felt somehow vulnerable to admit, as if they might hear what I was really saying: I'd never stopped caring about any of them. "It's so great to see you again so I can tell you in person. I'm just so proud of what you've accomplished. Truly."

"Thank you," Trace said, one of those genuine smiles coming out to play. For a moment, we were back in their crappy apartment in Chinatown, Trace in his workout clothes, giving Axel and me shit for being too lovey-dovey while we made dinner. The memory seared through me, nearly deafening me as Trace continued speaking. "I've seen you plenty in the news as well. You're slated to become CEO next quarter. That's big."

"Yes," I said and could think of nothing else to add. Which only proved that my coffers were empty. I'd lost every last modicum of joy I'd ever held.

Axel stood a few feet behind his brothers, making his emotional distance plain through his physical distance.

"Let's head back down to the lobby. And if you have any questions for me, please ask." I led them into the elevator, and once the car had started downward, I asked, "So what did you think of the building? Was it what you expected?"

"Well, let's have the engineer of this project answer that question," Damian said, jerking his chin toward Axel.

Axel tipped his head to one side. His stormy blues sent an indecipherable message to Damian. I only recognized it because I'd once been fluent in that language. His jaw flexed, and he cast his gaze over to me so briefly it counted as a slap. "It's what we've been looking for. Which do you prefer: cash or check?"

I gave a small laugh. "We need your final offer in writing, of course, and the sale does need to be approved by the board first."

Axel nodded. "You'll have it today. Then just get ahold of us once the drones have voted, yeah?"

The elevator came to a stop. When the doors slid open, Axel strode out, heading straight for the main doors. Over his shoulder he called, "I'll meet you two in the car." Which left me, Damien and Trace standing awkwardly in the elevator.

"I'm sorry about—" Trace started as we walked into the lobby.

"No, no." I held up a hand. "Don't apologize. I get it. I really do." I offered him a small smile. Damian had paused, as though he wasn't sure whether to join in our conversation or just follow Axel. "If I were Axel, I wouldn't be nice to me either."

"It was nice seeing you again, Cora," Damian said with a wave. He hurried toward the main doors, his shoes scuffing softly against the floor.

"I appreciate you fitting us in last minute," Trace said. "I really hope we'll be hearing some good news from you soon."

We shared a warm smile. Being around the Fairchilds again felt like coming home in a way that I'd never felt before. And there was something about the warmth—despite Axel's iciness—that had jostled loose something deep inside me.

"Trace, could I ask you for a favor?" My cheeks flushed once I realized I'd spoken.

"Sure."

"This is completely unrelated to the property. It's uh...could I..." I licked my lips, wondering how I could phrase this that wouldn't blast my dirty laundry into outer space. Hell, at this point, I couldn't afford to care. "I have some investment questions that I'd like to discuss with you in private. It's important that it stay discreet."

He nodded slowly, rummaging in his inside breast pocket. "Of course. Here's my card. It's got my direct cell. Just let me know when you're ready, and we can set something up."

I received the business card gratefully, my heart pounding. I hadn't planned on asking Trace for private advice, but here we were. I was crafting my exit strategy, step by step, on the fly. I'd started with a secret bank account two weeks ago; now I would make an appointment to discuss investments only for me. Even though I didn't know what the exact next steps would be, I could recognize a new door when I saw one. If there was anyone I could trust—despite the fallout with his brother—it was Trace.

"Thank you. Thank you so much." I slipped the card into my handbag and waved as he started for the door. "It was so good seeing you three again. I'll be in touch soon."

Trace headed for the Escalade. When the door opened, I tried to spot Axel one last time, but I didn't glimpse him.

Maybe today was all I'd get of him. A few stony glares. Business-related questions only. An emotional distance so great the Grand Canyon could comfortably fit between us.

I knew better than to hope for any sort of future with Axel. All I could do was quiet my heart's thrum, which constantly urged me toward him, and shun the memories that still whispered to me late at night about finding my way back to him. The painful ache in my chest would forever remind me: I'd chosen wrong.

If there was any way back to Axel, I'd take it in a heartbeat. But until I choreographed my exit from my sham of a marriage, there was no going anywhere.

And that choreography would need something a little bit more than just financial advice from Trace.

It would need a fucking miracle.

CHAPTER FIVE

AXEL

As a young and idealistic Axel, I had plenty of ideas of where future Axel would end up, and what sort of things I'd spend my time doing.

I never thought *real estate mogul* would be included on the list.

But as the week advanced, and I'd combed through my interaction with Cora and her ridiculous twatwaffle of a husband no less than a thousand times, I realized that I'd officially crossed over into a new industry.

My brothers and I had broadened our business interests once before. Last year, we'd become part of the tech startup world when we acquired a flagging business with an amazing vision but a despicable CEO. The acquisition had dual main purposes. Not only did we desire a standing within the tech world, but we wanted to send the company's CEO to hell, but the best we could do was buy him out and stop him from using the company to traffic underage girls.

The acquisition showed us we could expand, possibly infinitely—not just our physical holdings, but our moral reach. We conveniently set the former CEO up with a lifetime hacker monitor that would find out—and intervene—if he ever tried to participate in human trafficking again, thanks to Damian's freaky genius brain. The richest people committed some of the shadiest crimes, and most of these people were beyond the bounds of regular justice. So if we could tip the scales in some small way, well, we fucking had to.

And now, Margulis Realty was on my radar.

Allan Margulis was a target for personal reasons. He wasn't sending drugged-up girls around the world in private jets like some of these wealthy assholes, but he advanced his own brand of disgusting. I wanted Allan Margulis to go down more than I wanted to breathe some mornings. And trust me, I was really invested in breathing; I planned on sucking every last drop of life out of this fucking earth experience.

But now that we were poised to buy this building—provided Cora Margulis could be trusted even a little bit, which I still doubted—I realized I wanted in. I wanted to add realty to our holdings. I wanted Margulis Realty to become one of our flagship brands.

I'd always wanted to take down Allan, and maybe taking over his precious company was the best route to submission. Having Axel Fairchild in command of his brand was the best revenge I could imagine.

The idea pulsed through me like the bassline of a techno song. I couldn't avoid it. My knee bounced along to it, even without wanting to. Somehow, I'd make this work. I swiped open my investment app and tapped in MARGULIS REALTY. The company stats stared back at me.

I blinked. I could take over his company via hostile takeover someday, if I acquired enough stocks and could elbow my way onto the board. The idea spread through me like warm honey, prompting a smile. What a delicious little scheme. I purchased $50,000 of Margulis stock to start.

A nice beginning to my new weekly investment approach.

Knock knock. The sound on my office door stirred me from my thoughts. The door opened before I could speak, which meant it had to be one of my brothers. I tossed my phone onto the desk.

Trace's head popped past the door. "You busy?"

I gestured at my messy desk before clasping my hands behind my head. "Got all the time in the world for you, Trace. What's up?"

"Just wanted to give you a little FYI. Don't come to my side of the floor this afternoon."

"Why's that?"

He did the annoying hedging thing—the head tilt combined with "Ehhhh." He finally used his words. "Don't worry about it. Just avoid."

"You know that's an unacceptable answer." My hands dropped to my desk, and I leaned forward, pinning him with a stare. "Why do I need to avoid your office?"

"Reasons."

I palmed my desk and pushed to standing, not breaking my gaze. "Trace."

"Axel."

"Fucking spill."

He blinked, and I could see the gears turning behind his dark eyes. "There's someone coming you would rather not see."

"*Who?*"

His eyes narrowed. "Cora."

Silence stretched between us as we engaged in an intense eye war. I trusted he could feel all my questions via my gaze alone.

In case he wasn't clear, I followed up with, "Why the *fuck* is she coming into our building?"

He expelled a burst of air. "Listen, I know it's weird. But she asked me for some private financial advice after the showing last week. And...I dunno. It seemed urgent. I got the message, if you know what I mean."

All sorts of reactions flared to life inside me. Exasperation. Regret. Just to name a couple. But what won out was jealousy. "What message is that? Do you know what I'll do to you if you even look at her for too long?"

Trace groaned. "Jesus, Axel, not *that* message."

I flumped backward into my seat, a scowl settling into place.

"She sounded like she needs help. And what are we if not a bunch of patrons for charity cases?"

"Even my ex-fiancée?" I said, more than a note of challenge in my voice. "Who has access to all the resources in the world."

"Yes. Even her."

I couldn't go on, though, because I knew what he was talking about. I knew why he did it. If I could see past the hurt, I'd agree with him. But for now, I couldn't. All I could admit was that I was curious.

"What time is she coming?" I asked, clicking the nearest pen I could find. "So I know when to avoid."

"In forty-five minutes. She's slated for an hour, but it might take less. I can let you know when the coast is clear."

I nodded, sniffing. My mind spun. Though I was thankful for the heads up, I knew I'd be able to think of nothing else until that woman was gone from the building.

Trace retreated to his own side of the building, and I was left stewing and pacing.

I'd always envisioned so many possibilities for my life, despite the setbacks.

But one that would never materialize was husband.

After Cora, I didn't have it in me to let anyone else get even remotely close. Mirabella was the closest anyone had gotten, and I still didn't know anything about her family. I preferred it that way.

Between what happened with Cora and what I'd lived through during my childhood, I didn't have it in me to let anyone get that close ever again.

I started out a normal lower-class kid—two parents who loved me, my older brother Damian, and my two younger sisters. One present per birthday. Always dinner on the table, even if it took every last cent to put it there. Then when I was eight, my parents died in a car crash while they were out trying to find Christmas gifts for us. Yeah, we were the sad case of the kids whose parents died the day before Christmas.

Our granny wasn't well enough to watch us more than a night here or there, so we got kicked into the foster system. My baby sister Jordan was only two when we lost our parents. Imagine that shit.

I wished I could say we at least had each other to lean on. But we didn't. Damian and I got shipped off to one home, Kaylee and Jordan to another.

Damian and I saw it all in the first two years of foster care. Shit I still don't even want to talk about. Foster farms is what we called them—parents milking the system for the benefits while the kids lived like rats in a hovel. I learned real quick how to fend for myself. Damian and I stuck together like glue. We watched each other's backs in each new school or when the foster farm had older kids who were punch happy.

Damian was always on the front line, finding the compromise, negotiating for extra snacks, reeling things in when I got too mouthy with the new moms and dads or siblings. Even at age nine, he felt like he had to find the way. He was a year older than me, so he took the protector role seriously, like those eleven months between us meant he had to be the man of our broken family. But no nine-year-old should have to shoulder that shit.

By the time we landed in Trace's family, we were predisposed to fighting. To tension. To absolutely batshit unstable foundations. It took us a minute to adjust to the stability. Took us even longer before we realized Trace was an ally, not an enemy.

From love, to broken, to love again.

I wish I could say the same for my little sisters.

There's not much that'll make me break down in life. But when I get to thinking too much about the fate my little sisters were handed because of the foster system, it sends me into a spiral. Because that same system saved us.

How could the same system deliver both salvation and ruin?

These are the questions I don't share with a fucking hook-up. The questions I can't even bear to speak out loud. Cora was the only one who ever knew about my sisters, besides Trace and Damian.

My sisters were why the three of us diverted every spare investment dollar back into supporting foster kids, families in need, and children who'd lost everything and needed a North Star.

We got lucky and found North Stars. Jordan and Kaylee never did.

We were able to stay in touch with our sisters, but only sporadically. There was never any rhyme or reason to when we could make contact with them. Once we'd gotten settled in with the Fairchilds, Mama Deb and Papa Gary tried to track down our sisters and add them to our family—even though the addition would have pushed the financial scales way out of balance. But they tried. Bless 'em, they tried.

For a brief period in high school, the four of us were in the same school system. Damian and Trace and I were seniors, Kaylee was a sophomore, and Jordan was in seventh grade. Damian and I made sure to meet Kaylee every morning by the doors, walk her to homeroom, talk about what was going on in her life. But by that point, at fifteen, she was acting out like crazy. Coming to school looking wrecked or tweaked out, her blonde hair matted, eyeliner smeared. She'd brag about trying drugs or hooking up with men in their twenties.

But we didn't give up on her. Hell, I felt guilty because our foster parents rocked, and hers clearly sucked. Kaylee told us that her foster parents blamed her, but Kaylee was the true victim. She made one wrong friend or hooked up with one wrong guy. We'll never know who it was that finally pushed her into the sex trafficking world. But by March, she'd stopped coming to school.

The only way we could learn any information was when we were able to intercept Jordan at her middle school. We'd stop by early with donuts, hoping to run into her. Jordan barely recognized us the first time we caught her. We were only her big brothers in theory. She'd sit with us with the saddest eyes, picking at her donuts, keeping all her secrets wrapped up inside her.

Once Damian and Trace and I graduated, Kaylee's cell phone number stopped working, and we found out that Jordan had been transferred to another school system *again*.

We never found Kaylee again. Not until her obituary hit the newspapers our freshman year at Columbia. Jordan just disappeared. We never found an obituary, but we knew she might have met a similar fate. We suspected their foster parents had been the link to the sex trafficking world.

Where would they be now if they had somehow escaped the system?

Our success had to be doubly big, doubly grand. We weren't just building our own legacies. We were achieving for the family we'd left behind. No, the family that had been ripped from us.

I spent too long stewing in my thoughts. Some days, it felt like the past would never leave us. Fuck, I'd tattooed it onto my body. It *drove* us.

Even Trace. That big-hearted genius. Of course he'd adopted our mission statement without question: *help change the lives of the most vulnerable*. He hadn't suffered the way we had, but he would fight for the future of forgotten and abandoned kids all the same.

Once three o'clock rolled around—a full hour after Trace's appointment with Cora was slated to start—I started to itch. I waited for a text from Trace, but nothing came. I could feel down to my bones that Cora was still in the building, though the thought made me crazy. I had to get out of my office.

I told myself it was not because I wanted to glimpse her again.

I was fucking kidding myself. That traitorous siren was gorgeous, more so now than ever before. Which meant it was even more important that I stay the fuck away from her.

Even after all these years apart, she still made my cock sit up and beg. I'd never liked the looks of anything more than Cora Margulis.

I walked through the wide, airy halls of our office suite. My office was tucked into one corner, not unlike Allan Margulis's corner office that had wowed me all those years ago. Assistants nodded at me. Employees scampered. Everything was bustling. Active. Productive. Just the sort of thing you like to see when you take a casual stroll to Trace's side of the building.

"Hey, Axel, can you—"

"Not now." I held up my hand to quiet Francis before he could derail me. There was always something needing my attention. Right now, only one thing mattered.

I passed Damian's office. The door was shut, which meant he was probably balls deep in coding. As I neared Trace's office, my heart rate picked up. The door was closed.

She could be out the front door by now. Or maybe she was mere feet away inside that office.

All rationale left me. I was a sweaty-palmed mess, held hostage by my own desires even though my brain absolutely did not agree with this mission. Minutes ticked by. I paced the hallway until it seemed suspicious. Then I did a one-eighty and decided to leave and pretend I'd never given in to my curiosity.

Trace's door cracked open at just the same moment. The low undertones of his voice wafted out first, followed by the husky sing-song of Cora's. Sometimes her voice hit like the sigh of an angel. This moment was one of those times.

My skin prickled as I turned. My gaze landed on her.

She wore her dark, glossy hair pulled up in a loose top knot, and she'd painted her pouty lips maroon. She wore a cream silk blouse and high-waisted dark slacks paired with designer heels. Cora Margulis was the epitome of sexiness and professionalism. Mainstream beautiful on the outside, but with a sparkling, mischievous core that I'd known intimately.

"Oh. Axel." Trace's voice brimmed with confusion. He'd done everything he could to help me. He hadn't realized he needed to cut my legs off to prevent me from getting close to Cora while she was in my territory. "Everything okay?"

I nodded, glancing between the two of them. "I was just chatting with Francis." My resolve bottomed out, and I had no idea what I'd even wanted to accomplish. I swished my tongue back and forth over my bottom teeth as I struggled for a direction. "Cora, can you come with me?"

Her brows lifted. She looked over at Trace, as though tacitly asking if this was okay. "Oh. Sure."

I spun on my heel before I could catch Trace's reaction and led the way, my heart rate tripling as I wound my way toward my office. Cora followed close behind. I could feel it in the way the air pulled tight between us. The way every inch of my body prickled, expectant and alive.

I paused at my office doorway for her to step inside first. I shut the door quietly behind me, struggling to find clarity in the haze of my mind.

After all the shit between us—so much heartbreak—there wasn't much hope for seeing through the haze. It had grown thick and choking through the years. A noxious fog that needed to go—and stay—away.

Cora checked out the details of my office while I gnawed at my upper lip.

"Why the fuck do you think it's okay to come to my building?" I finally asked her, once the silence had become unbearable.

She looked taken aback. "I had a meeting with Trace. I assumed that him inviting me to your building meant that you'd be okay with it."

"Well, you're wrong."

She blinked, showing no emotion. "You came into my building first. How about we call it even?"

I crossed my arms, stepping closer to her. "That's a weak offer if you're trying to make things *even*."

"Can I ask why you're keeping score?" She mimicked me, crossing her arms with a look that raked down my body.

"Someone's gotta be on the lookout around your crew." I sniffed, gobbling up my opportunity to take her in. This was the only private moment I would allow myself. From here on out, the boundaries would be redrawn. "Can't let my guard down for a second around you people."

She hefted with a humorless laugh. "You're not wrong there."

The admission knocked me off track. Her gaze drifted away, something stony and unfamiliar sliding over her face. The waft of her clementine perfume almost sent me spiraling, but I managed to put myself back on track.

"I need you to stay the fuck away from my building."

Her nostrils flared, and she whipped her gaze back to me. The stoniness had melted away; emotion brimmed in her features, and she watched me so intensely for a moment that I had to look away.

"Axel, are you happy?" Her voice was soft, as if she hadn't meant to say it out loud.

I swallowed hard and walked toward the corner of my office. Two full walls were floor to ceiling windows, overlooking Manhattan from a dizzying height. I needed to get lost in the mess of life below us. Anything to distract me from the vortex I'd unwittingly opened.

"Why do you care?" I asked, shoving my hands in my pockets as I took note of whatever details I could latch onto: the puffy cumulonimbus cloud over Brooklyn. The glinting steel beams of the nearest skyscraper. The occasional sunlight sparkle from the waters of the East River.

"I'm curious. It's important to me."

I laughed bitterly. "Is it?"

"You might not believe it, but it is."

I frowned out at the beautiful day. Her attention sizzled over me, and I knew it was more important than ever not to look at her. Keep the boundaries drawn. "I'm extremely happy. I have everything I've ever dreamed of. Could not ask for anything else."

My words pinged hollowly inside me, bouncing through the hidden caverns of my heart. Because of course, that wasn't entirely true.

One dream had escaped me. And she was standing here in my office.

I cleared my throat, not ready to look at her. "What about you?"

"Am I happy?" She paused, as though the question did not compute. "I don't even know where to begin."

"Oh, come on. The Princess of Manhattan needs a better answer than that." I made the mistake of turning toward her. Her beautiful face was wrought with sadness. She looked more vulnerable, more distraught, than I'd ever seen her before.

"I'm not happy. I haven't been happy since the day we broke up."

Her words thudded through the room. My ears started ringing. This meeting needed to end. Because whatever path this conversation was leading down would not help either of us. I had fought for years to keep my head above water when it came to this woman. She was not allowed to waltz into my building and shove my head to the ocean floor.

These words were a fantasy. I'd dreamt of hearing them in my darkest moments. They were the words I'd forced myself to live without.

Maybe she regretted breaking up with me, but she'd still fucking married Eli. Which meant nothing could ever make sense.

I looked back across the complex swirl of Brooklyn beyond my window. "You mean when *you* broke up with *me*. The way you say it sounds like it was mutual." I cleared my throat. "And it wasn't."

"Right. When I broke up with you," she said softly.

"Well, you chose this life. You put yourself here."

"I did choose it. But it was for a reason. One that I believed in."

I clenched and unclenched my jaw. How had I become trapped in my own office? I'd wanted to scare Cora away; now she was holding *me* prisoner to the past that I very much wanted to leave behind us.

"Yes. Because your family has always prioritized excess wealth and vapid interpersonal relationships. I know." I looked at her over my shoulder. "Are we done here?"

Cora's gaze dropped to the ground and her back straightened. I could practically see her rebuilding her armor. Even though I knew how rare this window of openness and vulnerability was for someone like her, part of me wanted to erase this encounter from my memory.

It wouldn't lead anywhere productive. She had a wedding ring on her finger. And no amount of explanation or regret would change the fact that she'd fucking chosen *him*.

She drew a breath. "I'm sorry for coming into your building today. But it was good to see you again, Axel. I'm glad you're happy. You deserve all of this and more."

She toyed with a diamond earring, looking like she might add more. I spoke before she could.

"Stay where you belong," I told her. "And if you've ever wanted to balance the scorecard, get me that building and stay the fuck away from us."

Cora's mouth turned into a thin line before she spun on her heel and strode out of my office. When the door closed quietly behind her, I buried my face in my hands.

"Fuck fuck fuck fuck fuck." I pulled at my hair, allowing the briefest burst of the tempest within to come swirling to the surface. A gale force wind of emotion pummeled me. I slammed my fist into my desk, fighting to tamp down the feelings. Hold them back. Swallow them all until I could get to the fucking gym, or fuck it away, or anything.

Cora Margulis should not have this effect on me still. I hated that she could make me waver, that she could come into my space and ask me if I was fucking happy.

All it took was one glance at her heartbreaking beauty to reduce me to rubble.

I paced my office for a while, drawing deep breaths and ignoring the curiosity that sprang to life inside me. I had so many questions after that little interaction. How could she come into my office and tell me she wasn't happy since breaking up with me? That required a serious amount of ovaries, but I couldn't puzzle out her end game. All while wearing her wedding ring. Had this been an Eli-approved visit? Was she just making moves in the overall Margulis game of chess? I wanted all the answers, but I didn't want to want them.

It became clear that I needed something, whether a stiff drink, a punching bag, or the slightest of hints that could begin unraveling infuriating tangle of questions in my head. She was the only one who could cut me to the core, and I was determined to cauterize the wound. Once and for all. I stormed down the hallway to Trace's office.

I pushed open the door without knocking. He looked up at me, unsurprised.

"Okay. What the fuck was that meeting about?" I dropped into the chair facing Trace's desk and looked past his shoulder at the blue sky through his window.

"I thought you'd be here a little sooner." He checked his watch. "It's been a half hour since she left."

"Yeah, well, I'm practicing something called self-control. Now fucking spill it."

Trace leveled me with a look, judgmental eyebrow and all. "You sure you want to get into this?"

"I'm not getting into anything. I'm just asking for information."

He smirked. "Sure."

"Trace, just tell me. Why was she here?"

He leaned back in his seat, steepling his fingers in front of him. "She's setting up a worst-case scenario safety net for her investments. Wants help moving things around. She's gearing up to divorce Eli."

I ran my palm across my forehead, not a little bit relieved to hear those words. I wasn't okay with how good it felt to hear them.

"I can't say I'm not happy to hear that," I finally said.

"Same here. She seemed seriously miserable."

I sniffed. "She's not happy."

"How do *you* know that?"

"She told me," I admitted, looking up at him. "I meant to kick her out of the building but instead we...talked. Sort of."

The judgmental eyebrow returned. "Couldn't have seen that one coming."

I threw my hands wide. "So sue me."

"I'm sure Eli's lawyer will."

"Oh, no. Stop it. Stop it right there, Trace Fairchild, because I'm about to get angry, and I do not want to hold a grudge against my own brother for the rest of our natural lives."

Amusement curled at his lips. "Oh, really?"

"Yes. Now let's review the rules. First: do not ever mention that name in front of me again or I will punch you or puke on you, whichever happens first. Second: you know as well as anybody that Cora and I are done."

His smile spreader wider. "Done, huh?"

"Like the One Ring into Mount Doom-style done. That relationship has been cast into the fire from whence it came." If that was true, why did I see the word *LIE* flash behind my eyelids? "Furthermore, that disgusting fuckface would never have any reason to sue me. I've informed Cora to never set foot on our property again."

"Sounds about right, then." Trace shifted in his seat, looking somehow more pleased with himself than ever. "She needs to stay away because you can't."

I dropped my chin, mustering up my best death glare. "Do I need to review the rules again?"

"No, sir. I just know what I see. You were fucking stalking my office."

Discomfort churned inside me. I hated when either of my brothers had a point and used it against me. But I could talk my way out of anything. "She needs to know where she stands. Which is not on Fairchild property."

Trace still looked smug, and it irritated me. But he didn't need to believe me now. He'd believe me once I proved I was right. He didn't need to know that banishing Cora from our building was merely the way to prevent me from slipping closer to her.

I didn't fully trust myself, so I needed my brothers to trust me. I needed to borrow their trust in me to know I could really do it. But if Trace already doubted me, we were all in trouble.

With how smoking hot Cora Margulis still looked in a cream silk blouse coupled with rumors of divorce on the horizon, it wouldn't take much to start the avalanche of desire.

I needed to begin rebuilding my fortifications immediately.

"Besides," I added, "I've got a plan. I want to acquire Margulis Realty with a good old-fashioned hostile takeover."

Trace's eyebrow popped up, conveying his extreme disdain. "You don't say."

"I've already started buying stocks. I'll accumulate them on the sly until I'm as close as I can get to being a majority shareholder. You just fucking watch me."

"I guess I will," Trace said, leaning back into his chair. "Having Margulis Realty as a banner brand would be...intriguing."

"See? You like where I'm heading with this. I'll fill in Damian soon. We'll all be one big happy fucking family soon enough. With the Margulis side of the family kicked to the curb, of course. Because Cora and I are done. Would I try to capsize her entire livelihood if I believed in her?" I held out my hands, as though this was the last remaining piece of the irrefutable evidence puzzle.

"All right, brother," Trace finally conceded, dropping the judgmental brow of doom. "I believe you. You and Cora are capital D-O-N-E. I'll conduct all further meetings via phone or video call."

"Great. Well, back to work." I clapped my hands on my knees, ready to resume my previous life, the one I'd maintained just fine for the past eight years, without Cora in it, no sight of her, no mention of her fucking family, none of it.

The building deal just needed to close, and I'd be on my merry way to quietly ruining Allan's empire.

Before I could take a step away from the chair, a knock sounded on the door.

"It's Francis," Francis said, his voice muffled through the door. "Can I come in? It's urgent."

"Yeah, it's open," Trace called. I smoothed down the front of my pants and adjusted my cuffs as Francis stepped inside the office, worry etched across his face.

"I have some news," Francis said, nibbling on his bottom lip. "And it's not good. The Margulis camp called." He paused, grimacing, as he looked between Trace and me. "They rejected your offer."

CHAPTER SIX

CORA

"Hold it...hold it...hooooold it." The bright and encouraging voice of my private Pilates instructor, Jazz, was the only thing breaking through the burn of my abs. "Jazz" wasn't just a quirky name; it was necessary for this grueling shit. She needed to jazz me up, or I'd never make it through. I grimaced, my entire body shaking as I struggled to hold the pike position for what felt like the hundredth minute straight.

"You're doing so good! You got it, Cora! Woooow!" She slapped my biceps, which were also shaking. "Look at your alignment! This is incredible."

"Hnnnggh." I tried to respond, but the burn made it impossible. All I could see was the flashing clock behind her. Ten seconds left. Which equated to an eternity in Pilates Land.

"Almost there. Almost there!" My legs started to drop at the five second mark. "Nope! Hold it!" I righted my posture, and a couple seconds later the time went off. I collapsed to the mat like a deflated balloon.

"Pheeew, girl. That made *me* burn just watching you." Jazz chuckled as she walked around my living room, picking up equipment. I'd called an emergency session today and come straight to my condo from the Fairchild building, ready to sweat the pain away.

I needed some kind of release after that tense face-to-face with Axel in his office. If he wasn't going to fuck me—which would be the best route to dissolving all this tension I carried in my body—then it needed to be this masochistic exercise.

"Thanks for this," I said, gesturing weakly at my limp body and the props she had in her arms. "I needed it."

"No sweat. Or in your case, lots of sweat." Jazz chuckled. Her perfectly toned and tanned body glinted in the late afternoon sunlight streaming in through the wall of windows in my high-ceilinged living room. Six-pack abs winked at me as she bent down to collect the foam roller. She always came in the cutest sports bras and sleekest leggings. It was probably a law for in-home Pilates instructors to represent their physical strength during working hours.

"Think I'll have a six pack like yours someday?" I hauled myself to sitting, pinching at the belly flab that appeared.

"Only if you want it." She winked over at me. "What do you want?"

The question landed more heavily than she probably intended. I sighed, my gaze drifting toward the windows. The tops of the maples across the street in Central Park moved gently outside my window. The first thing that streaked through my mind was embarrassingly unachievable. *I want out of here, and I want Axel Fairchild.*

But no. I needed to be more realistic. We were only talking about six packs.

"I think I want you to come back tomorrow," I said with a laugh as she offered me a hand. I popped to standing, grabbing for my water bottle on the end table. "There are a few things I want to keep off my mind. And this is just the ticket."

Jazz giggled. "It's hard to think about what bothers you when you're planking for an hour."

While we went over possible times to meet up the following day, my front door clicked and slowly swung open.

Through the archway, I saw Eli strut into the main hallway, his face partially obscured by an enormous bouquet of white roses.

"Where is my gorgeous wife?" he called out, his voice echoing slightly.

I sighed, avoiding Jazz's gaze. He knew exactly where we were. He was just putting on a show for the visitor. "We're in here."

Eli's footsteps scuffed across the wood floor as he headed our way. His smile was ear to ear as he presented me with the bouquet, as if this was the first time any man in history had thought of such a thing. "These are *for you*."

"Thank you." I received them, offering up my cheek for a quick peck from him. While I carried the flowers toward the kitchen for a vase, I heard Eli chatting with Jazz.

"Hey, Jazz. Long time no see."

Jazz giggled. "You could say that."

The interaction struck me as odd, since Jazz had stopped coming to the Upper West Side brownstone after I moved out. Unless he'd started lessons with her too, which seemed unlikely. But even mild speculation about where they might have run into each other made my insides feel heavy. I couldn't force myself to care.

I caught a whiff of the roses as I arranged them in a glass vase. The scent always reminded me of home. Rather, my parent's house, which no longer felt even remotely close to my home. The scent of roses had long been baked into my subconscious as a harbinger of the anxiety my parents' demands and expectations provoked. And though Eli probably didn't know about that, it was only fitting that he'd brought me roses while expecting me to uphold our happy façade.

"I'll see you tomorrow, Cora!" Jazz poked her head into the kitchen just as I set the vase in the middle of the brunch table.

"Great. Thanks for the killer workout." We waved, and she headed for the front door. Eli appeared in the kitchen a moment later.

"Those look great." His smile lasted a second before fading. "So you took the rest of the day for a workout class?"

"I took the afternoon off," I reminded him. "Personal time."

"You haven't checked your emails, have you?" He shoved his hands into his pockets, keys jangling as he started a slow walk toward me.

"No. I might sit down later and get caught up." I sighed, pressing a palm to my forehead. Sweat still coated my skin, but there was no way I'd head for a shower while he was here. I didn't want any opportunity for a romantic overture to arise.

He tutted, pausing at the dinette. "Well, you'll read all about it later then. Such a shame the Fairchild deal was rejected though."

My brows knitted together. "What?"

"Yeah. Can you believe it? Somebody actually outbid them." He nodded, his gaze skating over my face, like he was analyzing me for information. "We still need to hold the vote, but you know the board's hands will be tied. They have to go with the highest offer."

I opened my mouth to protest, but I there was nothing I could say to argue. Eli was right. And this didn't make *any* sense at all.

"This is impossible," I sputtered. "What was the new offer?"

"Two point seven million over asking."

It seemed a little too convenient, just enough above asking price to beat Axel's price and avoid the sale to the Fairchilds. "Do we know who made the offer?"

"It's all in the email."

I sighed. "Great. Well, I appreciate the update."

He huffed. "Why are you so salty? Thought you'd be excited we're milking even *more* money out of that building. Wasn't that the whole point? Talk up the Fairchilds to get more money? We did that, and now somebody wants to pay more. This is money in *our* pocket, remember."

"You're right," I said flatly. The money in *our* collective pocket wasn't an incentive, since it was going to the company. Even still, whenever he mentioned that money was "ours," it meant it was really *his.* Which was why I'd started to secretly disentangle our finances. I needed money of my own, money that he wouldn't notice if I used or disposed of or acquired. "I was just...eager for this to be done."

"It'll be done on the same timeline as it was scheduled before," Eli said, his *duh* tone out to play. "Why do you care so much who it gets sold to?"

I knew better than to continue this conversation. "I don't."

"Right." He ran his tongue along the inside of his cheek. "That's obvious."

The same ache appeared in my gut, the slow pulse that served as a warning signal. "Any other news?"

"Nope. Just thought I'd drop by on my way to *our* house to visit *my* wife." He sniffed, fixing me with a disapproving look. "What about you getting changed and we go grab dinner? Make the rounds. Show our faces."

I wilted slightly. That was the *last* thing I wanted to do. "Eli, I'm tired. I just want to be alone tonight."

He nodded as if he'd been expecting that answer. "Yeah. Of course. Because you *always* want to be alone."

I had no response for that. It was only partially true. I wanted to be alone so much more than I wanted to spend time with him. My own company, at least, was tolerable.

"Too tired. Needs to be alone." He ticked off each excuse on his fingers. "Absolutely never in the mood."

"Eli," I started.

"Wife of the year award right here, folks." He pointed at me as though we had an audience he was performing for. "And on top of all that, claims to want kids but hasn't gotten pregnant in five years, despite nothing being wrong with her! Incredible how all those doctors say you're perfectly fine, yet you still can't conceive. Must be the only woman in America who literally can't make a kid. Easiest thing in the fucking world."

I cast my gaze down to the table, suddenly so tired I could have collapsed. Kids had been on the table since the beginning of our relationship. I'd admitted, stupidly, that I wanted them. But the truth was, I never wanted them with *him*. I'd taken great pains to make sure I never had his children.

I'd been quietly taking birth control since about year two of our marriage. In the beginning, I'd naively thought that a kid might actually help our arrangement feel more like a family and less a business arrangement with the occasional romantic interlude.

Our arrangement had been born from a very real desire of two families to produce more power and capitalize on two different industries, and now both Eli and I were trapped between the stark expectations of a business deal and the soft caresses of a romantic relationship. I never would have chosen Eli for myself, but since he'd been thrust upon me, I'd made a valiant attempt to cultivate some of those soft and sweet feelings for him in the beginning.

Eight years later, I could say those attempts failed. I harbored nothing soft and sweet for him. But his expectations and goals for our marriage existed beyond the regular dimensions of marital normalcy. He wanted the picture-perfect family. He wanted the business-shark wife and sexy-time lover—on his terms. He wanted me to be everything to him while giving nothing of himself. Eli would freak out if he knew I was on birth control; he was gung-ho about having kids to carry on the empire. But I couldn't stomach the possibility of being tethered to him forever like that. I wanted kids, just not *his*.

There was only one man I'd ever consider having children with, and he'd forbidden me from setting foot on his properties ever again.

"Though maybe it's a blessing in disguise, right? Not sure how you think you'd ever be a good mother when you aaaalways want to be alone," Eli went on.

My phone alarm went off from the living room, bringing me back to the present. When Eli went on his diatribes, it was easy for me to sink into a dissociative space. But I knew what that alarm meant. It meant I had real work to do.

"You'd make such a great father, with the way you support your spouse," I muttered, brushing past him as I headed for my phone. "Can only imagine the sweet things you'd say to our children."

"You're a real winner," he went on from the kitchen as I hurried to turn off my alarm.

Suicide Hotline in 30 minutes. I swiped the reminder off my screen and turned the alarm off. My weekly volunteer hours on the suicide hotline was the one thing I never missed. And another thing I'd never tell Eli about.

"Listen, you better go," I said, forcing the waver out of my voice. "I have an appointment coming up and—"

"And you need to be alone," he said snidely. "Got it. Guess I'll see you at the office, then, huh?" He strode toward the front door, his footsteps loud and purposeful. A moment later, the front door opened and closed.

Silence.

A shaky breath escaped me, and I sank onto the floor next to the couch. *Thank God he's gone.* I buried my face in my hands for a moment, basking in the warm sunlight entering the wall of windows.

Roses showing up almost always meant something was about to be knocked off-kilter. In the same way headaches preceded a storm. I hated how my anxieties always proved themselves right. I remembered the email Eli had mentioned and scrambled to standing, heading for my laptop in the bedroom.

I had a half hour until my hourlong shift on the hotline began. It was a commitment I'd never wavered on, not since I made the decision to do anything possible to honor my brother. It was one way I could live in the memory of losing my older brother Chris to suicide. He'd taken his life my senior year of high school, when he was a sophomore in college and on track to become the person *I'd* become instead.

I'd partly chosen this path—Margulis Realty, Eli, and all—because he'd wanted me to. Because he knew I'd fulfill the duties that had been expected of him.

My family had forbidden me from acknowledging his suicide publicly. Nobody could. The official announcement had called it a kitchen accident. I'd watched firsthand as Chris strangled certain parts of himself in an attempt to conform to what our father, our world, demanded of him. Chris had forsaken his true love, theater performance, after my father found out Chris was slated to headline a small, artsy play in Chelsea. It wasn't long after that that Chris's mental health started to go downhill. The closer he got to assuming the role my father had groomed him for, the faster he spiraled into the abyss of his depression. And I just watched it all happen as a seventeen-year-old, too confused to figure out how to help my brother escape.

And now here I was, equally trapped and groping for an escape hatch.

But I couldn't talk about it with anyone. If the real reason behind Chris's death came out, it would result in total exile and financial ruin. And what was I if not a compliant little doll?

I might have Margulis blood running through me, but I didn't have the legal team necessary to face down my father.

The master bedroom of the condo was decorated plainly, a mass-appeal catch-all room for whoever might be using the space. Eli and I had bought the condo as a place to put up guests. Emergency lodging for family. It had never been intended to become *my* home.

While the spartan decorations and neutral tones weren't my favorite, I had no plans to improve the place. My escape plan wasn't solid yet, but I knew I couldn't continue on *here*.

After all, Eli had keys, and he loved to just waltz in whenever the mood struck him.

I couldn't live with that type of access. I could barely stand seeing him in the board room at scheduled meetings.

I booted up my laptop, which rested on the tan comforter of the king bed, then navigated quickly to my email, seeing a whole slew of new messages. I skipped past all the Margulis correspondence and headed straight for the most recent arrival, an email from Fairchild Wealth Management.

"We are extremely disappointed to hear of the board's decision to pass on our offer. The 10th Avenue building in Chelsea is truly a unique fit for our needs, and we are committed to sharing our vision with you, so that you will better understand the intended use. Please see the attached invitation, so that your company might learn more about our vision and our mission. Signed, The Fairchild Brothers."

My heart raced as I reread the email then opened the attachment. YOU ARE CORDIALLY INVITED... lined the top of the invitation in a formal script font. Below, the details of an upcoming fundraiser were laid out.

The Fairchild brothers were hosting a fundraising gala this weekend for their charity organization, Foster the Future. Dinner, drinks, and live entertainment would be provided.

The brothers were trying to sway the board. *Good on you, guys.* It might not help, especially if the other offer was truly so much higher. But there was time until the final vote. I had information that could help the brothers make an effective counteroffer. And maybe I could somehow become part of the future of the building too.

As much as I tried to ignore it, the building was calling to me. I didn't want to strip the opportunity from the brothers. But could we work together? That way I could see my own ideas brought to life without invoking the ire of my parents. Something that nodded toward suicide prevention, without needing to include the Margulis name in the press release.

Since this fundraiser wasn't on Fairchild property—*and* they'd extended a formal invitation—I felt confident that I could attend. I'd also be honoring Axel's demands. Win-win.

I could already imagine the annoyed look on Axel's face when I pointed this out to him. And I absolutely planned to.

I planned to become the unofficial negotiation liaison. Except I wasn't negotiating for the best interest of Margulis Realty. No, this was strictly for personal reasons. And beyond that, I wanted any excuse to get near Axel again. Even if all he did was act annoyed and ignore me.

The brushes of warmth I felt from him and his brothers were more comforting than anything I'd experienced in years. I was starved for the familiarity. For genuine people.

My ecosystem in Manhattan was getting sparser and less nourishing as time went on.

Something needed to change. And the only way forward that made sense was to get closer to the Fairchilds.

CHAPTER SEVEN

AXEL

"Hey, Axel, you ready?"

Damian's voice floated into my bedroom, where I'd been spending far too long obsessing over which cufflinks to choose for our black-tie fundraising event beginning in an hour. I usually went with the sterling silver with the stylized F of our logo, but tonight, I wanted something different.

I kept telling myself it was not because Cora might be in attendance.

"Help me pick my cufflinks," I called out. Zero stirred from beside my dresser, slightly annoyed that my loud voice had awoken him.

Damian's groan traveled through the doorway, but he appeared a moment later. "You spend more time getting ready than anyone I've ever met."

"Oh, please." I rolled my eyes at him. He was just as concerned with his appearance as the rest of us, just quieter about it. "Your barber comes to the penthouse daily, so don't even start." Damian's longish, dark blond hair required more upkeep than my simple haircut, so he had no room to speak.

"Every *other* day," he corrected with a smirk, coming up to the wide surface of my dresser. "Now what are the options?" He jerked his chin toward my snoozing dog. "Oh, hey, Zero."

I gestured toward the mirrored plate that held every cufflink I'd ever purchased. There were Gucci lapis lazuli cufflinks, New York Yankees studs, knotted sterling silver, as well as five different styles of Fairchild links. Damian barely looked at my stash for a few seconds before snatching up a pair of silver bears.

"Here. Use these." He held them out in his palm. "Kids will love them. Adults will think you're referencing the current bear market. And both of us will know that really, it was Jordan's favorite animal the last time we saw her."

I nodded, taking them from him. "Always gotta make it meaningful, don't you?"

"Everything I do." He sent me a warm smile. The man lived and breathed meaning. He barely took a shit in the morning without dedicating it to someone out there in the world. He watched as I inserted the cufflinks. "You feeling good about tonight?"

"Of course I'm feeling good," I lied. I had been on-and-off anxious since Trace sent the invitation to the Margulis camp. I knew why he did it—I'd even signed off on it. But that didn't mean I wasn't terrified that Cora would actually show. "Why wouldn't I feel good?"

He inspected his own cufflinks. "No reason."

"I'm fine."

"Okay." Damian shoved his hands in his pockets then, affecting a casual smile. "I'm done henpecking."

"Thanks. You and Trace really suck at the ex-fiancée check-in thing, you know that?" I clapped him on his shoulder, taking a moment to look him up and down. "Dang, Damian. You clean up nice. You fixin' to go home with a purty girl tonight?"

He laughed, shoving my shoulder. He hated it when I used the exaggerated Southern accent. Though when we got drunk enough, the accent came out regardless.

"No girl on my radar."

"None on mine either." If there were a lie detector anywhere, that statement would have gotten a harsh *buzz* from it. Because there had ever only been one girl. "I invited Mirabella though."

Damian nodded. "She's nice."

"Yeah. Nice." I laughed. Our hookups had nothing to do with her personality. Damian knew that. What Mirabella had in spades was the intoxicating power of stirring up zero emotion. She wasn't someone I dreamt about nightly, unlike a different brunette I wanted to stop thinking about. "Let's fucking rock this fundraiser."

We left my bedroom, both wishing Zero a pleasant nap. I wouldn't torture him with the party, which would only make him skittish. Our expensive dress shoes tapped softly against the tile floors. Trace waited in the foyer, looking at his phone.

"There you girls are," he said, pocketing his phone. "We ready now?"

"Yes, dad." I grinned over at him, appreciating his black suit and tie. We all wore the same designer—Gucci—but slightly different takes. The lapels of my suit, for instance, had a subtle matte black check that you could see only when the light hit it right. A small detail, but one that delighted me.

My brothers and I took the private elevator to the ground floor. Our Escalade, Harry behind the wheel, awaited us at the curb, hazard lights flashing. We loaded up and headed toward midtown. The fundraiser was one of two we held annually for our charity organization. Everything we raised went to the kids. But we needed more space. More capacity to help. Which was why the new building was so important.

I didn't believe for a second that the fundraiser would convince anyone over in Margulis Land. If they even showed up. After all, Cora herself had promised there would be no problem with the vote. And here we were.

We arrived at the Manhattan Manor to find the party in full swing. A string quartet had already started their set list, backed by the huge windows overlooking the theater district. Huge explosions of fresh floral bouquets lined the entryway, with matching centerpieces in the middle of every table in the venue. Along one brick-exposed wall, the artwork of our featured students was on prominent display. Immediately upon entering, Francis waved us down.

"The men of the hour!" His smile was a mile wide. His own Gucci suit, which the company had paid for as a work expense, shimmered a deep purple under the moody lighting. What Francis wanted, Francis got. "Things are progressing wonderfully." He lifted his wine glass. "I've personally tested all the appetizers, and they are to die for."

"What's the best one?" Damian asked.

"The curry balls," Francis gushed. "You have to try them."

While Damian and Francis chatted about the food and we made our way into the thick of the soiree, I scanned the crowd. I saw plenty of familiar faces—lots of waving and nodding as my gaze landed on each new attendee. But every time my gaze landed on one of our kids, my cheeks hurt from how hard I smiled.

That was what made us different. What the "rest of them" didn't like about us.

We invited the kids to the soirees. We showed them this slice of life. We helped them in every fucking way we could.

But I didn't see Cora.

I couldn't tell if I was relieved or disappointed.

"Hey there, stud." A soft voice at my ear set my muscles tightening. A hand snaked down to my ass, and from the squeeze alone I could tell it was Mirabella.

"Hey there." I offered my cheek for her to kiss, barely able to look her way. As my perpetual plus one, she attended all our galas. But fuck, I didn't want her here.

"Grab me a pinot?" she asked, trademark puffy lips tugged down into a pout.

"Give me a minute," I said, wrapping my arm around her waist. But the intimate touch was more performative than anything. She was elegantly thin, and depending when the runway events were, sometimes lived only on alcohol and celery. I couldn't figure out why I wanted her to get back into the Uber she'd come in. "I've gotta go check on the kids."

"You're such a nice rich guy," she said with a giggle.

"I try." I detached myself from her. Trace and Damian had become engrossed in conversation with other attendees. Francis had disappeared. I headed over to the kids area, where our event coordinator lingered, overseeing the kid experience. It was mostly teens here, though some recently aged-out participants in our academic booster program had come as well. *Foster the Future* helped kids excel in school, no matter the level, and prepared them for the future via apprenticeship programs and unique grant and affordable housing opportunities. I made the rounds, saying hello to everyone, asking them what they thought. They knew who I was, but only as they would an inattentive celebrity godfather. One of the girls even asked for my autograph, which I gladly gave.

I happened to look up in the middle of a conversation with an older boy named Derick about his plans to go into social work. I don't know what made me turn toward the coat check, but there she was. Cora. Sliding a golden bolero jacket off her shoulders to reveal a strappy black gown beneath.

Time seized and shuddered to a stop. Across the mahogany floors, bathed in natural light and violin music, Cora was the only thing I could see or focus on. Her glossy dark hair had been freed from the top knot she'd worn the last time I saw her. It cascaded over her shoulders in soft, intentional, perfectly arranged waves. She was stunning, the type of beauty that could make my stomach drop even when I was determined to hate her. Even after eight years of avoiding her.

Worse yet, from the looks of it, she'd come alone.

She must have heard my thoughts, felt my attention, because she turned to look my way, revealing her smoky eyes and perfect lips. Her green gaze snapped to mine, and we were suspended there, paralyzed by the connection, floating through space as the entire world around us vaulted away and faded into obscurity. I couldn't even say how long we were trapped there. Two seconds? An hour?

Whatever it was, it was too much. I yanked my attention from her, focusing on Derick again. We talked about his potential paths, traded ideas, and I expressed my confidence he would succeed. Then it was time for a trip to the bar. Mirabella wanted her pinot, but now I needed some whiskey. I headed for the mirrored bar, letting the sights and sounds of the fundraiser sink into me. The place was alive with energy, thrumming with conversation and clinking glasses. Every type of attendee mingled beneath the vaulted ceilings—angel investors, bigwigs, CEOs of every type of business you could imagine. And though Allan Margulis and his inner circle hated us, plenty of people didn't. Those were the people we counted on for events like these.

Yet every pulse of my heart wanted me to look for Cora. I forced myself to focus on the task at hand. Order whiskey and wine. Chat casually with whoever was beside me. *Do not look around. Do not look for Cora.*

I made it back to Mirabella with my imaginary blinders on. We circulated, sipping our drinks, accepting appetizers, while my heart thumped.

"Did you get a room for tonight?" she asked as she eyed a passing platter of shrimp cocktail.

"Do you want some shrimp?" I asked, jerking my thumb at the tray. I didn't want to answer her question.

"Hmm. Maybe one. But only one. I have a fitting tomorrow."

I hunted her down a single shrimp. And through the crowd, I found Cora's eyes waiting for mine.

Electricity sizzled through me, and I frowned, snatching up the food and turning to Mirabella. "Here you go." I could still feel Cora's gaze on me, so I pressed a kiss to the top of her head. "Enjoy."

She giggled again, looking up at me curiously. "You're a nice *and* affectionate rich guy."

"Come on. You should know this about me by now."

"I know a few things about you," she said with a wink before taking a delicate bite of the oversized shrimp.

I milled around with Mirabella for a bit, pausing to go horse around with the teens before they began their presentation to the guests. The kids were putting together a long-term project they wanted specific funding for—a STEM-inspired sculpture project that would combine metalwork and art. The finished piece would be displayed in the lobby of Fairchild Wealth. The kids we worked with were the coolest.

One whiskey turned into two. By the time I'd drained the second, warmth licked through me. And this time when I caught Cora's gaze across the room, I didn't feel the urge to ignore her.

No, I needed to confront her.

She chatted with Trace and Damian, looking as breezy and gorgeous as ever. Part of me knew this was what I could have had if we'd ended up together—catching her eye from across the room at high-class gatherings, joining the conversation with her and my brothers. Bringing her into my arms, disappearing into a room on the top floor once dinner and drinks were finished.

Just thinking about the life we'd lost still made my stomach bottom out. Cora filled my head and it drove me crazy. I'd managed to reduce the memories to a dull hum over the years, but even this distant inter-action—this animosity-laced orbit—was still too much.

Eight years should have been enough time to move the fuck on. The fact that I hadn't just made me feel ridiculous. Was this what soul mates felt like, something just shy of a mental illness?

"What are you staring at?" Mirabella searched the room, trying to follow my gaze.

"Hm?" I barely heard her over the raucous party of my thoughts.

"Tell me a celebrity arrived. Oh my God, who is it?"

Her voice registered as an irritating buzz, the type of noise I would swat away like a fly if I could, now that Cora was within arm's reeach. If *this* was what soul mates felt like, then I needed to buck up for a lifetime of madness. Because even though Cora was headed for a divorce, my sense of justice would not allow me to drop this grudge I held. I could hold a grudge longer than an ash-encrusted corpse held onto pottery in Pompeii. I'd be holding this grudge until scientists looked at my remains a thousand years from now.

Cora did not deserve reconciliation. She would not get it from me, no matter how much she claimed to support our efforts.

And since my heart and my brain were not on speaking terms these days, I needed to physically remove her from my line of vision.

Except that I couldn't stop staring.

"Axel, are you even listening to me?"

"I'm listening, Cora."

Mirabella's brows drew together, registering my slip before I did. "Cora? Who the hell is Cora."

"Mirabella. That's what I said." I swallowed hard, dropping my gaze to Mirabella for the briefest of glances. "Bella. You must have heard wrong."

Her side eye told me she didn't totally buy it, but things were fine for now.

"I gotta go have a chat with someone real quick," I told her. "I'll be back in a bit."

"Okay. I'll go mingle." She batted her eyes at me and pushed up onto her toes to plant a kiss on my lips. I stiffened, unsure how to respond. We didn't often kiss in public. In fact, we rarely showed any affection, save the occasional ass grab. Everything else was reserved for the bedroom. But maybe my Cora-induced flirtation had accidentally opened that door.

I headed across the room. Cora laughed with her hand pressed to her mouth. Trace was deep in storytelling when I got there, and I waited politely until he was done telling her about the time he'd accidentally offended the King of Morocco.

Trace clapped my shoulder when he was done with the story. "Wasn't that awful?"

"It was horrifying," I agreed, my gaze fixed on Cora. She straightened her back, biting back a smile. "I was wondering if I could show you some of the ongoing projects our charity is working on."

Her eyes lit up, as if she believed it was the olive branch I presented it as. Little did she know. "I would love that. Thank you, Axel."

"He is better equipped to present these projects than anyone else," Damian said.

I offered my brothers a tight smile and jerked my head so Cora would follow. We wound through the packed ballroom, heading for the kids area where the presentations had taken place.

"So you really showed up even though our offer was rejected?" I asked once we were standing in front of the display laying out the STEM-inspired project.

"Of course. The deal isn't dead." She sipped her white wine.

"Seemed pretty dead to me."

"There are avenues. If you look hard enough."

I faced her, crossing my arms. "I don't trust Margulis avenues."

"What do you want me to say? I'm working with you."

"Seems like you're putting up a front." The way my heart thumped against my ribs and my entire body went warm warned me that we should probably move this conversation somewhere more discreet. An arched doorway led to a service hallway behind us, and I nodded toward it. "Let's go talk in private."

She smirked. "You just love talking in private, don't you?"

"I don't want my guests knowing that I have anything to do with you."

Her cool smirk flickered, letting me know my barb had landed. When I headed for the hallway, she followed. And then we were tucked into the moodily lit alcove just off the main service hallway. The sounds of the party were dulled to an indistinct hum. The music sounded more like a soundtrack than a live group. Cora looked up at me, her sea foam green gaze robbing me of my words.

"Okay. Let's hear it." She gestured at me. "Give it to me, Axel."

But I couldn't give it to her. At least, not what she was expecting. Being this close to her, with this amount of whiskey pumping through my veins, only reminded me of the fact that we were alone. She was divorcing. And not a day had gone by that I hadn't wanted her.

I shook my head, looking away. "I told you to stay the fuck away from us."

"Ooh! I've been waiting for this." She laughed, jabbing me in the chest with the index finger of the hand holding her wine glass. "*You* invited *me*. Remember?"

"I didn't. Trace did."

"Yes, well, the invitation was signed *The Fairchild Brothers*, which I'm pretty sure includes you."

"Don't get sassy," I warned. "You know what the rules are, and you still showed up."

She chuckled throatily. "Sassy, huh? I'm just sending back what you're dishing out."

I dipped my chin. She and I had always had a special talent for the back and forth. I hated that *that* hadn't changed. I had to bite my tongue to keep it from going further. "Do you remember the agreement?"

"There was no agreement," she retorted. "Only demands from an angry Axel."

I couldn't rip my gaze from her mulberry pout as she spoke. Every detail of her was utterly edible. All the way down to the pearl earrings and the black polish on her toenails seen through her peep-toe shoes. She wore the same diamond pendant around her neck that I'd seen her wear on the other few occasions. I was dying to find out all the tiny details: where did the pendant come from, if the black dress she wore was as silky as it looked, to explore the dips and curves of the terrain beneath. I balled my hands into fists. *Stay the course.*

"The agreement was," I spat, "that you get us the building and stay the fuck away from us."

"What if getting the building involves me *not* staying away?" she challenged, mischief lighting up her sea foam gaze.

"I don't have time for your technicalities," I growled. I'd taken steps toward her without realizing it. Her shoulders bumped against the wall of the alcove and suddenly, somehow, our faces were mere inches away. "Do what I say, or just forget the entire thing."

"I said I'd work with you, and I'm doing that. You're the one who wants the building. So you have to play by *my* rules, too, Axel."

I pressed my palm to the wall beside her head. My resolve was slipping fast. Her nearness was a dizzying slope. One wrong step and I'd be a broken mess at the bottom.

But Cora's lips were so close. And there was nothing I wanted more than one last taste of her.

"Respect our territory," I said through gritted teeth.

"Like you're respecting mine?" Her voice came out a husky whisper. "Having me backed up against this wall?"

Her words jarred something loose inside me. My heart rate had skyrocketed, and my cock strained against the zipper of my suit pants. I tore myself away from her, drawing in a deep breath of cool air.

Fuck. That had been close.

I headed for the party, intent on either losing her or leaving immediately. But her voice pierced the air.

"Axel! Wait!"

I paused, not turning back to her.

"I have an idea. For getting you the building."

I clenched my fists and stared out at the party. "What is it?"

Her heels clicked closer to me. "I wasn't lying when I said I believed in your vision. Even after the completely unproductive *tour* you claimed to offer me."

"Just tell me," I snapped.

"I say we up the offer. But not you alone. I'll pitch in enough to beat the competing offer, since I know how much you'll need. But if I do this, I want your word that I can also use a small portion of the building for my own project. Under strict confidentiality, of course."

I turned to her, the idea hitting like a breath of fresh air even though I didn't fully understand how. "What on earth do you want the building for? It's already yours."

"Not mine," she said, peering up at me through her thick, dark lashes. "It's the company's. And what I want space for doesn't jive with the Margulis mission."

A million questions burbled to life inside me, but I tamped them down. Curiosity might be construed as me wanting to know about her life. I could not have that.

"If we raise the offer by at least three million, all of which will be my money, then the board will have to reconsider the sale. The vote is next week. We have time to get it in." Her heart-shaped face looked so earnest, so dedicated, I couldn't help but be swayed by her. Her throaty alto lured me into the idea like a siren's call. "I'll transfer the money to you on Monday as a sign of my commitment, if you agree. Even if you wait for the transfer to complete, you can have your offer in before the board meeting."

I swallowed hard, studying the contours of her face. In the amber shadows of the alcove, she looked like a goddess. Tantalizing, with unknown depths that sang to me, begged me to learn more. Every inch of me craved her, which was why my heart knew the best answer: *no.*

But logically, the offer was sound. Since she was offering her own money, I doubted this could be a scheme of some kind. She'd be risking a lot, using insider knowledge to snag the deal in our favor and going against her father's wishes, I was certain. If word got out, everything would tank. Not just our chance at the building, but her own position on the board.

The only problem was that if I agreed, I'd be seeing more of her.

Possibly a *lot* more.

I opened my mouth, and the words flew out before I could think better of it.

"Let's do it."

CHAPTER EIGHT

CORA

A now-distant college friend had once said after a recent breakup, "My ex isn't an asshole, he's the whole ass."

That's how I felt about Axel as I drifted through his gorgeous soiree, tethered to him by forces beyond my control. He made sure to keep an eye on me, the intolerable ass that he was. Smirking at me across the ballroom while he slung an arm around his perfect model of a girlfriend. Though I doubted she was his girlfriend. Maybe more like a hook-up. If she was really his girlfriend, she didn't seem to mind the way he paid her almost zero attention, except when it was convenient.

Or maybe I was just reading too much into things and hoping there was some glimmer of a chance for our own love story, still tucked away into a forgotten cavern of his heart.

I needed to hope for as much, because those twenty seconds of being a breath away from him in the alcove off the service hallway had about killed me. I needed to change my panties. I needed more Axel. Not just immediately, but forever. He got under my skin in a way I couldn't explain, much less rationalize. I didn't know what the future held, but I prayed Axel would be a part of it.

It seemed like a laughable fantasy, too outrageous to even consider. I might as well wish to teleport. I probably could invent teleportation myself before Axel would consider forgiving me.

But miracles could happen.

I'd felt the catch of his breath as he leaned in. He'd wanted to kiss me. And if our history proved anything, I was willing to bet he could still feel how my body had lit up at his nearness.

He still knew how to hear me begging for it.

And every inch of me was begging.

I needed to leave the party. I'd come, I'd made my offer, and now I was just being tormented. Axel woke me up, all the way down to my aching core. But without any chance for satisfaction on the horizon, I needed to head back to the condo and take matters into my own hands. Literally.

Axel and his plaything were gone when I made the decision to bolt. I hunted down Trace and Damian, who were once again wrapped up in conversations with powerful and important people, to say my goodbyes. I wouldn't bother trying to find Axel. We were tentatively en route to a business deal, but I knew he wouldn't appreciate any unnecessary niceties.

I headed to the coat check to retrieve my sparkling, golden bolero jacket. I slipped it on, feeling the mood burst that came whenever I wore it. I considered having my driver take me to a swank little cocktail lounge for a solo drink, but the thought of Eli finding out put a damper on my plan. No, it was better to head home and avoid any tabloid speculation about why Cora Margulis-Rossberg was drinking alone on the weekend. If Eli found out, he'd give me shit about why I'd shown my face without him, and I just didn't want the drama. At least with this fundraiser, I had a legitimate excuse—this was business related. I needed to do damage control after the Fairchild offer had been rejected. Even though the true reasons for my visit were vastly different.

I texted my driver as I meandered toward the gilded doors facing a bustling 7th Avenue. I pushed my way outside, taking a deep breath of the intoxicating evening air. Dusk was just wrapping Manhattan in a dark velvet embrace, though it was almost nine p.m. I loved the ethereal, late-daylight evenings of summer in the city. It felt like we were all operating on borrowed time. Car horns honked, swelling like an orchestral moment.

And in front of me, Axel and his plaything were grinning like fools at each other. She swayed back and forth in front of him, her loose dress swishing seductively around her body. Though I couldn't hear them, I could only assume they were sharing sweet words with their eyes locked. The humidity of the night clawed at me. I was suddenly uncomfortable in my bolero, but it was easy to blame the late heat. I slipped my jacket off and hung it over my arm.

Axel cracked a grin, and I had to look away. It shouldn't hurt to see, because I'd not only dated someone else but *married* someone else. But if I'd had my way, Axel and I would have never been apart. We would be the couple on the sidewalk of 7th Avenue, staring into each other's eyes without a care in the world.

I feigned an intense search for my driver while Axel loaded up his arm candy—or maybe serious girlfriend now, I couldn't tell—into the car. The door shut, and he tapped the back window. The car drove away a moment later, and Axel sauntered back toward the building. His cool grin faltered when his gaze landed on me.

I watched him for a moment too long, paralyzed by indecision. I wanted to needle him. To tease him. To do anything possible to get him near me again. I was ensnared by his magnetism and repelled by his death stare.

"Thanks for the party," I finally said when he'd almost passed me.

He didn't stop walking. "Glad you approve."

"I'm sad to see your girlfriend go," I called out over my shoulder. What was I doing? He stopped walking at that one. He turned slowly, curiosity tugging at his features.

"Excuse me?"

"She seems really nice. I'm glad to see you've, you know, got someone." The white wine I'd consumed feverishly after the confrontation with Axel zipped through me, pushing me toward a wild abandon. Would I regret or relish this tomorrow? It was anybody's guess. "You guys are cute together."

"I don't care what you think. And I would rather you don't speak to me until you have some good news about the building," Axel said. His blue gaze acted like a whip against my skin. Even though it hurt, I couldn't look away. "Let's keep the dialogue to a minimum. And please don't comment on my life again."

He was so rude. The entire ass. But all I could do was laugh. God, it was refreshing. I deserved it, *and* he was so good at this. I wanted to return his hard edges, but more than anything, his coldness just made me nostalgic for all the warmth we'd once shared.

"Fine. I'll keep the dialogue to a minimum. Gosh, I'm going to need a pen and paper to write down all these rules." I pretended to search my body, as though I'd misplaced my notebook. "Give me a second to jot this down."

His eyes narrowed. "Shouldn't be hard to remember. All it requires is staying away from me, saying nothing, and fulfilling your end of the deal."

"How are we going to pull off this deal if we don't talk?" I flipped my hair over my shoulder. "Don't be ridiculous."

His gaze dropped to the shoulder my hair flip had revealed. His jaw flexed before his gaze snapped back up to my eyes. People filed past us on the sidewalk, oblivious to the lightning shooting jagged and hot between us.

"How about your phone number? Would texting better comply with the rules?" I suggested.

"You should have it. Unless it's still blocked." His face was a perfect mask of disinterested neutrality.

I swallowed hard. I didn't have it in my phone, but I still knew it. The numbers had been etched into my heart after all the times I'd had to subvert my father's phone plan in order to call him. I'd used friends' phones. Domestic employees' phones. I would have used a payphone if I could have found one on the Stanford campus.

My phone vibrated with a text from the driver. I saw him pull up to the curb a moment later.

"Great. I'll reach out that way then. Anything to make you more comfortable, Axel." I blew him a kiss. His nostrils flared. "Have a good night."

I headed for the car, heels clicking over the cement sidewalk. I could feel Axel's eyes on me as I walked away. Once I'd slipped into the backseat, safe behind the tinted windows, I searched the sidewalk for him.

He was gone.

The drive back to the condo was both dreamy and tense. Manhattan had a way of seducing me during my commutes, luring me into the flashes of life and light that throbbed from all angles. The city was bathed in the highs and lows of human turmoil and vibrancy. Anything you wanted to feel or see, you could tease out from the tangle of life beyond the window. Tonight, all I could glean from the streets around me was urgency.

The thumping of my heart pushed me toward an outcome I didn't know how to reach quite yet. I just knew I needed to get there.

I needed Eli out of my life.

And I needed *something* from Axel—whether it was one genuine hug or that wild fantasy of forgiveness.

Back at the condo, I let myself inside with tense expectation. Was Eli here? Would he be arriving later? I hated that he still felt like he could waltz in whenever he wanted. He couldn't be stupid enough to think that I wanted him here. And I doubted he actually wanted to make things better with me. He couldn't. Not with how disparagingly he talked to me and about me.

But my condo was dark and quiet. Light from the streets below filtered into the living room through the enormous windows, illuminating the edges of furniture, the sleek curve of a vase. I listened to the quiet for a moment, letting out a deep exhale.

I knew what I needed *now*.

I tossed my purse and bolero jacket onto the couch, and drifted toward my favorite chair in the living room. It was enormous, overstuffed, big enough for three people, with golden piping along the seams that matched the sectional.

And perfect for the pressing task at hand.

Getting my hand into my panties.

I kicked off my heels, settling back into the insanely comfy seat. I kicked my leg up over the arm, my dress gathering naturally at my waist. My hips bucked, my core already tight with need. I hadn't had sex in what felt like years, but it was closer to six months. The last time Eli and I had fucked, I hadn't wanted to. I'd done it to shut him up.

Now the stuff of my fantasies was raw desire. Unabashed sex and gluttonous horniness. I got off now by imagining what true, bona fide, mutually desired fucking felt like. It had been so long since I'd felt that. Actual years. The mere idea seemed like something pornographic.

Only one man had ever pushed me into raw abandon. And he'd spent the entire evening commanding me not to talk to him.

My fingers danced along the crotch of my panties. I was soaked; I had been since spotting Axel at the fundraiser. One look from that man was all it took. If only he'd known how badly I needed him, how much I'd have given to have one last night with him.

I whimpered as I plunged one finger inside myself, and then another. It wasn't anywhere close to what I wanted—the steel heat of Axel. Through the windows, the dark shadows of the Central Park treetops moved in the breeze, and I could almost imagine myself back in Kentucky with him. Every time we'd made love had been memorable, but for some reason, when we went to Kentucky it was fucking epic. Like some part of him became unhinged in his hometown.

I could practically hear the way Axel used to groan when he pushed into me. All the dirty things he'd whisper about how fucking wet I was, how absolutely tight and perfect for him. In Kentucky, we'd made love outside on a blanket, wrapped up in the sweet scent of wild grasses and hay. I could almost smell it if I tried. My eyes drifted shut as the memories took over, mingling with fantasy.

The Axel I pictured was the new Axel, the man who filled out his suits and growled when I came too close. He was a man who'd press me up against the wall of a back hallway and—in my fantasies now—threaten to have his way with me. All the images of Kentucky faded away as I imagined exactly how that encounter at his party *should* have ended. With his cock buried inside me. His mouth covering mine. His fingers tangling in my hair as he reminded me, just as he always used to, who loved me most.

My fingers slipped over the tight bud of my clit. I was desperate and clumsy, and I still came lightning fast. I cried out as my orgasm flashed through me, hot and wild. My leg spasmed, and I arched back into the seat.

My heart pounded as I drew deep breaths, watching the dark movements of the treetops over Central Park.

I hadn't been this turned on in ages. And the release was only the tip of the iceberg.

Thank God I'd started down the path of getting what I, and Axel, ultimately wanted. I needed to get closer to him. So much closer.

The only thing that would satisfy this desire was Axel himself.

CHAPTER NINE

AXEL

Mondays were usually my focus days.

There was something extra appealing about starting a week off right with a fresh start, goalsetting, and good teambuilding. Francis and my brothers and I usually had check-in meetings first thing in the morning, followed by a whole lot of motivational check-ins through lunchtime.

But on this Monday, I cancelled everything except the morning meeting.

I was only available for one thing: stewing in my office, waiting to find out whether Cora would make good on her plan.

I'd been pacing along my office windows, looking out over the city, trying to imagine what truly lay around this next corner. Part of me couldn't believe Cora needed the building for anything, especially since she already basically owned it. But a deeper part of me knew where her words came from. Her father controlled everything with an iron fist. If she needed it for something he wouldn't approve of, she needed to get crafty to escape his notice. And using me for cover was a surefire way to escape notice.

I hated how Cora could disrupt everything. My gala. My Monday. Even my chance to get laid. I was done with Mirabella after our too-flirty evening at the fundraiser. I couldn't even stomach the idea of fucking her again. Cora was an expert at destroying my peace.

Maybe I'd prove to myself that she couldn't destroy my peace any longer. Just because I'd wasted half a day pacing my office, mired in anxiety, it didn't have to be like this forever. Either the building deal would happen or it wouldn't.

And I had a weird suspicion that it would.

Francis delivered lunch wordlessly, knowing that I needed my space. I picked at my gourmet deli sandwiches—I always called them the "Lunchables with a retirement plan"—stuffed with microgreens and cured meats. I popped exotic cheese cubes into my mouth as I thought, sipped on sparkling water as I waited.

Finally the call came.

Francis buzzed. "Axel, you have a *visitor.*"

I knew by the drop in his voice that he meant Cora. "Send her in."

"You were expecting her?" he asked, but I didn't respond. He was probing for information, but he wouldn't get it. Not now. Not when I was torn up inside, waiting to see her again.

It had always been like that with her. One step short of a Slip 'n Slide. All it took was a gentle tap—not even a push—and I'd go tumbling down the slick chute.

I just couldn't tell if she'd pushed me or if I'd taken a running leap.

A soft knock sounded a moment later. "Come in," I barked.

The door creaked open. Cora's head popped in past the doorframe, a mischievous smile tugging at her mulberry lips. Her glossy dark-chocolate locks were pulled up into a smart bun. She wore dark frame glasses that were too trendy to be prescription. Besides, I knew she didn't need glasses.

"Permission to enter?"

I smirked. "Granted."

She strode inside, her smooth calves flexing atop designer heels. The door clicked shut behind her, and she took a deep breath once it was just us.

In here. Together. Alone.

Fuck.

"Permission to speak?"

"Cora, cut the crap." I tried my best to sound annoyed. I really did. But of course I was amused. God, I hated how refreshing it was to still catch glimpses of the woman I'd known and loved.

She pursed her lips into a strange smile as she sauntered toward my desk. "Well, I wasn't sure after the weekend. Do you remember? You told me to keep the dialogue to a minimum."

"Which I see you're not obeying."

"Oh. *Obeying*, huh?" She lifted a brow. "Do you want me to sit on command, also?"

"I don't know." I feigned boredom, blinking slowly as I struggled to memorize every detail about her. The form-fitting emerald green dress that went down to mid-thigh. Nude heels. The blush in her neck that told me she was loving this as much as I was. "How about you sit the fuck down and we'll find out?"

She grinned this time. "I don't think so, Axel. That's too blatant."

"Well, you're barking up the wrong tree if you expect me to be subtle." I came around my desk, my hands clasped behind my back. I didn't know where this was headed, only that I needed the challenge almost more than I needed air.

"Ahh, yes. Barking. That's what I should have come in here doing, since you've forbidden me from dialogue. My continuing use of words is allowed, then, right? Because this deal will require communicating, and I don't plan on using smoke signals."

I came to a stop in front of her, running my tongue along the inside of my cheek. She faced me, her back straight, as poised and confident as ever. I hated her for it as much as I loved her for it.

"To be honest, smoke signals do sound preferable to continuing this ridiculous conversation," I said.

She arched a brow. "Me ponying up three million dollars is ridiculous?"

"Where's the money?"

Cora blinked demurely. "Is that how you close all your deals?"

"Only the deals that I don't enjoy being in."

Her lips curled up at the corners. "I stuffed all the money into my bra."

I looked at the ceiling. I'd somehow gotten close—too close—to her again. But I wouldn't let the same thing happen here that had happened at the fundraiser. That had been because of *alcohol*. But now I had my wits about me. I could control myself.

"You said you'd have the money today, and I don't see it. So please, enlighten me."

She leaned against the edge of my desk, and I caught a whiff of her scent, that luxurious fruity and floral mix. Her satisfied smile irked me...but only because I wanted to wipe it off her face with my lips.

The longer she sat here, the harder it was to look at anything that wasn't her mouth.

Or that glinting diamond pendant dangling around her neck, heading toward the breasts I'd imagined cupping too many times over the weeks.

Or the impeccable emerald-green fabric covering the body I would have given anything to see laid bare.

Or the sleek thighs that I'd kissed my way up too many times to count.

"I don't know, Axel. I'm not sure I can tell you anything unless you back me up against a wall again." She cocked her head, mischief dancing in her gaze. "That really helped negotiations, don't you think?"

She was provoking me. Teasing me. Intentionally pushing all my buttons. But I couldn't resist. I stepped forward, bridging the small distance between us, placing my palms on either side of her ass on the surface of my desk.

"Whatever it takes to close the deal," I said, suddenly realizing just how close we were. The good girl/bad girl, fruity-floral mix of her scent was a mindfuck, and all I could see was the fullness of her lips. The mere inches that separated us. The delight in her gaze as I edged closer. My cock was rock hard already, and I hadn't even touched her.

"So?" I prompted. "I've got you cornered how you like. Now spill it."

A flimsy laugh fluttered out of her, but it faded quickly. She was reacting to the nearness as well. Her cheeks had flushed. Her chest rose more quickly now. And I could see the pebbling tips of her nipples beneath the dress.

Fuck. I surged forward, claiming the kiss I'd been fantasizing about. She'd been goading me enough. Now here it was—the final piece she needed to know she had me where she wanted me. I lied to myself, telling myself this was just a part of the negotiations. Cora wanted to somehow provoke me via seduction before moving forward with the deal. Sure.

Whatever I needed to tell myself in order to feel less like a chump who was a victim of his own desires.

Our mouths met hungrily. The heat surprised me. It had been so long, and for some reason I thought she'd have fangs by now. But no. She was silk and warmth, the sweetness and hunger of pure woman. She reached for my shoulder, digging her nails into the seam of my suit coat.

We kissed and kissed. And fucking kissed some more.

There was not a single blood cell in my body that was not heading to my cock. My head was spinning, completely derelict in its duty to rule my body with reason and logic. The only thing that made sense right now was Cora. And I'd be lying if I said I hadn't been waiting for this moment for eight fucking years.

My tongue plunged into her mouth. I wanted to taste her. I wanted to consume her. I wanted to fuck her into oblivion and then forget about her for the rest of my life.

She whimpered, the type of raw noise that served to quadruple the amount of testosterone thrumming through me. I took her face in my hands, fingertips digging into her scalp behind her ears. She was mine. For now. Right now. All mine.

Our lips danced in perfect union. We'd always known how to fucking kiss, and that hadn't changed. In fact, it was a little annoying. If anything, I'd have expected my memories to be better than the reality. After all, I'd had almost a decade to inflate things in my mind.

But no. It was as good as I fucking remembered. Like that realization helped things at all.

Cora wriggled her hips, her dress bunching higher. She pushed her hands inside my suit coat, groping desperately for my waist. She tugged me forward, bringing my body crashing between her spread legs. The haze of seduction grew thicker. A noxious fog that consumed me.

"Is this how you close deals?" I asked her, dragging my lips down the side of her neck. She bucked her hips, squeezing me between her thighs. She had to feel my cock by now. The warmth between her legs was the most intoxicating promise. Somewhere deep inside me, an alarm was going off. *Get away from her. Get out of this. Go.*

"Only the ones I *really* want to be in," she whispered huskily.

I tugged at her ear lobe with my teeth. "Fuck you."

"Will you?"

I squeezed my eyes shut. I'd fuck her a million times. Even though I shouldn't. But that part of my brain wasn't operating anymore.

Thud thud thud.

I looked over my shoulder at the door.

"Axel, you got a second?" It was Damian. God dammit. I could hear the proverbial brakes screeching.

I swore, tearing myself away from Cora. I glared at her as I went behind my desk. "Sit down."

She didn't give me any sass this time. She slid into the seat facing my desk and adjusted her dress. I sat behind my desk, adjusting my raging hard-on as I cleared my throat. I didn't know what I wanted more—to send Damian away and finish what I started with Cora or throw her out of the building and tell her to keep her money.

"Come in," I called, just as Cora fished a mirror out of her handbag to touch up her lipstick.

The door opened and Damian walked in, looking equal parts curious and elated. He jerked his thumb toward the hallway beyond the door. "So. This thumb drive of cryptocurrency Francis just told me about. Anyone care to explain?"

Cora fixed me with a satisfied smile before looking back at Damian. "That's part of the deal I made with Axel. I was hoping he would have explained the terms to you. But now, you three can make your offer to Margulis Realty, and this time, you won't be outbid."

My heart thumped in my chest as I looked between Damian and Cora. I still couldn't wrap my head around seeing Cora sitting in my visitor's chair. And I had to contend with the fact that I'd nearly sucked her face off, on top of it all.

This was what Damian had been afraid of, why my brothers kept checking in on me.

I hated that I'd given in to my curiosity. To the long-simmering desire. I didn't know where to go from here. I'd mouth-fucked her on a rumor that she wanted to divorce her husband. But she hadn't done it yet. And I had no idea what else was going on in her life. Whether it would be happening soon, or ever.

You fucked up.

"How much is on there?" Damian asked.

"Three million," Cora responded coolly. "A little over, based on the trading rate when I last checked. But feel free to keep the overage." To me, she said, "This is the Bitcoin you convinced me to invest in during my last year at Stanford. So thanks for the tip. I think it will serve us all well."

I clenched my jaw, determined not to let that little tidbit win me over. The full-circle use of cryptocurrency that I'd encouraged her to dabble in was heartwarming—of course it was. But I was not in a position let Cora warm my heart.

Damian blinked. "Does Trace know about this?"

"Not yet," I said. "I wanted to be sure this was happening before I told you two. And, well, it looks like it's happening."

Damian nodded, a genuine smile on his face. "Well. This is great news for a Monday. What's the stipulation?"

Cora laughed, because of course a thumb drive giving us access to the equivalent of three million dollars came with a stipulation. "I need to use a portion of the building for my own non-profit purposes. My use will not be attached to the Margulis name or mission and must be kept confidential."

His brows drew together. "Okay. Give me a ballpark of your intended use."

"LGBTQ Theater."

Her words hit my heart like an arrow. I knew exactly what she wanted to accomplish and why. And fuck if it didn't soften me up after I'd just decided to close myself off to her again.

"Sounds great to me," Damian said. "I'll go tell big bro."

"Uh, Damian, will you see Cora out?" Regardless of her altruistic endeavor, I needed her out of my office. Because two seconds alone with her would lead us right back to where we'd left off. And however much I wanted to go down that path, I knew we shouldn't. Couldn't.

Cora whipped around to look at me, something fierce in her gaze. "Shouldn't we talk over some of the details—"

"No, I think we've got everything clear." I sent her a strained smile. "I really appreciate you coming by." *Now get the fuck out, or I will fuck the shit out of you.*

Cora dipped her chin, sending me a dark look bathed in disappointment. But I couldn't afford to care. My cock was disappointed, sure. But now that my brain had rumbled back to life, I knew what needed to be done.

I'd gotten my taste. That had to be enough.

"Once you tell Trace, let's have Francis send over the updated offer," I called out to Damian while Cora gathered her things.

"Roger that." Damian waited outside my door as Cora checked her handbag and stood.

"Are you sure you don't want to—"

"We're good. It's been great doing business with you, Cora. Maybe I'll see you around sometime." I sent her the most genuine smile I could muster—which wasn't very successful—as she flattened the front of her dress. With a final intense look, she headed for the door.

My brother led her away, and I took one last look at her perfect figure in that emerald green dress.

It had to be my last taste of her.

Because no amount of stolen kisses in my office would erase the truth that at the end of the day, she was Cora Margulis-*Rossberg*.

CHAPTER TEN

AXEL

Our offer was in that Monday afternoon.

The board voted on Friday morning.

And Saturday night, my brothers and I were out in Manhattan, celebrating our status as the future owners of the building on Tenth Avenue.

We had opted for a French bistro in SoHo to celebrate. I couldn't believe the Margulis board had voted to sell to us, but Cora had been right. Her extra money had paved the way. Whether this would prove to be a scheme of hers was still up for debate, but it had been her funds, not ours, that got the deal done. And now all we had to do was wait for our legal teams to finish up the details.

Damian, Trace, and I waltzed into La Fève in our Wall Street finest. I'd opted for dark slacks, alligator shoes, and a light gray button-up with the sleeves rolled up, exposing all the colorful details of the tattoos on my neck and arms: Jordan and Kaylee's names, . As we stepped into the intimate, cluttered setting of La Fève, a hostess leading us to our reserved table, I scanned the restaurant for familiar faces.

There was always someone we knew when we went out. That was the nature of the Wall Street beast. We were incredibly connected—for better and for worse.

Usually my brothers made sure there was nobody unsavory on the premises before we sat down. And by "nobody unsavory," I specifically meant anyone from the Margulis family.

Maybe it was because Cora had been within a ten-foot radius of me on multiple occasions recently that my brothers let their guard down. Or maybe they'd simply forgotten to check. But for whatever reason, it was *me,* not my brothers, who first noticed the Margulis family, tucked into their little VIP table, set above the regular floor and protected by golden railing.

Cora, her parents, and the charming Eli.

"Oh Jesus," I muttered as my gaze landed on their little party. They hadn't noticed us yet.

"What is it?" Damian asked.

"The nation's foremost realtor is in attendance," I spat as we gathered at our round table. The hostess left us with menus, and we settled into our seats.

Trace looked around briefly before spotting them himself. "Should we go?"

Damian nodded. "I'm cool if you wanna go somewhere else."

"No, no. It's fine." A month ago, it would not have been fine. I would have demanded we leave. We had a history of executing one-eighties when anyone Margulis was on the premises. But tonight, I wanted to stand my ground. Even though I'd learned just how devastating it was to be around Cora again, I didn't want to back down.

"You sure?" Damian asked, in his stern but affectionate way.

"I think we should send them a round of drinks." I could feel the mischievous smile taking over my face. "To celebrate their outrageously overpriced sale."

I watched the Margulis table intently. Cora glanced over, and though a crowd of people separated us, I could feel the electricity snapping between us. Worse, I could still taste her lips from our incredibly hot make out session earlier that week. I might have used the memories of those kisses a time or ten while pumping my cock to ecstasy in my shower over the past week. But nobody had to know that. Cora would certainly never know.

Nor would I ever make that mistake again.

Because no matter how much the chemistry was alive between us, there was one simple fact. She hadn't divorced Eli, and from the looks of it, didn't intend to. You didn't dine out with your parents and the man you were separated from on a Saturday night in SoHo. Simple facts.

Eli's arm draped protectively over the back of her chair. Allan and his wife Bernadette looked around the room smugly while Eli the douche nozzle yammered on about God knew what—probably his fucking fleet of helicopters and how many one must own before they had the authority to speak to him about it.

If I'd had no intention of getting near Cora over the last eight years, I was even less inclined to get enmeshed in whatever *that* party was over there. But it didn't mean I couldn't fuck with them a little bit.

"Axel." Damian snapped his fingers. "I said what red do you want?"

I looked guiltily between my brothers. A server stood at the edge of our table, looking uncomfortable.

"Sangiovese," I blurted, the first thing that came to mind. "Whatever the best is."

Trace rolled his eyes as the server hustled away.

"Try not to be so blatantly absorbed in Cora next time," Damian muttered.

"I'm not," I lied. "I was just thinking about how much I'd like to celebrate with Allan, you know?" I rested my elbow on the table, angling my body toward the Margulis-Rossberg clan. "I'm thinking I might send them a round of shots. That way, we can all toast to our new future."

Trace leveled me with a stern look. "How about no?"

"Don't bother," Damian said, waving him off. "He's already made up his mind."

"Damn straight I have." I interlocked my fingers as I sent my brothers a devilish grin. "I just think that forcing Allan to sell to us deserves a toast. We know he tried his best to avoid this outcome, and he failed. We need to commemorate this momentous occasion."

When the server returned with a bottle of Sangiovese and three wine glasses, I lifted my index finger while my eyes stayed on Allan's table. Eli and Allan had their heads together, deep in conversation about something. I wondered why *they* hadn't gotten married instead. Cora and her mother weren't speaking, a similar melancholy pulled tight around them as they focused on their meals.

"I'd like to send a round of shots for this table and for that table over there." I smiled up at our server. "The Margulis-Rossberg party. The table with the golden rope, so we know how special and untouchable they are."

The server's eyes darted in the direction of Allan's table, and he nodded. "Absolutely. Any drink in particular you'd like to send?"

"We're celebrating the purchase of a very expensive building from Mr. Golden Ropes. What would you recommend?"

The server rattled off some options. I nodded along, picked the most exotic sounding whiskey, and leaned back in my seat. Mission accomplished.

Trace looked like he was fighting back a smile. "Mr. Golden Ropes?"

I laughed, and soon Damian joined in. But when I caught another glimpse of Cora, this time with Eli whispering into her ear as if they were moments away from heading back to the bedroom, my chest cinched tight.

I was not okay with this situation. Whatever she'd told Trace must have been a lie. And though she'd ponied up three million for the building, I couldn't believe for a second what she'd told me about not being happy since breaking up with me. She had an ulterior motive somewhere. I couldn't trust her. Even though I could feel the unhappiness radiating off of her with Eli at her side—practically like an oily film coating her—I couldn't allow myself to believe it. Because believing that we still had that connection would only lead to my downfall.

As long as she was at Eli's side, I couldn't afford to listen to that whisper inside me.

The server returned with our shots, setting them on the table one by one before heading to Cora's table with theirs. I watched as our server delivered them to the now bewildered-looking Allan and Eli. Cora's mother barely registered any expression as she received hers. But Cora's gaze found mine immediately, the start of a smirk on her lips.

"To the new building!" I called out loud enough for my voice to reach them over the din of the restaurant. I lifted my shot glass. My brothers followed suit while I amped up my smile. Allan glowered. I had not received such potent stink eye from anyone in my life. God bless that man's capacity for disdain. I downed my shot in a gulp; Damian and Trace followed suit.

"Do you think they'll drink them?" Trace set his empty shot glass in the center of our table.

"I couldn't fucking care less," I muttered, relishing the hot sting of the whiskey down my throat. "We should get some snacks, yeah? Maybe a steak?"

"Steak tartare," Damian said, pointing at something on the menu. "And more shots. That shit was good."

"Now, now, Damian. Don't go hog wild celebrating," I chided him jokingly.

"It's a Saturday in SoHo. I do what I want." He twisted, flagging down the server. We ordered a sumptuous dinner feast and another round of shots, and I relaxed into my chair sipping on Sangiovese. Life was pretty damn good, as long as I could keep my mind off Cora.

That had been and would continue to be one of the sad truths of my life. I just wondered how many more years it might take for me to accept it.

My phone vibrated with an incoming text.

CORA: Meet me by the bathrooms?

I frowned down at my phone and tapped out my response.

AXEL: No.

CORA: I thought we were celebrating the purchase.

AXEL: Celebration is over.

CORA: Fine. Then I have a complaint.

I tamped down my amusement. I would not look over at her table. I sipped my wine, eyes widening as the server returned with more shots.

"We're gonna be toasted before the bread is," Trace said, receiving his whiskey.

My brothers and I clinked glasses and downed our shots together. Afterward, we made varying grunts of appreciation.

CORA: Don't make me beg.

AXEL: Maybe I should.

Across the room, Cora dabbed at her mouth with a cloth napkin, set it aside, and stood. She wore a short, floral-patterned dress with a boatneck that showcased the ridges of her collarbone. The only way to prevent me from staring would have been to remove my eyeballs. She snagged my gaze as she stepped down from the VIP perch and wound her way through the carpeted restaurant toward the bathrooms.

Cora's gaze seared into me. I wouldn't be surprised if I found scorch marks across my chest later.

I didn't want to follow her.

Lie—*I did.*

I knew I *shouldn't.*

But a few of my vital organs weren't speaking, and this time, the one that shouted loudest was my cock.

"I'll be right back, guys," I said, setting aside my napkin. I took a fortifying gulp of wine. Between the whiskey and the Sangiovese, my body was abuzz with bliss and mischief. "I've gotta go do something."

Damien fixed me with a look.

"The bathroom," I said, standing. "I've gotta go pee. That's all. God, why are you two looking at me like that?"

Damian lifted his glass to me while Trace delivered another round of judgmental eyebrows. I left them behind and sauntered through the restaurant, adjusting the rolled-up cuffs of my shirt as I went. Every thump of my heart told me this Cora encounter wasn't just a bad idea, it was batshit crazy. Both her father *and* her husband were fifty feet away.

But who was I if not batshit crazy?

Jazz music wafted through the restaurant, barely noticeable over the clamor of voices and conversation. I tucked my hands into the pockets of my slacks and headed for the back of the restaurant. The air was warm and scented, notes of garlic mingling with onion taking me back to my childhood home, with my biological parents. Back to the contentment before the crash. The anticipation of dinner with my loved ones safe all around me.

Now, my anticipation was laced with something much fiercer, much more intense, than in those childhood days. I wanted Cora in a way I couldn't rationalize. In a way I refused to allow.

Yet here I was. Taking the bait.

I maneuvered toward the open doorway with a 1940's-style drawing of a toilet above it. I spotted her in the shadowed corner of the hallway. Half-lit and fully tempting. Cora's eyes nearly glowed in the dim lighting as she pressed one shoulder into the wall, watching me. I took a few steps toward her—the only confirmation she'd get for now that I intended to fling myself into whatever trap this was—and a smile tugged at her lips.

This was a cat and mouse game if I'd ever seen one. Cora disappeared around a corner. She could have been leading me into a poison chamber and I would have gone in behind her. When I rounded the corner after her, she stood with her back against the wall. Her cool hand shot out to grab my wrist, and everything that wasn't Cora faded from view.

It was just us. Alone. Again.

I didn't blink. I didn't breathe. I sure as hell didn't move. But somehow, we were pressed together against the faded floral wallpaper of La Fève . My palms were glued to the wall on either side of her head—though I wasn't sure if it was to keep her where she was, or prepping myself to bolt.

"What do you want?" I growled, my lips already dangerously close to her face. If I angled myself right, my mouth would graze her cheek. And there could be none of that.

"Talk to me," she said, her words floating on a gasp.

"I answered your texts. We don't need to dialogue," I said, my gaze bouncing across her face and gobbling up all the minute details. The silver shimmer of her eyelids. The gut-punch green of her eyes. The mischievous smile that I had dreamed of so many times after we broke up that I'd probably still see it when I was dead. "In any format. Remember?"

"Okay. Then why did you follow me?"

"I got lost on my way to the bathroom."

She laughed sharply, her breath hitting my nose. I caught a hint of wine there. Every inch of my body constricted, wanting more. Wanting to cover that mulberry mouth with my own. Wanting to hoist her into my arms and have my way with her, back hallway etiquette be damned.

"We should finish what we started in your office," she said, arching herself so that her chest brushed mine. My fingertips curled into the wall.

"No."

Disappointment flashed across her face. "Why not?"

"Your sweet and understanding husband is here."

She crumpled slightly.

"I heard you were getting a divorce, but it seems like that's not really the priority."

Her eyes sharpened to gemstones, practically drawing blood as they whipped across my face. "This is a delicate departure. I thought maybe you could appreciate that, at least. I can't just serve him papers and be on my merry way. I need to have a fucking plan."

"And your plan is to fuck around with Axel Fairchild until we get caught?" I laughed snidely. "No thanks."

"Then go."

I clenched my teeth. What a delightful way to call me on my bullshit. When I didn't leave, her smile spread like a wine stain on white cloth.

"You shouldn't be back here with me," she whispered huskily, arching her body toward me again.

But her words were pure posturing.

She just wanted to push my buttons. And I was the dumb sap who wanted her to push them.

CHAPTER ELEVEN

I knew this was wrong.

Everything I was doing—luring Axel to a back hallway, stoking this passion while Eli and my father were so close by—was wronger than wrong.

But hell if I could stop.

My desperation knew no limits. Every time I committed to tamping things down, here I went again.

It was just...I needed to taste him again. To feel his hands on my body. I needed his cock buried so deep inside me that I wouldn't be able to walk the next day. I needed to remember what it felt like to be desired. To be with someone who knew the depths of my soul and didn't tell me to fix something. That had been Axel, before I'd detonated everything.

Axel was the only person in my life who'd seen my softest and most-scarred parts and didn't ask me to hide them.

I needed Axel Fairchild in every conceivable way and then some.

"Don't look if you can't handle the show," I told him. My heart raced so fast I thought I might pass out. Why wouldn't he touch me? I was seconds away from throwing myself on him. I rolled the diamond pendant between my fingers, the only way to calm and control myself.

"What show?" he growled.

"The show I'm putting on with Eli," I told him.

"You guys looked pretty fucking content," Axel said, and he pushed away from me. My arms shot out to grab him by the waist. He couldn't leave now. Not when we were so close to a breakthrough. To something *more*.

"I told you, it's delicate." I swallowed a knot in my throat. "I'm biding my time and getting things ready until I have everything in order. We've been living apart for the past few months, but he still doesn't get how serious I am."

Axel's sky blue gaze focused in again, his pupils widening. "Living apart?"

"I've been in our condo at Central Park." I swallowed hard, wondering how many details I could share before I ruined the vibe altogether. "He's stayed at our brownstone on the Upper West Side."

"Fine. So what do you want?"

A whimper escaped me. I fisted his dress shirt and brought him closer to me, until our bodies were flush. The masculine scent of him wafted over me, cedar and that intoxicating scent of a wide-open Kentucky night. That was what Axel represented to me. Manliness. Freedom. Safety. He was a beacon for me. One that would never dim or dull. "I just want *you*."

My words washed over him in visible waves. His edges softened, like butter on a hot plate. Axel dipped his head, bringing his mouth closer to mine.

"Just me, huh?" He paused, his lips a breath away. I could almost taste him. I yanked at the sides of his shirt again and he came crashing toward me, a practiced tumble against my mouth. Our lips met with precision, a dance we'd perfected and never forgotten. I welcomed him, relishing the warmth that snaked through my limbs, the sense of coming home. When Axel was near me, my body eased, my muscles unknotting for the first time in years.

His rough palm cupped the side of my face. Our kisses grew deep. Consuming. Electric. I whimpered for more, because no amount would ever be enough. I'd pushed him away all those years ago for his own good, but only because it had been the better of two evil options. Only a lifetime of these kisses could hope to restore the balance.

Axel kissed me hungrily. I felt the passion in my numbing lips, in the yank of my hair at the base of my neck, in the way his kisses migrated to the hollow of my neck. His teeth sank into the flesh there, a move we'd always called the hangry vampire. But Axel wasn't hangry anymore. He was famished. Just like I was.

He growled through his kisses as he bit and sucked at my neck. I hoisted a leg, eager for him to fill the space there. I needed him against me. Filling me. Reminding me of the one solid thing I used to have in my world: his commitment to me. To *us*. Axel gripped my face possessively, his fingers curling around the back of my neck while his thumb brushed over my chin. His other hand burned a trail down my body, tracing the curve of my waist, until he found the hem of my dress at the top of my thigh.

He pushed his fingertips beneath the fabric, his burning gaze issuing not so much a request as a demand. I arched myself closer to him, inviting all of it. The clock was ticking, and I didn't intend to waste a precious second as his hand moved higher.

Axel hooked a thumb beneath the edge of my panties, at the same time tracing my bottom lip with his tongue.

"That's where you want me, huh?" he asked, tugging at my panties. The fabric stretched tight against my pussy, flattening against my throbbing clit. When I didn't answer, he tugged it tighter. I gasped.

"Right here?" he asked again.

"Please, Axel." I writhed beneath him, desperate for more.

"What makes you think I even want to give it to you?"

I couldn't help the husky laugh that rolled out of me. I reached between our bodies, finding the thick ridge of his arousal. I palmed the length of his cock through his slacks, even though it threatened to unravel me. "Yeah. Seems like you don't."

The air went taut between us. His fingertips dug into the back of my neck, and he jerked me forward into another sloppy tongue kiss. He bit my bottom lip so hard I almost cried out.

And then he plunged a finger inside me, unyielding and assured. He palmed the top of my mound, grinding the heel of his hand against my aching clit. Another finger pushed into me, and then he was pumping them in and out while his gaze danced over my face. The slip and slide of his fingers inside me sent me to dizzying heights. I'd only been fantasizing about this for an eternity.

"You're dripping wet, Cora," he murmured, his voice a guttural dream. "How fucking long have you been waiting for this? Hmm?"

I drew a shuddery breath, trying to find the strength to respond. "You know how long."

In and out. He curled the fingers as he pushed inside me again, grinding his palm against my clit. I cried out as my knees wobbled, but he held me steady. I wasn't going anywhere while I was in his arms.

He dipped down like he might kiss me. But instead he said, "I bet you want something else inside this tight little cunt, huh?"

I squeezed my eyes shut, nodding like my life depended on it.

"You want me to fuck you?"

I arched against him. He pumped his fingers into me faster. Giving me just a little bit more of the friction I was begging for.

"You want me to push my cock into you so fucking slow, just like I used to, huh?" His breath was hot at my ear. "Remember when I'd take you from behind? Your perfect little ass in my hands, at that perfect angle. I'd fuck you until neither of us could walk." He pressed his forehead against mine, his fingers making slippery circles around my clit now. The man hadn't forgotten how to play me like an instrument. I was close now.

With Eli, he'd never once gotten me off with his fingers alone.

With Axel, all it took was a minute.

"Ohhhh, Axel," I moaned, burying my face in his shoulder. My hips locked. My pussy throbbed. Every inch of my body sucked inward, waiting for the explosion of heat and bliss. "I'm so fucking close. I need you. I need you inside me." I grabbed at his shirt, looking to anchor myself in preparation for the tidal wave that crested.

Axel laughed and withdrew his fingers. But he didn't plunge them inside again. Instead, he disconnected from me.

Entirely.

He stepped. The fuck. Away.

Storm clouds roiled in his blue gaze, chest heaving like we'd been running a marathon instead of parked against the back hallway of La Fève.

"Axel," I started, my voice thick with emotion. He couldn't be done. Not when I was so close. Not when I'd been needing this for so fucking long.

"Your husband can finish you off." He pinned me with a cold look, but I witnessed the play of emotions across his face hardening into that practiced neutrality. He tore himself away, storming around the corner before I could squeak a protest.

I tugged down my dress, suddenly aware of how far we'd gone and what we'd put on the line. My heart hammered in my chest as reality sank in.

I was alone in the back hallway of the restaurant, the almost-orgasm screaming through my veins. All the dreaded what-ifs and possibilities bore down on me. But more than that, a new type of feeling zipped beneath my skin. Something powerful and angry. Something absolutely fucking over it.

I balled my fists. *Fuck you, Axel, for that little stunt.*

I stormed around the corner, bolstered by the lingering electricity from my encounter with Axel. I pushed my way into the women's restroom, took a moment to touch up my face and make sure I still looked presentable, and headed back into the clamor of the restaurant.

I spotted Axel first. He was back at his table, chatting with his brothers, looking as unaffected by what had just happened as if he'd stopped by the post office after work. Dropping my chin, I beelined for my parents' table. Eli and my father were still deep in conversation about a new investment strategy they wanted to tackle. I'd been checked out of this dinner since the second Axel had shown up. Not like I could distract myself in conversation with my mother, either. She spent every outing scanning the room for people she knew, angling for a social interaction with anyone who wasn't family.

At the table, I downed the rest of my wine without sitting down. Then I grabbed my handbag.

"I'm leaving," I announced.

My mother blinked with absent surprise. "Do you have a different engagement?"

"No. But I'm full and bored. So I'm going home."

Eli furrowed his brow, turning toward me. "Honey, you don't—"

"Drop the act, Eli," I hissed. "I'm going alone."

Three sets of glowering gazes followed me as I stepped off the podium of our VIP table. I'd catch flack about this later. From all of them. But I didn't care. I could barely breathe after Axel's torture, and I needed to clear my head, submerge myself in ice water, or both.

I didn't look at Axel as I left. I knew Eli's eyes were on me, and I didn't want him to have any ammunition. No more than he already had, at least. I wove through the busy restaurant, bumping shoulders with a man as I crossed the threshold onto the sidewalk.

Outside, I took a grateful gulp of air.

It helped. But not enough.

I called for my driver while I started off down the street, my heels clicking against the sidewalk. It was a humid, dreamy evening in SoHo. Fashionable people filled the streets, angled shoulder pads brushing up against me as a crowd of models filed past. Surely some event had just let out—or was about to begin—nearby. I smiled after them, admiring their unbridled expression. All my fashion choices were restricted to certain racks, specific designers. Nothing too flashy. Nothing too provocative. I had my followers in the way that Jackie Onassis had hers. And they loved to make sure I colored inside the lines.

The brief escape into the bustle of SoHo didn't last long. Randall pulled up to the curb moments later, able to see where to meet me via my phone. And then the texts from Eli began.

ELI: Way to embarrass me.

ELI: What the fuck was that all about anyway?

ELI: You really have got to learn to control yourself.

Control myself. That was the funniest thing in the world. I lived controlling myself. I'd wasted my entire life controlling myself.

It would never be good enough.

I slid into the back seat of the company sedan, asking Randall to take me to the condo. I sank into pensive silence, watching as we passed the fashionable group I'd noticed before.

Emotions boiled inside me like an untended pot. What I'd done in the restaurant was risky because it invited commentary and backlash from everyone who'd been at our table. And I was so incredibly tired of hearing their fucking opinions.

Sometimes I felt like if I heard one more thing from any of them, I'd combust. I wanted to get back to my own opinions. When had they ever taken precedence? And more than that, I wanted to correct someone else's opinion of me.

After the past few weeks, one fact had become glaringly clear: keeping Axel in the past was no longer an option.

CHAPTER TWELVE

Hours floated by in a restless, unmoored state. I'd changed into comfy shorts and a tank top with no bra and cranked electronic-infused jazz to as much of the condo as the speakers would allow. Worry lurked in the back of my mind: would Eli show up? Would someone come to interrupt this me time, as they always did?

But I didn't want to inhibit myself tonight. For the first time in maybe forever, my patience had worn thin. I had increasingly fewer fucks to give. With any luck, I'd get to zero. Just like Axel and his rottweiler.

Even in a house all to myself, I tended to color inside the lines. Nothing had ever felt truly mine—except for this evening, apparently. So I tried masturbating in the living room with my vibrator, something I would normally never dare to try; I'd always believed sex toys were for *the bedroom*, to be hidden away.

But my vibrator didn't cut it. Nothing would cut it except more Axel. I threw my vibrator to the other end of the couch and left it there.

Because all fucks were off tonight.

Midnight crept closer, but the itch beneath my skin wouldn't leave me. I was horny as hell and adrift in this sea of sexual need that Axel had created and elevated. He was the only one who could satisfy it.

I took out my phone, drawing a deep breath before I initiated a video call with him. I stared at the dark screen. *Ringing.* What the hell was I doing? My heart hammered as I awaited the inevitable disappointment. He wouldn't pick up. And I'd go down in history as the desperate ex who had lobbed an unanswered video call hours after he'd edged me and run away.

I almost swiped to end the call.

He answered.

Axel's evil grin and boxy shoulders filled the screen.

He was bare chested, backed by the dizzying skyline of Manhattan from his perch on some rooftop in some corner of the city. His expertly arranged dirty-blond locks had loosened since dinner. Waves threatened to spill out of his immaculate style. And that sky-blue gaze was just as piercing through the screen of my phone.

"Why the fuck are you calling me?" Axel was eating this up. He almost couldn't contain himself. He certainly couldn't contain the grin.

"No reason," I said, trying my best to look casual. To sound unaffected. To pretend I wasn't absolutely, perpetually dying for this man.

"You're getting desperate, huh?"

I blinked slowly. *Nailed it.* "This is just a check-in call. To make sure we're on the same page."

"Oh, don't worry. We are." The background shifted, and he turned to look behind him. I watched as his location flashed around him. People milled in the background. Women everywhere. He was at a rooftop party. "And that page is that you are completely desperate for my cock."

Giggles floated up from somewhere nearby. I couldn't tell if it was in response to our conversation or something else. I pressed two fingertips to the side of my head, feigning annoyance. But he was so right it hurt.

"We must be reading different books. It kind of seemed like you were the one who couldn't keep your fingers out of my pussy."

He laughed—one of the genuine Axel laughs, the kind that made me fall in love with him all over again. I couldn't fight the smile it prompted. On his end, he was still walking somewhere, people flashing by in the background.

"Listen, my fingers wouldn't have gone anywhere near you if you hadn't been harassing me via text message. And now the harassment continues on video call! When will this end?"

Hopefully never. "Maybe when you've finished what you started."

A low rumble of a laugh escaped him. And then he opened a door and entered what must have been a dressing room. I heard the *snap* of a lock. The lighting was low, gauzy. He was pixelated and darkened, but when he set the phone down, I saw all of him.

Every inch of his perfect frame.

His belly creased as he bent to check the phone's placement. When he stood, he raked a hand through his hair, replacing some of the escaped waves. He wore the same dark slacks from dinner, but no shirt. His broad chest was on display, the hills of his biceps more pronounced than I'd ever seen before. He palmed the front of his pants.

"You mean you want to watch me jack off?"

I licked dry lips. "I wouldn't say no to that."

He cocked a grin. "In your fucking dreams."

I held the phone with one hand while the other drifted between my legs. I began absent-mindedly stroking my pussy. My lips were already swollen, ready for more attention.

"I'm touching myself, Axel," I said.

"Show me."

Anxiety streaked through me, but I ignored it. This could end poorly in so many ways. But my Axel-inspired insanity pushed me deeper. I leaned forward, moving the end table and arranging my phone so that the camera could see all of me. I returned to my seat on the couch, spreading my legs for him.

"Take those fucking shorts off," he growled.

I did as I was told, my heart thumping wildly as I stood and shimmied out of the cotton shorts. I tugged my panties off for good measure, watching as he came closer to the camera. My almost-bare pussy faced the camera, and I slowly turned, enjoying the stunned silence from his end.

"Don't you want to get this perfect ass from behind?" I teased, wiggling my ass cheeks for him. I faced away from the camera, bending over for him. Spreading my cheeks a little. He groaned from his rooftop SoHo party.

"Are you wet, Cora?" His face filled my screen. The heartbreakingly blue eyes were all I could focus on as I allowed my hand to drift between my legs. I made sure he could see as I rubbed my fingers back and forth across my pussy. I was dripping. Absolutely drenched and swollen and needing him.

"What do you think?" I dipped two fingers inside myself. "I've been wet since you pulled your fingers out of me."

Axel stood up, crossing his arms over his chest. I couldn't read his face. He was somewhere between engrossed and calculating. I didn't know where this journey would take us, but I had to find out. Consequences be damned.

The only shred of inner struggle I could glean was in the way he cleared his throat. The flex of his jaw. Yes, he was battling to keep himself in line. Under control. I'd seen the same struggle plenty of times during our relationship, when I'd been intentionally provocative in public spaces. He dipped his chin, his gaze lasering through me, even though we were over a mile apart.

"You wish it was me." The way he said it wasn't a question.

"So bad, Axel." I bucked my hips, spreading my legs wider. "Look what you do to me." My pussy was slippery. Juicy. I'd never bared it like this before, least of all for a video chat. Doubts nagged at me, but I could barely hear them over the roar of my desire. "I've never been this wet before."

He cleared his throat again, and he stepped away from the camera, walking around the room in a slow circle with his hands interlocked on top of his head.

"Don't you want to play?" I asked him.

A bitter laugh was the only response I got. The tenting in his slacks suggested he did want to play.

"You have no idea how much I miss wrapping my lips around your cock," I breathed, meaning every word. I'd particularly loved sucking off Axel. I'd thought of it countless times over the years. "Do you remember how much I loved it?" I ran my fingers in a slow circle around my clit, loving the jolts of pleasure. "Jesus, Axel, I would choke on your cock right now if I could."

"Taste yourself," he commanded, running the heel of his palm over the front of his pants. I did as I was told, bringing my fingers to my lips. I ran my tongue back and forth across the tips before I sucked them both. Exactly as I would have done to his dick.

"You should taste it too."

"Not unless you put a gun to my head."

I wasn't swayed by his attitude. I knew to expect this, since I was on his shit list. It would take a lot of creative maneuvering to get off that list. "I'm open to new kinks."

He laughed bitterly again, his stormy eyes focused on me as his hand lingered at the fly of his pants. He palmed himself again and then, as if thinking better of it, interlocked his fingers above his head. He was keeping himself at a distance. He would play, but only so much.

I plunged my fingers inside me again, my eyes fluttering shut as I picked up a pace that I knew would take me to the edge.

"Imagine me, Cora," he said, his voice gritty. "Imagine me pinning you to the wall of your office. Tearing off your panties. Pushing my cock inside your wet pussy."

I squeezed my eyes shut, moving my attention to the tight bud of my clit. I made slippery circles around it, my insides going tight as the orgasm crested.

"Imagine me fucking you up against the wall of your office. Everyone would hear it. They'd hear our bodies hitting the wall like my bed used to in my dorm room."

I gasped as my thighs tensed. A whimper escaped me as his words took me higher.

"Nobody's cock ever filled you as good as mine, huh? You just can't forget about it."

Fireworks burst and my vision faded to sparkles. I cried out, letting the orgasm whisk me away. Everything on display for him. His smile stretched a mile wide.

"Mm-hmm." He sniffed, something dark lining his attention. "You got your fill, Cora? Are we done here?"

I drew deep breaths, trying to bring myself back to earth. "I think it's your turn."

He placed his palms on the table where his phone stood, bringing his face closer to the camera. "No. There will be none of that." He was about to say more, but something clanged on the door. He abandoned the phone, pulling open the door. Giggles floated into the room. A hand pulling at his wrist.

"Giovanna, hang on. I'll be there in a second." The warmth had returned to his words. Only when it wasn't directed at me. He sent a smile to whatever plaything awaited him and then returned to the phone.

"Well, your time is up," Axel said with a sigh. He rejoined the party. The sky vaulted across the screen for a moment and then righted on his face again. His jaw flexed as he scanned the crowd. A group of entirely naked women flashed on the screen behind him. "Hope you got what you wanted out of this, Cora. Because this is the absolute last time you'll get what you want out of me." He sent a tight grin to the phone. "Happy dreaming about my cock."

The video chat ended abruptly, leaving me in a painful silence. I stared at the ghostly reflection of my face in the screen of my phone, both stunned and sated.

As time ticked by, logic caught up with me. *Why on earth did you do that?* I couldn't make sense of it, only that Axel was shaking something inside me loose. I didn't mind.

Even if he refused to ever speak to me again, he'd gifted me something in his brief reappearance in my life. I just had to continue to unwrap the present.

After I'd spent enough time poring over my actions and staring at the ceiling, I slowly dressed, ready for bed. I snatched up my vibrator at the last second, almost forgetting it in the crease of the couch. Part of me was still irrationally jealous of whoever accompanied Axel at his rooftop party. *Giovanna.* The man probably had a rotating door of women. How could he not? He was funny, smart as hell, and built like a god. He was my dream man, which meant he could seduce any fucking woman in Manhattan.

I stewed over this fact as I shuffled into the bathroom and washed my face. I had no right to him. I'd broken up with him, forced him out of my life, and married another man. I was the last person who had any bearing on his life.

Except I'd done those things to protect him.

The soft underbelly of my heart didn't care that I'd taken the wrong path for a higher good. I just wanted to be back in Axel's arms.

A rustling sound caught my attention and I straightened, listening over the rush of water in the sink. It sounded again, almost like footsteps. I turned the water off and listened harder.

Thud.

Anxiety slithered through me, making my limbs hot and heavy. I hurried out of the bathroom, almost afraid of what I might find.

Eli.

He stood with his palms pressed against the kitchen island, a smarmy smile stuck to his face. He'd always been classically handsome, but tonight in the bright lighting of the kitchen, his features were twisted. Ugly. He watched me with uneven eyes. Drunk as fuck.

"Eli, what are you doing here?"

He hefted with a humorless laugh once and then again. "Can't a man come home to his wife?"

"Oh, please." I wanted to add more, but I swallowed the words. "You should head back to the house and go to sleep."

"Should I?" He took a few uneven steps toward me. "I think you owe me after what you pulled tonight."

"Eli," I said, ready to roll my eyes and serve him this grief right back to him. But something behind his words made me tense, told me to tread carefully. Maybe it was the quiet whisper of my intuition, but I made an effort to keep my tone neutral. "I'm sorry for leaving like that."

"Yeah, fucking right you're sorry." He swiped at the decorative vase on the island, and it soared into the backsplash behind the oven. It burst into pieces, the loud smash making me jump. "All you are is sorry anymore. A sorry fucking excuse for a wife. A sorry fucking excuse of a woman."

Panic clenched me, a crushing grip that rendered me immobile. I opened my mouth to respond, but nothing came out. Maybe he was right. I was a sorry excuse for a wife and a woman. Even though we hadn't married for love, I'd promised to collaborate with him. And I'd spent the entirety of our marriage figuring out ways to escape him. To avoid having his children. All the way down to hiding my birth control and pretending to be confused or upset when I didn't get pregnant each month.

"Unless you're ready to prove that you aren't," he spat, lurching toward me. "That would be fucking nice, wouldn't it? A wife that puts out." Eli was in front of me before I could even consider moving away from him. He grabbed my arms so roughly that I cried out.

"Eli, you're hurting me." My voice shook with my attempt to remain neutral.

"Oh, come on. Don't act like that. How fucking long has it been, Cora?" His breath washed over me in a sickening wave of alcohol. I didn't even want to imagine how many drinks he'd had after dinner. Where he'd gone. How many hours he'd spent bathing in his resentment. "When's the last time you let me fuck you?"

I tried to jerk my arms from his grip, but he held tight, his fingertips gouging into my biceps. "Eli, just let me go." It was impossible to hide the panic in my voice. He'd sense it like a shark after blood.

Because for however new this arrangement was—my living in the condo—his drunken rage wasn't. This wasn't the first time he'd asked for more than I was willing to give. His pasttime over the last couple of years was talking down to me and then acting like it had never happened.

But tonight was different. It was worse. No, the worst. My heart hammered as I tried to spot an exit route. Eli was normally adept at keeping the drunken abuse just this side of negotiable. Brazen but still within the bounds of "Oh come on, I just drank a little too much." But this time, fear flooded every inch of my body. Just how far would he take it tonight?

I'd been playing it too fast and loose with him. The guilt had been slowly accumulating, threatening to swell up and drown me. Now with Eli here, part of me believed I deserved whatever he gave me. Because even though I hated him and had never wanted to marry him, he was still my husband.

"Maybe we just need to get it over with." He hauled me down the hallway toward the bedrooms. "Break the seal, you know?"

I tripped and stumbled behind him, unable to follow his drunken gait. But even in this state, he could overpower me. Hurt me. Make me wish I'd never fought back.

"Eli, you are way too drunk for this right now." My voice trembled as he led me into the bedroom. He shoved me toward the bed. I lurched forward, falling face first into the bedspread. My heart pounded against my ribs. Every inch of my body was on high alert now.

"Just stay there," he grunted. I heard the clank of his belt buckle. *Zzzziiip* followed soon after. "It'll be easier."

I turned over, finding him looming over me, freeing his limp dick from his pants. Bile rose in my throat, and I scrambled off the bed. His arm shot out, gripping me by the forearm so hard tears came to my eyes.

"Eli!" I shouted. "Get off of me!"

"You owe me after what you did tonight," he growled, pure venom in his voice. My entire body quaked, fear turning me to jelly, but I yanked my arm free. I slipped out of his grip and bolted for the bathroom before he could turn on his unsteady legs.

I slammed the door shut behind me and locked it, my heart hammering in my throat as I sank down against the cool wall and curled into a ball.

Waiting. Praying.

Thud thud thud. "Cora! Open the fucking door!"

I gathered my knees against me, burying my face there. I would not respond, react, or invite more. I just prayed that he would leave without forcing his way in here. I didn't know what would happen if he actually made it in.

Nothing good. I knew that much.

"Cora!" He pounded again, louder and harder this time. I jolted, squeezing myself into a smaller ball. "Cora, I said open. The fucking. Door!"

The door vibrated with every slam. His rage boomed and filled the condo. The bedroom was positioned so that no neighbors would hear through the walls. This attack was hidden. Nobody would come knocking. Nobody would check on me.

After all, this was just a routine interaction between husband and wife.

"Please please please please," I whispered into my knees, squeezing my eyes shut as he released another round of angry pounding. I'd dropped my phone in the bedroom. Which meant he could find it. He could see that I'd called Axel. He could begin piecing things together, which would only make him angrier.

"Please please please." I was too scared to even pray properly. I just wanted out of here alive. Unharmed.

"You can't hide in there forever," he shouted gruffly.

But I could. I would. If I had to.

He pounded on the door again, but it lacked the previous vigor. Maybe he was getting tired. He grunted from the other side of the door. "Cora, can you hear me?"

He sounded sleepy almost. Or maybe that was sadness. I couldn't tell. And there was no way in hell I was going to investigate.

"You can't stay in there forever." His speech was slurred now. Heavy footsteps fell outside the door. From farther away, he said, "I'll just wait here until you decide to come out. Watch me."

Challenge accepted. I stayed in my spot, huddled and alert, for what felt like forever. Every whir of the HVAC or flutter from the pipes jolted me. I didn't doubt he'd be sitting out there on the bed, waiting for me to come out. Ready to finish what he started as soon as I unlocked the door.

I listened to the in and out of my breaths, my eyes squeezed shut, for so long I couldn't remember if I'd been doing it for ten minutes or two hours. Time melted away in my quest to disassociate. The aches in my body were the only sign I'd been curled up here for too long. I stretched out a little bit, my body grateful for the chance to stand down. I took a deep breath.

"Eli?" I called out. Testing the waters.

No response.

"Eli, I'm ready." Though it was a lie. I would never be ready for *that*.

Silence filled the bathroom once more. Wincing, I shakily pushed to my feet, pain blossoming along my forearm and in my shoulders from where he'd grabbed and yanked at me. But I'd deal with that later. As silently, slowly as I could, I unlocked the bathroom door and pushed it open. I could hear every thump of my heart as I peered past the door.

I spotted him splayed out on my bed. Fully clothed. Fully asleep.

Relief pounded through me, tears pricking my eyes. *Thank you, Lord.* I let myself out of the bathroom, my legs tingling from how long I'd sat hunched up and fearful. But there was no time to let them recover.

I didn't plan on being here when Eli woke up. Which meant I needed to pack my things and get the fuck out of here.

Immediately.

CHAPTER THIRTEEN

AXEL

Days churned by in an irritating blur of everything but giving in to my basest desires.

I'd always had a hard time saying no, especially when it came to women who were begging me to fill their pussies with my cock. But I had to make an exception for Cora. I had to draw a line *somewhere*.

Since Cora had reentered my life, things were not going well. I'd given into too much. Fuck, I'd hate-fingered her in the back hallway of La Fève. I deserved an award for maximizing how much I'd tasted of that women under the guise of denying her what she wanted.

It had to stop. She was on my schedule again—to talk about *the building plans*—and I was so tired of wanting her, acting like I didn't, hating her again, only to repeat the whole cycle.

I did hate her. As much as I still loved her.

And that was where the fissure lay, the gulf that threatened to swallow me whole every time we came too close.

We were slated to meet at the building on Wednesday afternoon, which meant I was sitting in the back of the Escalade on Tenth Avenue, forbidding myself from looking, breathing, sniffing, or sneezing too close to her. God forbid my lips got the memo that hers were within a ten-foot radius. My fingers were already planning a revolt to inch their way back into her panties. And my cock? Forget about it. I'd been hard since I'd noticed her name on my schedule that morning.

Truth was, I didn't know how much longer I could put up the I-hate-Cora front. And I worried that with yet another meeting, *just the two of us*, it would crumble altogether.

While I waited for her, I dicked around in my investment app. Scooped up another few thousand shares of Margulis Realty. Then I circled back to a crowdfunding plea I'd seen an old friend in Kentucky post on his social media account. His eight-year-old daughter was in the hospital after a car crash with a drunk driver. I put up his entire asking amount plus a few thousand extra and drew a deep breath.

My phone buzzed.

CORA: Just pulling up. Meet you at the front.

My stomach pitched to my feet, and I pinched the bridge of my nose. Here went nothing.

Her classy sedan pulled up to the loading zone a moment later, four-ways flashing. I alternately gripped and released the back door handle, prepping myself for what needed to be our final encounter.

I didn't know how much more of this twisted cat-and-mouse game I could play. While fun and sexy as hell, it came at a steep price. I'd spent all of Sunday in bed with a hangover because I'd picked my favorite numbing agent of choice, whiskey, for the rest of that delightful rooftop SoHo party. I hadn't even bothered to get laid that night. Cora had already stained me. Warped me. Penetrated the barriers of my heart. My brothers were right to be worried about me.

Now I was worried about me.

And once we stepped into that building together, I didn't know what would happen.

I thanked Harry and hopped out of the backseat, shutting the back door gently. The sidewalk was calm, which meant only a slow stream of passersby at this hour of the morning. The scent of coffee wafted from down the street on a humid breeze, joined by the shouts of some people wandering nearby. Cora stepped out of her car a moment later, wearing a fitted cream dress. A teal scarf was draped over an arm, along with her handbag.

And there it went. The internal explosion. The deafening roar of my heart opening up, wanting to bring her into my arms, to eliminate every inch of space between us until we could fuse and heal and pick up where we left off. I straightened my back, rolling my neck in a slow circle. *Stay strong.*

But it was hard to stay strong against her mulberry grin and that glossy dark hair pulled up into a sleek high ponytail. When she stood in front of me, looking picture-perfect and every bit the upper-class professional, I caught the mischief in her gaze.

That sparkle was reserved for me.

"Long time no see," she said.

I hated that she was still so wry. So whip smart. So fucking perfect. "I'd say the same about your pussy but that's not true."

A genuine laugh rolled out of her, husky sweet and angelic. She swatted at my chest, and I caught her wrist.

"Hands to yourself, Cora," I warned. But it was too late. I'd broken the rules already. Not only was she too close, I'd touched her. All bets were off. She pursed her lips.

"What can I say? Old habits die hard."

But I didn't release her wrist right away. The scarf over her arm slid back to her elbow, revealing mottled bruising on her forearm. My gaze fastened there as I tried to figure out what I was seeing.

Cora snapped her hand out of my grip and spun on her heel. "Let's go inside."

I followed her perfect figure at a safe distance. We were always dancing on the edge of a slippery slope, and I didn't want to be the one who pushed us down.

Cora fished the building keys out of her handbag and spent a moment turning the lock. Once the door was opened, we walked slowly through the expansive foyer, our footsteps on the dusty floor echoing in the empty space.

"So when is it officially ours?" I asked. My eyes dropped to her forearm again, but her scarf hid the area. I couldn't help wondering. She seemed embarrassed, so of course I wanted to know more. That bruise was nasty. And it sure as hell hadn't been there at La Fève.

"Formal closing should be in about two weeks," she said, smoothing a hand across the top of her head. "I'd give you the keys today, but I think your brothers would be upset they missed the ceremonial passing of the keys."

I cracked a grin. "You know them well."

"I know all of you well."

My smile faded, and I jerked my chin toward the elevators. "Let's go up. I want to hear your stipulations before I get too deep into the blueprints."

"Of course." Her heels clicked over the floor as we moved toward the elevator. The air between us felt a lot different than the first time we'd come here. Then, it had been tense with anger. Now, it was tense with expectation.

Who would make the first move?

The elevator doors opened as soon as she pressed the button. Inside, Cora pressed the button for the eleventh floor.

"So floor eleven is where you're hoping to set up?"

"That's what I had thought. Why, do you want it?" She lifted a brow.

"I'll let you know when I see it. If it's a good floor, I might want to keep it for myself." I cracked a grin to let her know I was teasing. She returned the smile. We watched each other for a few moments as the elevator soared upward, something hanging unspoken between us.

"So...what's with the scarf?"

Her brows knit together. "What do you mean?"

"Why do you have it? It's like eighty degrees outside."

She shrugged. "In case I get chilly."

"The air is off in the building."

"I had it more for the car ride."

I sniffed, holding out a hand. "Can I see it?"

The elevator reached the eleventh floor and the doors slid open. She looked at me like I was crazy. "Why do you want to see it?"

I followed her off the elevator. "It's pretty. Now give it to me."

She gave me a side-eye as we started down a blue-carpeted hallway. "Can we focus on this? I need to show you my idea."

I left it for now. She smoothed her hair again. Something was off about her today, but I couldn't pin it down. There could be a million different reasons, not the least likely that I watched her masturbate herself to shuddering orgasm via video call while I was at a friend's house on Saturday night. And anyway, what did I know about her anymore?

The answer was: nothing. I knew the ghost of Cora Margulis. I didn't know a thing about Cora Margulis-Rossberg.

Cora played with the tip of her ponytail as we walked. This was a former office suite, though it looked caught in the nineties. Sky blue Berber carpet stretched beneath our feet.

"So this is currently just offices," she said, her voice unnaturally soft. "But I'm thinking that this would be the easiest level to convert to what I have planned."

I nodded, watching her intently, trying to figure out what was going on beneath her surface. Wondering if this was truly spidey senses or just the effect of my certifiable delusion that we were somehow meant for each other.

"I wanted to preserve some of the layout, in fact. Like probably this entire side here." She swept her arm in the direction of a bank of offices. "But I do think this whole floor needs to be gutted and revamped."

"Sorely needs an update," I confirmed, crossing my arms.

"So what I'm planning on executing first would be a community drama school."

I blinked a few times. "So how does office space work for drama?"

"Some of these office spaces would be preserved." She cleared her throat, her gaze darting between me and the open office door behind me. "We'd need the offices for the teachers and administrators. Then we'd convert the rest of the floor into workshop space. You know, for classes. Get-togethers. Whatever might make sense, whatever is needed. And then down there"—she pointed toward the far end of the floor, which looked like it held an empty conference room—"I want to build out a stage."

"A stage?"

"Yeah. Like an actual black box *theater*." Some of the excitement returned to her face, and whatever I'd unearthed by prying had been temporarily forgotten. She started toward that end of the building. "Can't you just see it? I'm thinking we could make it modern, like a black box theater. There won't be red carpeted steps or concessions stands, but something functional to do rehearsals. A space that can be dressed up to serve as the performance area. And we could put in a small box office there." She pointed toward an area closer to the elevators. "So people who come for the performances won't miss it."

"The theater should have some sort of sign, too," I said, nodding along with her vision. I loved it, but I was hesitant to let her know how deeply it touched me. I probably didn't need to tell her though. We shared this wound, the deep cut of losing a sibling. "And you'll have to name it."

She laughed, still looking around like she could actually see the gold letters on the wall and the theater behind it. "Yeah. I will."

"You should name it the Christopher B. Margulis Auditorium," I suggested. Because that's who this was for.

She looked over at me sharply, something pained sliding over her face. "I can't."

"But it's yours," I told her.

A bitter laugh slid out of her. "That's not very on brand for the Margulis mission, now, is it? No, Axel, this has to stay completely anonymous. I can't be attached to it. *At all.*"

"Fine. But wouldn't you like his name to be on it?"

She sighed, exasperated. "Of course I would. But that's not the world I live in. And you know it."

We somehow always had a way of coming back to this point. At least we had when we were together. So I wasn't sure why I was surprised that we'd made it back here all these years later.

"I think it *could* be the world you lived in," I said, because I couldn't help myself. Apparently Cora was right—old habits died hard.

She dipped her chin, sending me a dark look. "I'll be sure to tell my father's legal team that it was all your idea, when I get sued for violating the NDA."

Silence settled between us.

"You've never been able to understand this about my family," she murmured. "Or maybe you just refuse to."

Sure, it was hard for me to imagine a world where my own father would sue me for talking openly about the fact that a sibling had committed suicide. But Allan Margulis defied any definition of *father* I'd ever dared to imagine. His version of paternal affection consisted of the relentless pursuit of more money, more prestige. From what I'd learned from Cora, there had never been tenderness there. Only cashflow.

"It's not that I don't understand," I shot back. "I just never wanted you to be so stifled."

She sent me a sad look, and for a moment, it looked like the entire weight of the world was on her shoulders. She'd lit up while talking about the auditorium plans, but now the joy had receded, and hollowness had replaced it. Gray pulled at her edges, the thing that I couldn't name but that lurked just beneath the surface.

"If it weren't for you," she said softly, "I wouldn't even know that non-stifled was an option."

My fingers twitched with the urge to get closer to her. Bring her into my arms. Help dissolve whatever was hurting her. But I didn't know how to do that without falling face first into the abyss. So I had to stay away.

"Well, it's a noble project." I crossed my arms again, reminding them to stay away from her, and jerked my chin toward the imaginary auditorium. "Maybe you'll help save some other kids. That's all we can hope for."

Her brows drew together, and she nodded, emotion clouding her features. She was normally put-together, her expressions carefully schooled and practiced, but today all of that was gone. She sagged slightly, and the scarf dropped. She sighed, reaching down for it, but not before I caught an unobstructed glimpse of the state of her arm.

"Jesus, Cora." I bent down, snatching the scarf up before she could. I gestured toward her arm. "What happened?"

Her face fell and she shook her head. "It's really nothing. I just didn't want to spook you."

"Spook me?" I took her wrist in my hand, tipping her arm from side to side as I inspected the damage. "It looks like you got hit with a baseball bat."

I glanced up at her face, finding tears shimmering there.

"Would you believe that I ran into a door?" She tried to make it a joke, but her laugh cracked halfway through, exposing the emotion beneath.

Whatever had happened, it was the iceberg in the water, cracking her ship. And hell if I wasn't gonna pull her out of the water.

I tugged her into my arms, overcome by the need to hold her. She fell into my embrace easily, as if she'd been waiting for the chance, and she clung to me like her life depended on it. Cora buried her face in my chest, her fingers knotted in the back of my dress shirt. I squeezed my arms around her, resting my chin on the top of her head.

"Are you okay?" I asked a few moments later.

She shook her head then looked up, sniffing. She brushed away some spilled tears with a shaky hand. "I'm not. But I will be."

I swallowed a knot, daring myself to ask the question that had been lingering since I first spotted the bruises. "Did Eli do this to you?"

The tears shimmered again in her eyes, and she looked away. "He got really drunk the night we saw you out. And he was just...upset. I don't know why. But he came to the condo where I've been staying, and we fought."

Her words landed like icicles down the back. "Did he hurt you anywhere else?"

A shaky sigh escaped her, and she gripped my waist as if she might float away if she didn't. "Just my arms. From how hard he grabbed me and—" Her voice cut out again. "It could have been a lot worse." She lifted her chin, emotion swimming in her green gaze. "I'm just glad I was able to get out that night."

All the alarms were going off now, anger swirling alongside the need to solve this. Immediately. My hand drifted to the side of her face. I swiped my thumb over her cheek to catch a stray tear. "Where are you staying?"

"A hotel." She offered a flimsy smile. "I'm fine."

I nodded, searching her face for more. She didn't seem fine at all, but I had no idea what my role was anymore. As much as I wanted to scoop her into my arms and carry her off into the sunset, I knew that wasn't the answer. There was too much at stake here. This was unbearably complicated. And that didn't even take into account all this lingering resentment and anger I had toward her.

But none of that mattered when she looked like this.

Her light was dimming, and that scared the fuck out of me.

"You promise me you'll let me know if you need anything?" I asked softly, searching out her gaze. We'd started the inevitable drift closer. Having her in my arms felt like coming home, and I was ready to stay here forever.

"I don't deserve that," she said, more tears spilling out.

"You heard what I said," I repeated, cinching my arm around her waist. "Promise me, Cora."

She nodded, her bottom lip trembling. "Okay."

"And don't act hard when you really need help," I warned her, brushing my lips over the top of her head. The sweet clementine fragrance there wrenched at my heart. "Because I'll find out."

I almost couldn't believe I was saying these words. Yet again, my resolve to keep both physical and emotional distance from Cora had completely crumbled. Not only had I eradicated every inch of distance between us, if I wasn't careful, I was going to insist she come stay with me.

Tread carefully, Axel.

Cora laughed feebly, burying her face in my chest once more. She squeezed her arms around me. "Thank you, Axel. You have no idea how much that means to me."

"You're welcome." I pressed another soft kiss to the top of her head. Cora just needed tenderness. The exact thing that nobody in her life was willing to extend to her.

We hugged for what felt like an eternity. I was in no hurry to end it. Cora and I had always spent so much time hugging—for our health, we'd always joked.

"This is not how I expected the building planning to go," she murmured against my chest. I couldn't tell if ten minutes had passed or an hour. Time was fluid in her embrace.

"I think we got a lot accomplished today," I cracked.

"Yeah. Thanks for the hug." She propped her chin on my chest and smiled up at me. It seemed like some color had returned to her cheeks. The hug really had been for her health. She'd needed it more than I could have imagined.

"You want me to drop you off at your hotel?" I asked, checking my watch. "I'll give you a ride. I have to get back to the office for a meeting."

"I'd love that."

I released her awkwardly, only because my arms did not want to break the seal. Nothing made sense right now. Reality vaulted beneath me, and I couldn't find anything to hold onto. Something big had shifted—I just couldn't figure out what it meant for either of us.

I called for my driver as we headed for the elevator. Cora drew deep breaths and smoothed the front of her dress, the top of her head. Once I got confirmation that Harry would be arriving within five minutes, I pocketed the phone.

"Have you seen him since that night?" I asked.

Cora shook her head. "I'm not speaking to him right now. I can't. I'm just so disgusted."

My heart twisted in my chest. *And she chose him. She chose him over you.* I swallowed the angry feelings and stuffed my hands in my pockets. "Do you think he's going to try to reach out?"

"I don't know. But he doesn't know where I am. So that, at least, is a comfort."

We rode down in the elevator in intimate silence. I felt closer to her than ever, which didn't make sense. Because the gulf of Eli and her current life still stretched between us.

I was nothing if not loyal. Even to the woman who'd hurt me most.

Which was why I escorted her out of the building, and into the back of my Escalade. Harry only tipped his hat to us as we got in, thank God. Harry knew everything about us. The good, the bad, and the *we'd rather forget*. Which meant sometimes, when he was being saucy, he loved to bring up embarrassing moments. And he had plenty of dirt on just how heartbroken I'd been over Cora.

He'd joined our team way back in the beginning, just as our business started exploding with big-ticket clients. At that point, the pain of my breakup with Cora still resurfaced on occasion, which meant he'd heard a drunken rant or fifty about how much I hated her and anything Margulis. Harry was old-school—he insisted on wearing the black suit, the chauffer hat, all of it. I wasn't gonna argue with his ancient ass, as long as he continued acting as a vault for the occasional Fairchild messes and drunken confessions.

"Cora, meet Harry. He's been with us for a long time."

"Seven years," Harry piped up. "Though it feels more like a hundred."

"You mean because time just flies with how much you love us?" I cracked, meeting Harry's amused gaze in the rearview mirror.

"Yeah, we'll go with that," he said wryly.

"It's great to meet you, Harry." Cora sent him a genuine smile, some of the sparkle of her regular veneer returning. "I appreciate you taking me home."

"Where to?" he asked, and Cora rattled off the name of the hotel. Once the SUV was in motion, Cora busied herself with getting to know Harry. Where was he from (Scranton, PA), what did he love most about working with us (our annual Christmas party), where had we all met (repeat drunk taxi rides after grad school).

I smiled out the window, content to fade into the background of their conversation. It was nice to just listen to Cora. Her voice was like poetry, even when she didn't try. Especially when she didn't try. Being in my own space and hearing Cora laughing at something Harry said—it felt surreal. I wanted to lap it up before the fantasy ended.

"Looks like we're almost there," Cora said, peering out the window. She smiled over at me. "Thanks for the ride."

I reached out to take her hand, swiping my thumb over her knuckles. "Any time."

Her gaze dropped to our hands, then she looked back up at me. I could almost hear the request on her lips. Unspoken sentiments swarmed the air between us like invisible bees. But when Harry pulled up to the curb, the big doors of a Westin hotel visible through the passenger side windows, she pulled her hand away.

"Don't forget what I said," I told her once she pushed the door open. "My brothers and I, we're here for you."

She smiled over her shoulder at me, then stepped onto the sidewalk. "I'm in room 1046," she said. "If you ever want to visit." She waved at Harry and me before shutting the door and heading for the gleaming doors. People streamed past her on the sidewalk, but I kept sight of her until she was swallowed up inside the building.

A sigh escaped me as Harry eased back into traffic.

"So that's her, huh?" he asked.

"Yeah." I dragged a hand down my face, already wondering what the fuck I'd gotten myself into. "That's the one."

CHAPTER FOURTEEN

CORA

It felt wrong to float up to my hotel room the way I did.

I was in the middle of a personal crisis. A complete unraveling of my life. I shouldn't feel *happy*.

Yet I did. Axel had that way about him. He filled me up, even when he didn't mean to. Maybe especially when he didn't mean to.

And I was grateful for it. Because I wasn't just running on E. My entire life was a wisp away from shuddering to a stop altogether. And here I was, floating up to my hotel room on the top floor of the Westin, on cloud nine.

I had a whole mess of a tangle ahead of me to sort out, but I felt secure for now. For the first time in a long time.

Someone out there supported me because he cared. Not because he was legally obligated to do so. Not because it would be bad press if he didn't. Not because people would talk if he didn't show the world a certain image.

The taupe-and-shadow floral pattern of the carpet carried me toward my room. I'd selected this hotel on a whim, the first place my rattled brain could think to go after I'd thrown my things together and left the condo Saturday night.

I was living with the bare bones now. I had some undies, a few dresses, lounge wear, work heels, and bathroom stuff. That was it. I was too scared to send for more, because I knew Eli would find out where I'd disappeared to if I sent someone. I'd opted for remote work this week as well. I wasn't ready to talk to anyone. Not Eli and not my father.

Eli hadn't contacted me yet, but the onslaught was coming.

I fished my keycard out of my purse as I came up to room 1046. The door clicked softly, and I pushed it open, welcoming the sterile breeze that floated out. I appreciated the neutrality of this place. It wasn't mine, but it certainly wasn't *his*.

It was just a place to get my bearings. Until I could figure out the next step.

I hummed a nameless tune to myself, pushing into the hotel suite. My skin prickled, though I didn't know why, like the electricity before a thunderstorm. It wasn't until the door clicked shut behind me and I rounded the corner that I spotted the threat.

Eli was here. Draped over the chaise longue, one knee propped up, looking absolutely wrecked.

"About fucking time you got here," he spat, sitting up. Today, he was every level of disheveled, from his hair to his clothes, as if he'd been tossing and turning for days and had forgotten where his closet was.

"Eli." I swallowed, my tongue nearly sticking to the roof of my mouth. "What are you doing here?"

"Just trying to find my fucking wife." He balled his fists, resting his elbows on his knees. His caramel gaze was unsteady again. Shrouded. Even though it was barely four p.m., it looked like he was completely fucking drunk.

"What's wrong with you?" I asked, but my voice came out a whisper. "You look..."

"Distraught? Because I am." A humorless laugh slid out of him, and he pushed to standing. Despite the glassiness of his eyes, he rose steadily. And the steps he took my way were level, powerful. Fear pinpricked through my limbs, and the low thrum of a warning began pulsing inside me. "You just fucking disappeared for days. From *our* home. *Our* condo. You think it's funny to pull a stunt like that?"

"Eli, you were so drunk," I started, but my voice failed me. I was backing up toward the small foyer of the suite, my legs turning to jelly. Nobody knew I was here. The hotel phone was behind Eli. I didn't know what he planned, but I worried it was the same thing he'd wanted Saturday night. "You hurt me."

His laughter came out booming, sardonic. "Like you didn't hurt me?"

I suddenly remembered my handbag. I fumbled to open it, groping blindly for my cell phone. Everything I touched inside felt foreign, strange. I could only recognize that nothing was my cell phone.

"What are you doing?" Eli snarled, lunging forward and snatching my handbag away. I stumbled away from him.

"I-I-I was checking that I had—"

"Don't." He tossed my bag to the other side of the room, continuing his slow prowl in my direction. "I've been talking to your father. He thinks we need to mend fences."

My head was spinning now. My high heel wobbled, and I stumbled, my ankle twisting. I sucked in a sharp breath, but I couldn't feel the pain, only fear.

"Don't you think we need to mend fences?" He held out his arms, as if beckoning me into a hug. "Come on, babe. It's been so long since we fucked. I know if we just fuck, everything will feel right again. And maybe we can finally have a kid. You know we need a kid."

"Eli, I—*no*." I blurted the word before I could think better of it. "I didn't ask you to come here. You can't be here."

Darkness filled his face, and he slammed his fist on the wall as he passed by. I was almost backed up to the door now, but I struggled to calculate how I could execute my escape without him grabbing me or worse.

"I don't understand why you're being like this all of a sudden," he spat. "We're married. This is not how it's supposed to work. Our marriage has always had rules. I want something, you give it to me. You want something, I get it for you. We're in a mutually beneficial relationship here, Cora. Or have you forgotten?"

"I don't want you here," I said in a shuddery voice.

"And that's what needs to change," he said. "Remember how it works? I want something, you give it to me. I want *you*. Now you need to give it to me."

"Why did they let you in?"

A condescending grin twisted at his lips. "Because we're *married*. You're my *wife*. That's what they *do* for people like us, Cora. This is how the world works. Hello? Are you new here?"

I could barely process what he was saying to me. Not when I could sense that the door was within reach. I whipped around, my focus lasering in on the doorhandle. One step. That's all I had to cross in a half second. And I could be free.

Go!

I lunged for the door. Hand outstretched. *Please please please.*

Eli roared, surging up to block my reach. Our hands landed on the doorhandle at the same time.

But he was stronger. He was quicker. Eli grabbed my wrist and whipped me around to face him so hard that my neck snapped backward. I sucked in sharply, fear pounding through my veins.

"Knock this shit off!" He gathered me closer to him, not as an intimate maneuver, but as a punishment. "I don't want to have to tell you again. You need to fall in line, Cora. This partnership can work. But only if you fucking try a little."

I struggled to release myself from his iron grip. "Let go of me, Eli! This isn't right!"

Pounding broke through our scuffle. At first, I couldn't tell where it came from. Was Eli pounding me against the wall and I was just too shell-shocked to realize? But when Eli looked toward the door, the pieces clicked together.

"Who are you expecting?" he asked.

His question gave me a window of opportunity. I ripped my arm from his grip and flung myself toward the door. I gripped the handle, tugging it open before Eli could intervene. Whoever was on the other side was my ticket to safety. I didn't care who it was or what they wanted.

I just needed out.

I watched as a wide hand pushed open the door in slow-motion. I couldn't even utter a cry for help before the boxy frame I knew too well filled the doorway.

Axel.

I opened my mouth to say something—anything—but all that came out was a squeak of relief. Axel surged inside the doorway. Realization crashed over his sharp features in waves—first confusion, then recognition, followed by seething rage. His lips curled, something primal sliding into place. His brawny shoulders stretched at the seams of his button-down as he grabbed Eli by the front of his shirt, hauling him against the wall. Eli landed with a thud.

"Oh, what a fucking treat!" Eli spat. His eyes were wild, the only thing betraying his fear. "Should I even fucking ask why this loser is on the property?"

"Cora, go into the other room," Axel said, his voice gritty, eyes focused on Eli.

"Why should she leave when the circus is just starting?" Eli's gaze grew twisted and dark.

"I don't want her to see what I'm about to do to you," Axel growled, his face inches from Eli. I didn't know how Eli could be locked against the wall and still find it in him to talk shit to Axel's face. Eli's razor sharp tongue was his main weapon, but it wouldn't do much if Axel put his fist into Eli's face. Physically speaking, Eli had always been soft. That's what growing up in the board room created. His muscles were merely for show; just another part of his presentation, like the silk ties and chemically whitened teeth.

Axel drew his fist back. *That* wasn't for show. I knew how many fights he'd gotten into as a teen. As a young man.

"You're such a fucking piece of shit," Axel snarled, spit hitting Eli's chin. "You never deserved her in the first place."

"And you do?"

My heart pounded against my ribs. "Eli, just leave! Please!"

"No. You're my wife," he said, gripping Axel's closed fist as if that could somehow prevent the impending punch. "Who's to say this heathen won't try to fuck you in the other room once I leave?"

The irony was almost funny. The only heathen in this room was Eli. The only man I'd ever feared trying to fuck me against my will. The true villain who'd always expected the world around him to bend to his will. Tears pressed at the corners of my eyes as the realization washed over me. My father, too, had always forced me to bend to his will while maintaining the illusion of choice. And maybe that's why he saw such a great colleague and co-conspirator in Eli. He was just as ruthless. Just as dedicated to the outcome, no outside participation required. A gaslighter in Gucci. Part of me wanted to laugh, but the rest of me was stuck watching what unfolded by the door.

"Watch your mouth," Axel warned him, a few wisps of his hair coming undone from his hairstyle.

"That's what you came here to do, right?" Eli goaded him, struggling against Axel's grip. "Fuck my slut of a wife?"

Axel slammed his fist into Eli's jaw with enough force I heard the sick *crrrack* of shifting bone. Eli's eyes rolled up into his head for a moment, and a whoosh of air left him.

"Is that all you got?" Eli taunted, struggling against Axel's hold. He broke through and lobbed a punch, but it didn't go far. Axel dodged it easily and slammed his thick forearm against Eli's collarbone.

"I said watch your fucking mouth," Axel shouted, spit flying. "You don't talk about her like that. Not now. Not ever again. And if you fucking try, I'll make sure you can't show your pretty face in the board room for a fucking month."

"Ooh, is that a threat? You want to give me another love tap?" Eli nearly cackled.

"Eli, you are acting insane!" I shouted, my voice hoarse from all the emotions he'd brought to the surface.

"Looks like I have good reason, huh?" Eli laughed bitterly, wrenching himself out of Axel's hold. He lunged for Axel, landing a punch into his cheek. Axel stumbled but recovered quickly, pinning him back against the wall.

"Eli, just leave," I pleaded. But my words withered in the flames of the conflict between the two men.

"As soon as you leave, we're calling the cops," Axel said in a low, threatening voice. "You're getting a restraining order put on your ass."

"Good luck with that. Besides, I think *you're* the one who should be worried. They'll arrest you for being a disgusting hillbilly." Eli barked out a laugh.

Axel grabbed him by the front of his shirt and banged Eli's head against the wall again, another hard thud. "You need to get the fuck out of here before a hillbilly ruins your perfect face."

Eli cackled. "Say it again, but in that deep Kentucky voice this time."

Axel drew his fist back and unleashed another punch. His fist cracked against Eli's nose, and I would be lying if I said I wasn't secretly cheering. Eli groaned and crumpled slightly. Blood formed a dark rivulet down to his lip. I hoped it turned his entire face, from his chin all the way to his microbladed eyebrows, a delightful blend of blues and purples.

"Say another fucking word and you'll need to call a plastic surgeon," Axel growled. He threw open the door and tossed Eli into the hallway like trash. Eli stumbled, touching his nose gingerly.

"Man, you're really fucking dedicated to that pussy, aren't you?" Eli staggered down the hallway and out of sight, his goading voice still audible. "Probably need to get checked, if you know what I mean. There's no telling what you could pick up."

"Get the fuck out," Axel shouted, starting after him.

"Just bros looking out for each other, you know what I mean?" Eli's voice grew fainter. I crumpled against the wall in the foyer, prickles of relief beginning a tentative path through my body.

Axel stormed back into the hotel room, shutting the door behind him and turning the deadbolt. His arms were around me a moment later, gathering me against him.

"Cora," he said, and that was all it took to unleash the tears I'd been holding back. All the fear and anxiety spilled onto the front of his dress shirt. I clutched at his sides and sobbed.

It took me a few minutes to be able to speak. When I could finally form words, I asked, "Why did you come?"

Axel reached into his pocket and held up my phone. "You left this in the car. I came to return it."

This prompted another wave of tears. What would have happened if I hadn't forgotten my phone? The thought terrified me. Axel had been my savior purely by chance.

"He's so vile," I said through tears. "I'm so sorry."

"Cora, you can't stay here." He gripped my arms, searching out my gaze. "If this is supposed to be your safe house, we've got to get you somewhere safer."

"I don't know where to go," I whispered, rubbing the heel of my hand across my tear-stained cheek. "I never told him I was here. He must have tracked my credit card. Or-or—"

"Shhh." He pulled me back into his arms, wrapping me in a hug that dissolved the hard edges of my grief. "We'll figure something out."

He drew a deep breath, the sound of the air rumbling through him practically a balm for me. It reminded me of evenings in his apartment, when we'd lie on the couch, me curled into his arms, paying more attention to the rise and fall of his chest than whatever was on TV.

"Thank you," I said weakly. "I can't express how grateful I am."

Axel squeezed tighter around me. "You don't have to. I can feel it."

His simple words prompted more tears, but not the kind born from grief. This was something pure and light. His nod to the incredible bond we shared was a relief. Because for however complicated things had grown—however messy and unrecognizable—there was still this tether between us that had never frayed.

Axel's hand made a lazy circle over my back. His lips found the top of my head again. "Why don't you come stay with me?"

I pulled back to look him in the eye. "What?"

"I have more than enough room," he said. "And if there's one place Eli won't show up, it's Fairchild territory."

I searched his face, relief warring with guilt. I didn't deserve such kindness from him. I didn't deserve this helping hand that had the potential to not just help but heal.

"A-Are you sure?" My voice came out a hoarse whisper. "I can't...I mean, I don't deserve that. From you, of all people."

"I'm offering it to you," Axel said softly, running his thumb along the edge of my jaw. "You don't have to accept. But if you don't, then I'm going to personally find you somewhere acceptable to stay."

I swallowed hard, allowing myself to get lost in his stormy eyes. But there was clarity there, too, amid the storms.

In fact, Axel was the only clear, bright thing I'd ever encountered in my life.

"I'll go to your place," I whispered.

The warmth that flooded Axel's face when I said those words was hard to ignore. Just like the swell of my heart that followed it.

Because here we were, staring at the impossible. A complicated, uncertain, treacherous thing. A doorway to the future.

CHAPTER FIFTEEN

AXEL

Certain moments are sewn together from dreams.

That's how it felt, at least, to see Cora drifting through my penthouse.

I'd never once even imagined this could be my reality.

Not just her presence, but the whole complicated and painful package.

I ran my hand along the edge of the kitchen island. Firmly marble. Not at all gauzy dream stuff. This had to be reality.

"So what do you think?" I asked, tapping my knuckles along the edge of the island. She'd walked over to the wall of windows in the dining room and stood looking out over the city. We had a spectacular view up here, one that both grounded me at the same time it made me dizzy from sheer complexity.

"I remember when this place went on the market," she murmured, her gaze lost in the city. "I wanted to scoop it up for myself, actually."

"Sorry, not sorry."

She smiled back at me. "It's an incredible place. But far too big for you alone."

"All three of us share it," I told her. "And Zero. It's our Manhattan place. It keeps us brotherly, you know? We each have our own houses outside the city too. And back in Kentucky."

She nodded. "That sounds about right. Where's your getaway house?"

"The Hamptons."

She smiled, but it looked sad. The Hamptons had always been our place when we dated. I'd taken her there, an overzealous, broke college student, promising her the world when I could barely afford a cross-town cab ride. In my mind, using the Hamptons as our special place was a way of reinforcing my imminent wealth. I thought that if I faked it, I'd make it.

I'd been right. But the reality I envisioned wasn't quite the one I'd received. In those days, I'd imagined building my empire with Cora at my side.

My phone vibrated, and I pulled it out to see if my brothers were responding to the message I'd left in our group chat.

DAMIAN: So are we talking a new roomie in the Manhattan place?

I'd given them the heads up that I'd pulled Cora out of a sticky situation. But even I didn't entirely know what this meant. For her. For me. For us.

For any of it.

AXEL: Let's call her a temporary house guest. She'll stay in the guest room in my wing. Cool?

TRACE: Are YOU cool with it?

AXEL: I can feel your eyebrows.

I pocketed my phone. They'd be back to the penthouse soon enough. We could hash out details then. "Let's continue the tour."

"I'd love that." Cora turned from the window, following me out of the enormous dining room. I took her into the two-story great room with the black brick fireplace that cut through the middle. Low, boxy furniture complemented the room in shades of slate and black. From there, we visited the gym and peeked into Damian's wing, and then Trace's.

By the time we made it back to my end of the penthouse, Damian had just entered the kitchen. He loosened his tie before setting his briefcase on the kitchen island.

"Hey there," Damian said, nodding toward Cora. She offered him a shy smile.

"Hi, Damian. I take it Axel has told you...?"

He nodded. "He has."

"I'm sorry to impose. I promise this will be temporary. Just until I can find a more permanent place to go."

"Stay here as long as you need," Damian said. "We have more space than we know what to do with. When was the last time anyone used that guest room, anyway?"

"Maybe a year and a half ago?" I wagered.

"See? It needs someone to be an actual guest," Damian said. I squeezed his shoulder, emotion making my chest tight. He always went out of his way to help and to make people feel like his help wasn't a burden. He was a miracle worker on the downlow.

"Speaking of, let's go see it." I jerked my head toward the hallway leading into my wing. "I promise you'll love it."

She followed me, the air thick with unspoken words. When I pushed open the door to the guest bedroom, she let out a dreamy sigh. The room was opulent, excessively comfortable. A king-size sleigh bed was the focal point, with slate gray pedestals on either side of it. Roughly one million unnecessary throw pillows were heaped on the bedspread—a touch my interior designer had insisted on.

"I love it," she gushed.

"It's just a guest room."

"No. I mean everything." She turned to me, her green eyes electric. "Everything you have, everything you've done. I'm just so incredibly proud of you."

I blinked. "Well...thanks."

"I'm so happy you and your brothers have gotten exactly where you wanted to be. Honestly." She touched her chest, looking around the room again. "That is all that matters to me."

I appreciated the statement, however odd that it was possibly inspired by the excessive throw pillows on the bed. "Thanks, Cora. I'm glad you're rooting for us."

"I always have been." Her gaze cut back over to me. "Ever since I met you."

I gnawed on the inside of my lip, feeling like I needed to give her some space. Or was it me who needed the space? Truth was, my head was spinning. It had been since she set foot in the penthouse, and I needed to get my bearings.

"Do you need anything?" She'd come with the embarrassingly small bag of things she'd had with her at the hotel. "I can send for someone to get whatever you need from your condo."

"No." She waved away my offer. "I don't need anything. If I've learned anything over the past eight years, it's that I don't need any of it."

I nodded, recognizing the intensity behind her words but unsure where to store it. We'd have to circle back to that later. "I'm going to coordinate with my brothers on dinner. You relax, okay?" I pointed at her as I backed toward the door. "And let me know if you do need anything."

I shut her door gently behind me, rubbing the back of my neck as I hurried back to the main portion of the penthouse. When I got to the kitchen, I found Trace and Zero had joined Damian.

"There's my buddy." I knelt and held my arms out as Zero bounded toward me, his tongue hanging out the side of his mouth. He showered me with doggy kisses. "Did Uncle Trace take good care of you this afternoon? I'm sorry I couldn't come get you myself from doggy daycare. Sometimes Daddy has to go places you can't come along."

Trace smirked, fiddling with his wristwatch. "So I take it we have a new guest?"

"She's all settled into her room." I petted Zero's head and stared intently at his dark, glossy coat. Then I stood and faced my brothers at the kitchen island. I drew a deep breath, looking between their concerned faces. "This isn't a horrible idea, right?"

Trace and Damian shared a look.

"Not horrible," Trace started.

"Just...unconventional," Damian finished.

"I couldn't let her stay where she was," I said firmly. "That guy was unhinged. He said the most offensive shit. Not just to me, but to her too." I shook my head. "I don't even want to think about what would have happened if I hadn't gotten there when I did."

"From the sounds of it, Eli is an alcoholic, or worse." Trace rolled up the sleeves of his dress shirt. "She definitely needs to find someplace safe. But you need to be careful, too."

"I will," I said, though I wasn't entirely sure of it.

"I would do the same as you," Damian said. "But she *is* still married. And we can't forget who her father is."

My brothers were right. I clenched and unclenched my jaw, staring at the marble swirl of the kitchen island.

"I don't want you, or any of us, to get caught in something sticky," Trace said, glancing over my shoulder toward Cora's room.

"I promise the least amount of stickiness possible." I raised my right hand like it was a Boy Scout's honor. "There's a solution here, and I'm gonna find it."

My brothers looked placated, at least temporarily. Their concern was more than valid; I just wasn't entirely sure that avoiding stickiness was even possible. I'd wanted to promise to keep my heart out of it altogether, but even I knew that was a lie.

Keeping my heart out of anything involving Cora was about as likely as me calling up Eli for a friendly game of *Mario Party*.

Butch the chef joined us soon after, carrying his leather satchel of sharp-ass knives. We all conferred about what should be on the menu tonight, and after some back and forth, settled on scallops. Butch got to work prepping dinner while Damian, Trace, and I migrated to the sitting room.

"I'm ready for a visit to Louisville," Trace said with a sigh as he eased into his favorite spot, the pewter velvet barrel armchair.

"Oh yeah?" I settled into the chair facing him. My brothers and I usually traveled to Kentucky when we were in dire need of a reset or when we got too far embedded in the lifestyle of the rich and famous. Kentucky grounded us. Kept us real. "We were just there a couple months ago."

"Yeah. But I need to get out of this fucking city again." Trace dragged his palm across his forehead. "I'm tired of managing all this money, you know?"

We all laughed. It was one of our oldest inside jokes. Managing this money was the key to our lifestyle. But it came with its own costs. We each bore our own burdens within the business, which meant we all got a free pass to complain about our roles. But all of us equally bore the burden of our extra-vestments. The larger our business grew, the more often we convened to analyze our approach.

Trace managed the investments because he was a genius for that shit, but Damian had invented the algorithm that siphoned off a fraction of a penny from every dollar of return and reinvested the accumulated amount silently into noble causes. We were funding the foster care system across the entire country, and nobody even fucking knew, along with a few other altruistic endeavors. It made us nervous sometimes, being Robin Hood and all. But it was what we signed up for, now that we were wealthy beyond measure.

"You should take a trip this weekend," I suggested.

"Maybe I will and go say hi to Mom and Dad." He twisted in his seat, looking toward the small bar in our sitting area. "Are we having whiskey yet?"

"Allow me." I sprang to my feet, arranging three tumblers on the glass bar near the windows. The churn of Manhattan fifty floors below distracted me as I poured three equal neat whiskeys. And then I thought better of it and poured a fourth.

The scent of garlic and onion mingled with the sizzle of scallops as my brothers and I relaxed. Cora joined us just as the smell of dinner had reached mouthwatering levels. The sight of her emerging from my hallway in soft lounge pants and a loose shirt was almost too much to bear. Despite the loungewear, she still wore that diamond pendant. I knew it had to have a story behind it. One I planned to hear soon enough. I tipped more whiskey into my mouth, gobbling up this moment.

"Hey Trace," she said, joining us sheepishly. "Sorry it took me so long. I jumped on the Suicide Hotline for a half hour to take some calls."

"Look at you," I murmured, my heart swelling. She still did it, even all these years later. I hated to admit how much knowing that affected me. Whatever parts of me remained cold or closed-off toward her, she was rapidly forcing her way inside to every last corner of my heart.

She sent me a shy smile. "Hope you guys don't mind that I dressed down for dinner."

"We have no dress code at El Restaurante de Hermanos," Damian teased in a fake Spanish accent.

"But you do need reservations," I added. "Which luckily, I already secured."

Trace snorted. "They're hard to get, aren't they?"

"At least for someone with my last name," Cora added with a wry smirk. She slunk toward the open armchair.

"Yeah, Margulis doesn't show up too often on the guest list," I cracked. The four of us shared amused looks. A warm and familiar feeling blanketed me. This, right here—it felt like home. The four of us, hanging out, catching up, chilling in the living room.

Of course, the surroundings were different now. Instead of threadbare, hand-me-down couches from the streets of Chinatown, we had insanely expensive custom furniture. We'd swapped Thai takeout paid for with cryptocurrency for our five-star personal chef. But despite the differences, this moment felt the same.

Butch called us for dinner, and we followed the tantalizing scent of grilled veggies and seared scallops. Cora lagged behind, and I matched her pace, the two of us falling into step. There was nothing I wanted to focus on more than the rich mahogany gloss of her hair and her tired but smiling face, freshly washed, stripped of the business veneer.

This was the Cora I'd follow forever. Drunk, idiotic, smarmy-faced, Ken-doll-hair-wearing husband on the sidelines or otherwise.

"Thanks, Axel," she said quietly, snagging my gaze like she'd been waiting an eternity to find it.

I took her hand without thinking about it. Without even meaning to.

"Anytime," I whispered. It was true, no matter how much I didn't want it to be. I'd take her in after a break-up. After eight years. After she married somebody fucking else.

My brothers were right. This wasn't just sticky.

We were drowning in honey.

CHAPTER SIXTEEN

AXEL

Ever since my stint in the Kentucky foster system, I'd been a night owl. Damian too.

In the beginning, it was an anxiety thing. We didn't know what lurked around the shadowy corners of each new house, so we were too scared to fall asleep. And then as we grew older, the night anxieties solidified into habit. Now it was a concrete part of my foundation, these night-xieties, and life only kept serving up more things to worry about once the moon rose.

Tonight was no exception. It was the second night with Cora in the penthouse and the world still turned. But every hour with her under my roof begged for...something.

A decision. An update from the Margulis camp. Maybe even just divorce papers.

Whatever it was, the rock in my gut grew larger, wanting some direction. Because Cora was a magnet for me, now that she was within arm's reach. My only recourse was work. Getting out of the penthouse. Forcing that distance until dinnertime or after.

However much I wanted to erase the distance between us, that rock in my gut was the barrier. I'd caught up with her at dinner. Said a polite *sleep well* around nine. And then I disappeared into my bedroom with Zero until the pounding of my heart had subsided.

Having her this close felt like a fist holding my head underwater, forcing me to face down the past, to swallow it all until I choked. Memories I'd thought long dead and buried had started creeping out of the woodwork of my brain now that Cora was roughly twenty feet away from me. I paced my room, trying unsuccessfully to turn off the memories. To stop replaying the night I'd asked her to marry me and the pure joy I'd seen on her face. The way I'd gotten her off with my fingers alone as she sat draped across my lap on that rooftop patio.

Those were the dangerous memories. The ones that had promised a future full of light and opportunity that never materialized. The good times of the past became self-inflicted wounds in the present.

I drifted to the closet, tugging back the big, mirrored doors. In the back corner of the walk-in, I pushed aside last year's suits to reveal the ultimate memento of those days. I tugged the worn leather jacket from the hanger, my gaze washing over it like it had a million times before.

This jacket was long past wearable status. But I'd never get rid of it.

It was a reminder of who I was. Where I'd come from. This jacket represented what Eli and Allan hated about me. This was what I'd hidden in the fern eight years ago when I went to tell Allan I planned on marrying his daughter.

I slid it on, a grin tugging at my lips as the familiar weight settled over my shoulders. It fit a bit tighter these days—that was the virtue of having the in-home gym, which my twenty-year-old self couldn't have even imagined when I'd first spotted this coat in the bargain bin at a Chinatown second-hand shop. I looked at myself in the mirror, searching my reflection for signs of the Axel Fairchild from before all this wealth.

Looking for a sign of Axel Haynes, who I'd been before the Fairchilds adopted us. Before our entire lives had been upended.

It got harder every year to spot the roots of myself. But I wouldn't let them become covered up and eventually misplaced beneath the attractive trappings of wealth. That was one of the non-negotiables in my life. It went along with spending every waking moment in service to the under-served, even if we couldn't talk about it. I'd not let one sister's death and another's disappearance be in vain. I would work to change the course of the future as long as I was breathing.

It was well after midnight when I felt strong enough to shuck the leather jacket, venture out of my room and resume my typical ghostly roaming of the penthouse. I couldn't fall asleep most nights until at least two a.m., not even if I was dead on my feet. And even then, I naturally awoke around seven. There was too much to do in this lifetime to sleep.

Zero only lifted his head, sighed, and then collapsed back into his dog bed at the foot of my bed when I headed for the bedroom door. He didn't usually join me on my nightly wanderings, but I left the door cracked for him in case he changed his mind.

The penthouse hummed in its stillness, stretching shadowy and sepulchral. City lights filtered in through the floor-to-ceiling windows in the dining room, illuminating the edges of the armchairs, the curve of a vase, the tassel of a rug. I headed for the kitchen first. I didn't like lighting the place up at this time of night. I liked pacing in the shadows. Keeping to the recesses of my thoughts. Stumbling upon answers in forgotten corners.

I chugged a glass of water and then wandered. I headed to the gym first, to see if anything inspired me there. It didn't. I stopped in my office, listening to the hum of the electronics. I paused in the back hallways, staring out over the organized mess of Manhattan.

And the whole time, my mind churned, poring over the challenges of the day, reworking the sticking points of my life to see if I could conjure a different fit. Wondering when the Cora puzzle would finally be solved and ready to triumphantly frame.

One question always returned, the fist holding me underwater: *Why the fuck did she choose Eli?*

My brothers had tried to hide the news from me when news of their engagement circulated around Manhattan. But there was no way of dodging a family merger like that. Not in our world. Not when everyone lived, breathed, and ate Margulis and Rossberg bullshit on the daily.

The pieces of the puzzle had never quite fit together. I'd offered her everything I had. Promised her the world. She'd said that it was never about the money. Of course her father would have cut her off. But we would have been fine.

And we wouldn't be *here* right now. Hiding out from Eli. Pulling ourselves out of the stickiest mess I'd ever encountered. What sense did any of this make? It drove me nuts to board this train over and over again. It only went in a circle. *Why had she chosen Eli?*

Drowsiness nipped at me finally. Blessedly. I'd had my fill of the day, which meant I could lay my head down and actually drift off. Some nights, that moment never came. So I considered every night that I could yawn a success.

"No...no!"

Cora's voice wafted into the hallway as I passed her room. It was faint, and I wondered if I'd imagined it. I slowed, listening more intently.

The air conditioning clicked to life, the low hum of cool air pouring out of the vents.

When I heard nothing else, I started toward my bedroom.

"No, Eli!"

My forearms prickled, and I turned back toward her bedroom door. Now I was worried. There was no fucking way Eli had somehow broken into our penthouse...was there? I strode toward the guestroom door, then pressed my ear to it. Was it possible he was in there? Maybe she was engaged in a quiet struggle. I didn't want to be on the wrong side of a bad situation. Fear won out. I turned the knob and pushed the door open.

Darkness filled the room, and the dim hallway was the only source of light spilling in. The bedcovers rustled. Like she was kicking.

"Eli, no!" she called out again.

I searched out the light switches, feeling for the switch that would light up the moody lamp in the corner. The amber lighting revealed the room and the situation.

Eli wasn't in here. She was only dreaming.

My heart receded from its perch in my throat. As I was about to flip the switch and retreat to my own room, she whimpered again. And then she started to sob.

I swore under my breath; I had no idea what typical protocol was for something like this. Leaving her to cry into her pillow seemed wrong. But it was two a.m. I wasn't trying to insert myself into her bed when she was unconscious.

I drifted closer. Maybe I could just wake her up. Maybe this was just a nightmare.

"Cora."

She stilled, sniffling softly. "Axel?"

I swallowed hard. "Yeah. It's me. I was just checking on you."

She frowned, half-sitting up. Her cheeks were damp from tears as she ran her palm back and forth across her forehead. "Why did you get up?" Her slurred words told me she wasn't fully awake. Maybe even still dreaming.

"I was just walking by—"

"Come back to bed," she mumbled, her head dropping back to the pillow.

"You should go back to sleep," I told her.

"Please," she said, an arm flopping out onto the empty space beside her. "I need you, Axel."

There was no mistaking the emotion in her voice. The gut-wrenching sincerity there. God, it was so hard to walk away from. But I needed to.

Right?

"Cora, I should go back to my own bed," I croaked, not even half-meaning the words.

"Just hold me," she whimpered.

I was a strong man, but not strong enough to resist those words. Not from *Cora*, of all people. I sighed, heading for the door, giving myself the steps between the bed and the light switch to make my decision.

What we'd been doing up until now had been fun and games, born from very real chemistry, shadowed in heartbreak, and bursting with witty resentment. It hurt as much as it was fun. But this? This promised to be so much more than that. So much deeper than that.

If her coming to the penthouse was drowning in honey, this was someone throwing our jar off the side of a cliff.

I rested my forehead against the doorway. Every inch of me wanted to go to her.

Which meant I had to.

There was no choice. Not really.

I flipped off the lights and went to the vacant side of the bed. The bedcovers rustled as I debated how to show up for this unexpected sleepover. Undressing to my boxer briefs, as I normally slept, seemed presumptuous. Or at least shocking if she woke up with no memory of this. I chose to play it safe and crawled into bed as I was: in sweatpants and no shirt.

As soon as I hit the sheets, she was in my arms. Cuddled into me as if not a second had passed without us in each other's embrace. Her silky hair hit my cheek, and all the night-xieties dissipated. A big sigh rumbled out of me as I cozied up to her. Sleepiness licked at me.

It didn't matter how complicated things were. How tangled or terrible.

This was fucking bliss.

I only knew I'd fallen asleep when I jerked to consciousness and saw sunlight straining behind the drawn shades. Cora clung to me for dear life, but her eyes were open, and oh, how she looked at me. Like I was the only thing she wanted to see. Clarity and tenderness swam in her gaze, sending me stumbling into the past.

My lips ached to find hers. I drew a cleansing breath, and she extracted herself slightly.

"I'm sorry," she said quietly.

"For what?" I rubbed at my eyes, twisting to see the bedside clock. Just after seven a.m.

"I-I don't know," she admitted sheepishly, her gaze dropping to my bare chest. "Part of me can't even believe this is real right now. I thought I was dreaming when I woke up. Am I dreaming, Axel?"

My eyes opened and shut lazily, and I watched her, mesmerized by her just-woken-up perfection. I reached for her chin, swiping my thumb over it. "You tell me. You're the one who made me get in here."

"Did I?"

"Mm-hmm." I wet my bottom lip, gaze dropping to lips. All I wanted was to taste her. No, consume her. From top to bottom. Head to toe. Over and over and over again.

"Then if I'm dreaming, I don't want to wake up." She reversed the distance she'd placed between us, snuggling closer.

I grinned, wrapping my arm around her back. And yes, my cock was already at attention. How could it not be? Inches away from the best kisser in the world. This astute siren. The former woman of my fucking dreams. But doubts from last night crashed over me as the inches between us disappeared.

I needed to know the answer to my question.

I needed it more than I needed air. Especially if this woman was going to be sharing my house for any length of time.

"What, Axel?" she asked, tipping her chin up to find my gaze. "You just went somewhere."

"Yeah. I did." I closed my eyes, prepping myself to say the words that had been heavy on my heart since I heard the news they were engaged. When I opened them, her gaze waited for mine. "Why did you choose Eli?"

She blinked a few times, squinting as if she didn't understand the question.

"Instead of me," I clarified.

This time, she was the one who closed her eyes. She drew a deep breath.

"You still care to hear the answer?" she asked in a watery voice. The tears weren't far off.

"It's why I'm asking."

Her throat bobbed. "Will it change anything?"

"Probably not," I said. "Though I guess that depends on the answer."

When she didn't say anything, I added, "What's done is done. I'm over it. Your answer will give me nothing but peace of mind."

She nodded, licking her lips. Then she said, "My father promised he'd ruin you if we got married."

Something bulky and strange slid through me. I felt both hot and cold at the same time. Completely unnerved but also strangely relieved. "Ruin me?"

"Yes. You, your future, your business. Everything you and your brothers were striving for. He promised me that you'd never be able to achieve anything if I stayed with you."

I stared into the space beyond the bed as her words sank into me. I'd always assumed Allan had threatened to cut her off. That the possibility of losing her lifestyle had ultimately made her reconsider, even though she'd told me she could tough it out. In my darker moments, I considered the possibility that our three solid and unfathomably deep years together had somehow been a farce she'd executed. Fooling only me into thinking that I was the type of man she wanted, when really she craved the banality and slimy superiority of someone like Eli.

But I'd never considered *this*.

"My parents always wanted me to marry Eli. They made no secret of it. So somewhere during that first year after I broke up with you, I just decided to let them have what they wanted. I don't know. It seemed easier to just go along with it. I knew I would never love him. I knew we'd never have what I had with you. I didn't even try."

I shook my head, swallowing a lump in my throat. "You shouldn't have done that. We could have found a way."

A sad smile crested her face. "That's the least surprising thing I've ever heard you say."

"I'm serious." Now the emotions were cascading over me, pushing me so far into the past I could have drowned. All I could think about was all the time we'd wasted. All this fucking time apart because of Allan. As if I needed more reasons to hate the man. "I would have found a way, Cora. I swear to fucking God."

"I don't doubt you would have tried," she said softly, running her hand over the ridge of my shoulder. "But we both know it wouldn't have worked."

I shook my head, the anger burbling fiercely beneath my skin. "It would have. Trace and Damian and I, we would have come up with something. Allan could close doors on us, sure, but—"

"Axel." Her cool hands cupped my face, drawing my gaze into hers. "If I had told you the truth then, you would have detonated your life to make us work. And then where would you three be? Not in this penthouse. Not with all this success you're enjoying. It was too important to me, and to you, to take that away from you."

I clenched and unclenched my jaw. She was so right it hurt. Pain blossomed like a poison flower though my chest, its toxin sinking slowly through my veins. This just made everything worse.

"But at what cost?" I asked quietly. "You sacrificed your own happiness, for what?"

Her eyes closed for a few moments. When she opened them, a tear trickled out. "I never had a real shot at happiness, not with my family. You gave me more happiness than I ever thought possible."

"Cora." My voice cracked as the weight of her words settled over us. "This isn't right." I scooped her hand into mine, pressing her knuckles to my lips. "You deserve to be happy. You know that, right? You fucking deserve it."

She let out a shaky breath, a few more tears trickling down her cheeks. "Maybe. But I certainly don't deserve *you*."

I gathered her against me, the need to hold her outweighing everything else. Because the longer the truth of her sacrifice sank into me, the deeper I entered the ocean of love that had always existed between us. There was no turning back now.

And I'd lied. I'd said the truth wouldn't change anything,

It changed *everything*.

"Don't talk like that," I murmured into the top of her head. "You deserve me. You deserve happiness. You deserve to be treated with some fucking respect for once. To have some autonomy. This shit can't continue, Cora. I'm not gonna let it."

The tears were coming faster now, as she nodded and searched my face. I'd never seen her so open. So raw. So absolutely stunningly beautiful and pure.

This was Cora Margulis. The woman I'd always known. The woman I'd never stopped loving.

The woman whose happiness I'd fight for until the end of my life.

"Me and Zero are gonna protect you," I told her, kissing the top of her head. She squeezed her arms around my waist.

"Thank you."

"You know how many fucks he gives if Allan or Eli think otherwise?"

She shook with laughter in my arms. "Zero?"

"Exactly." I kissed the top of her head again, my lips drifting down over her temples. Each kiss was a new chance to discover her. To remember who I'd always loved, and to learn who she'd become since we'd broken up. I planned to create a map drawn strictly from kiss tracking. If I had my way, I could create this map in no time. When my kisses drifted lower, I noticed she still wore that diamond pendant. Even in her sleep.

"Why do you still have this on?" I asked, tracing the thin chain with my fingertip. "You always wear it, but even to bed?"

"I forgot to take it off last night," she said, her voice hoarse. "But it's the most important thing I own. The only physical possession that matters to me." She paused, licking her lips, searing me with a look so intense I wasn't sure how to process it. "These are the diamonds from the engagement ring you gave me."

The truth from this admission seeped over me, warm and intoxicating. I'd seen this diamond pendant on her from day one. And who knew how long she'd been wearing it religiously in front of Eli?

"Are you serious?" An incredulous laugh escaped me. It was the sweetest and sexiest thing I'd ever heard. "I'm not gonna lie, Cora," I whispered, my mouth pausing at her chin. "Thinking of you wearing my diamonds in front of Eli all this time is a major turn-on. I want to fucking eat you alive."

Her lips quirked up in a smile. Clarity had returned to her gaze. The tears had dried. And that old mischievous sparkle had returned.

"Then why don't you dig in?"

CHAPTER SEVENTEEN

CORA

Time moved around us in stop-motion, definable moments that I could pluck from the air like static memories. Axel plunging forward to claim my mouth with his. The flood of warmth when his tongue pressed past my lips and found my own. The solid steel heat of his body, fusing into mine.

Every movement from him heightened my awareness. His full attention sizzled across me, his stormy blue eyes acting like a whip to draw my attention. I wanted to drown in this sensation. To serve myself up on this altar and be worshipped by him forever.

It wasn't just because it had been years. It wasn't because he'd edged me and run last week.

It was because admitting the truth to him had lifted the burden I'd been carrying since the moment I broke things off. Even though I'd done it for him, keeping the truth from him had always eroded my center. None of the other complicated tangles of my reality mattered right now. Axel was undoing them simply by kissing me. Accepting me. Listening to me. This, right here, was all I'd ever needed. The only prescription for my ailments.

Axel's strong hands smoothed up my sides beneath my shirt, leaving a pair of scorching trails. He broke our kiss to help me sit up. With hooded eyes, he gently tugged my T-shirt up and over my shoulders, his gaze lingering over my exposed skin. Maybe it was his attention that made this feel like we'd tumbled backwards through time, back to our first time together. Despite how much time had passed, innocence shivered between us. A curiosity that came from the newness and the unknown.

He tossed my shirt aside, and his heated gaze moved to my breasts. He cupped them and placed a sweet kiss over each nipple, looking up at me for confirmation. When I smiled, he returned to each breast with greedy bites. My nipples pebbled, moisture surging in my panties.

"Ohhh, Axel." My eyes drifted shut and he silenced me with a kiss. Axel piled pillows behind me then and guided me to lie back. He smiled, satisfied, when I was in position.

"Comfy?"

"Incredibly." My heart swelled. This was the Axel I'd always known. The man who was always looking to make my life better. Always serving me. Always loving me.

He covered my mouth with his, eliciting a greedy kiss. Hunger swirled between us, threatening to devour us whole. He dragged his palm down my chest, through the valley of my breasts, over my belly. He paused there, deepening the kiss, tongues tangling. Then his hand dipped further, smoothing over the top of my panties, hooking his fingers beneath the soaked fabric. He brushed my swollen lips, a tease that felt more like a breath. I arched toward him and he swiped his thumb over the fabric of my panties, nicking the tight bud of my clit.

I shifted beneath him, vaulting to get closer to his touch. He fisted the top of my panties, drawing the fabric tight across my mound, pinching my lips together. His hungry gaze dipped between my legs, his attention leaving scorch marks. With all the pressure gathered around my swollen lips, he dove down and covered my mound with his mouth. Biting. Suckling through my panties. Giving me the sweetest, most delicious teasing touch I'd never known I'd always wanted.

My hips bucked, and I grabbed his head with my hands. "More, Axel."

He bit again, giving my needy clit the attention it craved only through the pressure of my swollen lips around it. It was a delicious torture. I rocked against his head, needing more. So much more.

Axel growled, biting harder one last time before slipping his fingers past the soaked crotch of my panties. He slipped two fingers inside me.

"You're so fucking wet." His teeth sank into the softness of my hip.

"For you."

He plunged his fingers deeper and flattened his tongue against the front of my panties. I hated that he was being so calculating, so teasing—but it fucking worked. "Always for me."

I moaned, thrusting against him. The need built inside me at a frightening rate. I wanted his fingers, but I wanted his cock buried inside me more.

"Please, Axel." I nearly thrashed against him. After so many years apart, the desperation might kill me. "I need you to fuck me." I swallowed hard, knowing exactly what I needed to begin healing the hole in my heart. "I want to come with you."

He held my gaze, pumping his fingers inside me again before he withdrew them slowly. He sucked on his middle finger and then gave me a sloppy tongue kiss, the sweetness of my own juices on his lips. When we broke apart, he pushed to the edge of the bed and stood. His hard-on formed an impressive tent in his gray sweats. He pushed them down along with his underwear, his cock springing free. I hurried to slip my panties off as he climbed back onto the bed, cock bobbing gently, framed by tightly trimmed dark hair.

He hovered over me, strong and reassuring as always, but completely divested of his Wall Street veneer. This was the real Axel, the southern farmhand transplant. I could see it in the brawny stretch of his shoulders, the powerful ripple of his washboard abs, mussed hair, and rough hands that knew their way around a farm as well as a board room.

That was where he surpassed any man who could ever be considered competition. I'd always felt safe around him. Safe to air my fears, my worries, my silly thoughts. Safe because I knew if I couldn't find a solution, then Axel would. Whatever life threw at us—from a blown tire to a botched deal—Axel could brainstorm with me and share the load.

I reached for him, relief flooding my body as I fisted the familiar length of him. His abs went tight, and he sank onto his heels, squeezing the tops of my thighs, his equivalent to waving me closer.

"Climb on, cowgirl."

Another ancient inside joke. I laughed. I was the farthest thing from a cowgirl, and he knew it, but it made sense for this Kentucky boy. My pussy pulsed in anticipation. We'd always come together like clockwork when I was on top. I moved to all fours on shaky legs, and he helped me climb on top of him. The heat of his skin against mine was both provocative and a balm. He steadied me above him as he maneuvered himself into place.

He tipped his head back to look up at me, searching my face. "You sure you want it like this?"

I nodded. I needed the feel of him. Nothing obstructing us. For this blessed break from reality, I wanted to pretend nothing would ever obstruct us again.

Axel gripped my hips, guiding me downward. "Take me, Cora." His swollen cockhead nudged for entrance between my slippery folds. I rocked against him, and he slipped inside. "Take all of me."

My eyes fluttered shut as I did what he said. I sank down on him, the steel length of him disappearing inside me. Every cell in my body was on high alert—expectant, euphoric. He cupped the small of my back as I sank downward, a groan escaping him. He latched onto the side of my neck, teeth pressing gently. Claiming me as his.

I was his. This fact had always been apparent. Had always been true, even when I married someone else. There was no room in my heart for anyone but Axel. Our gazes met, energy crackling there as I rocked my hips and swallowed the final inches of him. The pebbled tips of my nipples smashed against his chest as he squeezed his arms around me, closing whatever space remained between us.

Tears pricked at my eyes, and I buried my face in his neck. This. Right here. This was my safe space. The place that felt like home.

Axel ground up into me, sending pinpricks of light fluttering behind my eyelids. I rocked against him, starting a slow rhythm that soon evolved into something frenetic and needy. Nobody could fill me like Axel did. This wasn't just sex, this was communion.

His fingertips dug into my ass cheeks as he matched my rhythm. The noises of our lovemaking were slick, juicy. Axel grunted softly, a few locks of his hair falling into his eyes as he searched out my gaze.

And oh, the way he looked at me. I wanted to capture it and save it forever. He watched me with an intensity that threatened to unravel me on the spot. Like he would never let go of me now. Like he had never fully let go to begin with.

I didn't need to say the words that were on my heart. The air between us was thick with love and a tenderness so deep that it threatened to devour us.

Electricity sparked and swelled as our hips collided in a perfect rhythm.

"Axel," I moaned, clinging to the sinewy ridges of his arms. "I...It's too good. You're too good." I was helpless now, a victim of our passion. My breasts jiggled every time he drilled up into me. Sweat prickled at his temples, the blue storm of his eyes a raging tempest now.

His fingertips dug into the flesh of my hips as if they planned to root there, pulling me into him with every thrust. I squirmed against him, something powerful and cataclysmic around the corner. There wasn't just an orgasm waiting in the wings; this climax was going to split me open and change my life.

That's what Axel did. What he'd always done. Opened me up and showed me what else was out there.

"Ohhh, Axel. Please. Please. Please." I didn't even know what I was begging for, just that I needed more of it. More of him. As the desperation within me rose, his eyes glazed over. He fucked me until I was squirming against him, fisting the top of his hair, begging for it to never end.

My climax hit in a shuddering wave, lava hot and fast. I screamed his name. Louder than I thought possible. He yanked at my hair, forcing my head backward.

"Say it again," he growled, still grinding into me even though my pussy was a throbbing, sensitive mess.

"Axel." I wrapped my arms around his neck, my heart pounding as my climax stretched through me for round two. Everything felt broken open, vulnerable, volatile. So maybe that's what pushed the words out of my mouth. "I've never stopped loving you."

I captured his mouth in a kiss before he could respond. He slammed me down on his cock again and kissed me so hard that my lips buzzed. Axel erupted into me, the heat of his release coating my insides. We stayed like that for a long time, kissing hungrily, as though we were beginning all over again.

He squeezed his arms around me, his wet cock sliding in and out of me leisurely. I wished I could preserve this moment forever. Everything felt good again. No, it felt perfect. At least for a few blissful moments.

Axel pressed soft kisses to my neck, along my jawline, up to my lips. He tugged at my hair again, but this time it was gentler. It was just so that I'd meet his gaze. Our chests heaved as we stared at each other.

"Me neither, Cora," he said.

Tears pricked at my eyes, and I surged forward for another kiss. I'd never stop needing more kisses from him. We had eight years to make up for. And who knew how much longer I could get them?

We fell back onto the bed together, his body covering mine. He propped himself up on an elbow and gazed down at me, the words swirling unspoken between us.

I was his.

And he was mine.

CHAPTER EIGHTEEN

CORA

The weekend dissolved between us, a blur of sex, good meals, and more sex.

It was an escape. I knew it. He knew it. But we both just wanted to press pause on life for a minute.

Because good things came to an end. And in this case, the end was on Monday. I had to return to the office. I'd been working remotely long enough, and I had to show my face at Margulis Realty for a meeting. I didn't know what awaited me, other than it put me within arm's reach of Eli. I hadn't heard a peep from him since he'd broken into my hotel room, which was as relieving as it was unnerving.

Bright and early Monday morning, I pulled on a new black form-fitting dress that Axel and I had picked out together from the comfort of his king-size bed. I appreciated his desire to help me replace what I'd left behind, to get back on my feet. I even let him pay. These things represented the start of a new life.

I wasn't sure how long this new chapter could last.

"Hey. You call me when you can, okay?" Axel leaned forward to press a kiss to my lips as I rushed past him, gathering my work things. Today's suit du jour was Armani in slate gray with a black tie. When he looked like this, perfectly pressed and every inch a businessman, I had to do a double take. But then when I noticed the tattoos peeking past the collar and cuffs of his shirt, he became impossible to resist.

"I will," I promised, smoothing down the front of his tie. "And good luck with your meetings today."

"Thanks." He flashed me a devilish smile. "Though I don't need regular luck. I just need Zero luck."

Zero rumbled at the mention of his name, lifting his head to look at Axel briefly before resuming his sprawled-out position on the enormous dog bed.

"He's a great helper," I admitted, pausing to stroke his silky dark fur. "I'd say he stole the show at the Margulis pitch."

"You hear that, Zero?" Axel said as he stood in front of the mirror, tending to the last details of his appearance. "You stole the show."

"Actually, on second thought—*you* stole the show." I pinched his waist as I stood beside him. He gave me a suspicious sidelong look. In the mirror, we were an impressive pair. He was exactly the man I'd always wanted at my side, on my arm, in my life. "Even though you wouldn't look at me."

"Because you were sitting two feet away from your husband."

I quirked my lips. "Fair point."

He smirked at me, dipping down for a quick kiss. "But I still saw you. I couldn't not see you, Cora. I just couldn't look for too long. For my own sanity."

"I know." I smoothed my hands over the lapels of his suit coat, Axel's words burbling inside me. "It's weird to say, but I've never felt like he was my husband. Not really."

"Not even after your wedding day?" Axel asked.

"No. I always had some other idea of what a marriage should be." I swallowed hard, looking up at him. It was just after seven thirty and we both needed to be heading out the door, but this moment had swollen too big and important to walk away from. "The fairy tale must have gotten to me, even though I never saw anybody in my family living it."

He frowned, squeezing my arms. "The fairytale might not actually exist, but whatever your parents have going on isn't even close."

"I think you're wrong."

He lifted a brow. "About your parents?"

"No. About the fairytale not existing." A smile slowly lifted my lips. "Because you're my Prince Charming."

"Aww. Now don't go making me blush, Miss Cora." He allowed his Kentucky accent to lilt the edges of his words, which *did* make me blush. "Or should I say Princess Cora?"

"Let's go live in a castle somewhere."

"I'll hire a magic carpet," he added.

"And we'll live happily ever after." We said it in unison, which caused us both to break down into laughter. He squeezed my sides, pressing a kiss to the top of my head.

"Sounds like a plan. You ready?"

I nodded, grabbing for my handbag and briefcase. "Let's go."

I followed him out of the bedroom. Axel snapped his fingers as he crossed the threshold, and Zero sprang to life, trotting behind us. In the front sitting room, we found Damian and Trace in similar states of business readiness.

"Morning, you two." Trace picked up his briefcase. Damian gave us a withering smirk. He'd never been a morning person from what I remembered.

"Morning," Axel and I said in unison, which caused us to share a secret look. Then we burst into laughter again.

"Too chipper for this hour," Damian muttered.

"Because hackers are modern day vampires," Axel retorted. "The sun makes your skin melt off."

"That, and they require steady amounts of blood or alcohol to survive," Trace quipped.

"Exactly." Damian scowled. "Now take me to my darkened chariot that doubles as a coffin."

"Sheesh. These vamp-hackers are demanding," Axel muttered, jostling Damian by the shoulders.

The brothers continued ribbing each other while I just laughed and watched. They had a special knack for teasing each other, above and beyond typical brother rapport. There was so much love behind their ribbing. Even after so many years as not only brothers but colleagues, they still wanted to do life together.

"Okay, guys," Trace said while checking his watch. "It's time. Cora, are you coming on the helicopter with us?"

"No, I'll take cross-town traffic today, thank you." My smile dropped a notch, remembering what awaited me. "I think it might make things worse if I show up at Margulis in a Fairchild helicopter."

"You're probably right." Axel's hand settled in the small of my back, drawing me closer to him. "Let me at least send you in my car, though."

I smiled up at him, much closer to his lips thanks to my heels. I gave him a quick peck. "Thank you."

Once the brothers had said their goodbyes and headed up to the helipad to leave for their meeting in the Hamptons, I took the private elevator to the ground floor. The Escalade awaited me outside, blinkers flashing.

"Hi, Harry," I said as I slipped into the backseat. He sent me a warm smile. He was dressed as always in his black hat and coat with the silver buttons.

"Good to see you again, Cora."

"I feel the same way," I told him, allowing myself to dream about what it might feel like if this were my actual, regular reality instead of a one-off that had the potential to detonate my life.

It was time to decide what I wanted. I wanted out of my marriage—that much was certain—but I wasn't sure beyond that. The future I pined for—freedom from the Margulis machine—seemed unattainable. I could envision life away from Margulis, but no maps showed how to get there. The only path forward seemed to be to throw the road map away and just jump headfirst into the abyss.

Was I ready for that?

I couldn't answer that question yet. But I trusted I would be able to soon. I drew a deep breath as Harry pulled up in front of the Margulis building and I returned to that world of anxiety and roses. I was barely ten steps into the executive office suite when my phone buzzed with a message.

ALLAN: See me in my office. Urgent.

My stomach pitched to the floor, and I looked around guiltily, as though everyone might somehow know what was going on. Only a few pairs of eyes flitted my way. I assumed that the employees of our business at least suspected how little I cared for Eli, even though we'd put on a decent show over the years. But there was no way they could know what had happened at the hotel room. Most of them probably had no idea I'd even moved out from the brownstone on the Upper West Side, even though I felt like the truth was visible to the world, like a bright shawl over my outfit.

I counted the steps to my father's office, trying to rally my neutrality, my stoniness. The immediate summons wasn't good. But I was ready to confront whatever came my way. Because finally, I had ammunition.

For however doubtful I felt about my path, I knew that staying with Eli was impossible. Nobody in their right mind could expect me to stay.

"Hey, Brooke," I called out to my father's receptionist as I breezed past her desk. "I'm going in for a last-minute meeting."

I didn't hear her reply as I pushed open the door to my father's office. His expansive suite greeted me, the immense wall of windows the first thing to catch my attention. But I didn't spare the Manhattan morning a second glance as I focused my attention on my father.

He sat behind his desk, looking somber, already facing me as though I'd entered the room minutes ago.

He'd been waiting.

"Morning," I said, not bothering to inject any enthusiasm into my voice. "What's on the agenda?"

"Sit down."

I ignored the slow thump of my heart that served as a warning signal. He'd always been good at unbalancing the competition, the enemy, whoever it was on the other end of the negotiations. And with him, everything was a negotiation.

I suppressed a sigh as I settled into the leather armchair facing his desk. He cleared his throat, the flecks of gray hair at his temples moving as he clenched and unclenched his jaw. Even as he prepared to step down from his position as CEO, he was formidable.

"I've caught wind that you spent the weekend on Fairchild property," he said in a low, threatening voice.

I swallowed hard, making sure to keep my gaze steady. "I did."

"In fact, I've heard a lot of worrying information regarding you from Eli lately."

I hefted with a humorless laugh. "Have you?"

My father dipped his chin. "What is going on?"

I knew better than to think he was asking about my wellbeing. No, this was a business meeting, pure and simple. Emotions weren't to be considered. This was all about strategy.

"I'm preparing to exit my marriage," I told him, hoping the words came out as steel-edged as I intended.

"And you think running away to a pathetic ex-boyfriend is going to somehow help you in that?" His laughter was so caustic it nearly burned me. "You clearly have no clue what you're doing. You will reconsider."

"I will not," I responded, keeping his steely gaze. "Eli has become abusive. He's left bruises on multiple occasions." I wanted to say more, to dive into this with any expectation of compassion from him, but I knew it wouldn't come. So I had to relate to him on his level. "My husband leaving bruises isn't a good look for the Margulis brand. And besides, you don't have a say in my personal life anymore. I did what you wanted me to do. Now I need to save myself from the consequences of complying with your wishes."

This seemed to give him pause. His jaw flexed as his gaze shifted to something behind me. And because it seemed like I'd actually gotten through to him, I took this opportunity to share more.

"I cannot compromise my safety. Eli has been increasingly aggressive, and it's terrifying. I don't feel safe in my own home anymore." I swallowed hard. "I don't feel safe *anywhere.*" Except with Axel, but I wasn't about to tell him that.

"There are always two sides to the story," my father said, in an annoyingly diplomatic tone. "Have you considered giving it a fresh start?"

A fresh start. I wasn't sure whether to laugh or just walk out. My mouth parted but nothing came out. A fresh start was the last thing I'd considered.

"I can't believe you have the gall to say that to me."

"Well, maybe things wouldn't have gotten so out of hand if you'd tried harder."

Something shut down inside me. Whatever engine had been thrumming, trying to keep this charade afloat, finally stumbled to a halt. Yet again, it was my fault. The solution required *my* sacrifice. My heart was so incredibly tired of the letdowns from the people who called themselves family.

"What do you honestly expect from me?" I asked him, beyond outrage. Beyond shock. At this point, I had no room left for more emotions when it came to my father. There was just a blankness swelling inside me. Threatening to capsize even the good emotions. "To get beaten to death by a drunk just so you can have your picture-perfect empire? How's that going to go over in the tabloids?"

My father didn't respond but his scowl deepened.

"Honestly, why isn't sacrificing everything I love and desire enough for you?" I shook my head. "Now I have to sacrifice my body, my mental health, and possibly my life?"

"You are being excessive and dramatic," my father began.

"No. I'm not." I sliced my hand through the air. "And I'm done. I've had e-fucking-nough. I've given you and this company more than enough. I'm not giving you that." I stood up on shaky legs and headed for the door.

Before I could pull it open, my father said, "So what? You're ready to leave it all behind? Just because that sleazeball of an ex showed up again?"

"I never said I was leaving anything behind except that marriage," I told him. "There's no way in hell I'm not going after a divorce."

He glowered at me; that was not the news he'd wanted to hear. But he'd have to get used to it. I wasn't resigning. I wasn't stepping down. I simply needed to end my marriage, immediately.

I strode out of his office. I didn't need to hear anything else he had to say. Nothing could have been worse than what he'd already said, than what he'd spent his entire life telling me.

The Margulis family subsisted on a steady diet of outward perfection and inward turmoil. For my family, home was synonymous with conditions. "You can be a part of the family *if...*" If, if, if.

I wanted to exist in a place where home meant unconditional. Where my headaches weren't going to signify happiness-destroying storms whenever I dared to venture off the path they'd plotted for me. A place where white roses weren't a sign of worse times to come.

I'd spent my entire life being told that love was something you could buy. Love was something you could purchase off the rack or in the carefully drawn property lines in an exotic locale. But Chris and I had learned how false that lesson was together; meeting and loving Axel had only reinforced it.

Love wasn't something you could hand over and take back. It wasn't some capricious fancy of the heart.

Love was something that soaked into your bones. Steadfast and solid.

An unconditional truth that existed with no *ifs*.

I tucked myself into my office, which almost felt foreign after so many days working from the hotel room and Axel's penthouse, and tried to get into the groove of my workday.

Less than an hour passed before Axel texted.

AXEL: *You still alive over there?*

CORA: *I've got a pulse.*

AXEL: *That's how I like my women.*

I dissolved into laughter. He always knew how to take the edge off. And now that he'd beaten back the gloom from my predictably terrible meeting with my father, I could see that there was hope for us. Not just for us, but for the reality I'd always pined for. Balancing my job with the family business and being with Axel. It could still exist.

After all, my family couldn't force me to be with Eli. Not like this. Not anymore.

I wanted hope to flourish. If Eli would sign divorce papers, then the future would be my oyster. Axel and I could figure out whatever came our way.

Save the company meeting I was required to attend, I didn't leave my office for the rest of the day. I called my assistant to bring in lunch and spent the day poring over emails, strategy calls, and team chats. From here on out, I'd show my father that I could exist on my own terms while still preserving the stability of his precious company.

I could be CEO *and* be with Axel.

I began researching divorce lawyers. I was done pretending this separation was a long-term solution. Clearly, Eli and I could no longer continue. By the time four o'clock had come and gone, I had reached out to three lawyers, and I was ready to head back to Axel's. We'd been texting on and off all day: trading sweet words, planning for dinner, figuring out what else I might need for my stay.

One of my assistants knocked on my door. Tatiana poked her head in, her white-blonde hair in an expert messy bun.

"Cora? You got a package." She sounded excited, which caused me to perk up. "Do you want it now or should I leave it out here?"

"You can bring it in." I smiled as she walked from the door to my desk. She handed over a white box with a red ribbon around it. I could see why she sounded excited. This looked like a classic surprise-during-the-workday gift. The tag simply read *To my beloved.* It had to be Axel.

"I wonder what he sent you," she murmured, reminding me we weren't excited about the same person.

"I think I'll have to open this later." I patted the red ribbon. "I told myself I'd finish this last email before I moved on to anything else."

She wilted slightly, which made me wonder how much of a fairy-tale romance they really thought I had with Eli. Or maybe it was less fairy tale and more financial. Either way, I didn't want to reveal that this gift was most likely from someone who wasn't my husband.

No, that information needed to leak in a slow and controlled fashion. If it came out any other way, it would explode across the headlines like the Hindenburg. I'd have to manage that myself to avoid the messy alternative.

"Let me know if you need anything, okay?" Tatiana asked as she bounced back toward the door. She sent me another smile before shutting the door behind her.

I took out my phone to send a text to Axel.

CORA: You really didn't have to send me a gift.

And then I dug in, pulling at the silky ribbon, grinning as childlike excitement came over me. Axel knew how to pick up my spirits. Axel was unfailing. Axel was the man of my dreams.

AXEL: I didn't send you one...?

My smile dropped, and I pulled open the white lid. Inside, amid white fluffy filler lay a familiar package. I picked it up, confusion slithering through me, and then noticed a handwritten note beneath it.

Thought I'd make you a care package for your romantic getaway with your hillbilly lover. Gonna need this, huh?

It was my birth control. The package I'd left behind. The prescription I'd been hiding from Eli for the past several years.

Eli was playing dirty.

CHAPTER NINETEEN

AXEL

The helicopter was waiting for us when Cora made it back to the penthouse. I planned to surprise her with a dinner we'd discussed via text message during our workdays, but in my Hamptons house. It was time for her to start meeting my properties.

But when she met me on the top floor of the building, in the vestibule just outside the helipad, she didn't look nearly as enthused as I'd expected. Worry tugged at her features as she came toward me.

"Cora, what's wrong?"

The helicopter sat silent on the helipad, the pilot awaiting my signal. She stopped in front of me, nibbling on her lip. "Eli was the one who sent me a surprise gift today. And this was it." She tugged a white plastic sleeve from her purse. I turned it over in my hands, not understanding what I was looking at.

"He's always wanted to have kids. It's been part of his business strategy since the beginning," she said, her throat bobbing. "But I always knew I didn't want to have his children. So I started sneaking birth control."

"Sneaking?"

"Yes. If he found out, he'd get upset. I've always wanted children..." Her voice faltered. "But I only ever wanted them with you."

The truth of her confession ran into me like a train. I melted at her feet, coming down to one knee, gathering her against me. The pain I felt on her behalf was only balanced by the tenderness of knowing she'd waited for me. She'd still tried to honor our connection, even when she was trapped in that awful marriage.

"Cora, I don't even know what to say." I kissed her belly. If this was how I reacted to news that she had lied to her husband for years in an effort to not bear his children, I didn't know what would happen once she and I actually fucking had kids. Move over, overprotective meme dads. Axel Fairchild was coming for ya. "I hate that you had to hide this from him, but I fucking love that you even remembered me while you were with him."

"Remembered you?" She laughed, wiping at a tear that had fallen. "Axel, I was fucking haunted by you. There was no forgetting. There's only *you*."

I kissed each knuckle of hers in turn, my heart thumping with something so intense I thought it might shake me apart. I took the birth control package from her hands and tossed it aside.

"Fuck this stuff, then," I told her. "Take birth control if you want, but not this stuff. It's tainted. By him."

She laughed sadly. "In the beginning, I tried a few different methods that would be easier to hide, but they all made me feel bad or too weird to function. The only type that worked was pills. When I moved out of our house, I thought I'd taken it all. But I forgot my emergency pack. Which clearly, he found."

"Okay. But you know what?" I could see she needed reassurance. Grounding. Another eternal hug. "It's gonna be okay."

She nibbled on her lip again as I pressed my lips to the back of her hand. "Is it? He's upset. No, he's beyond upset. I'm worried about what he might do."

"It doesn't matter what he does," I reminded her, coming to my feet. I wrapped my arms around her. "Because we have resources."

She laughed slightly. "Axel. Please. Whatever resources you have, he has them too. If not more."

"You're wrong." I stepped back to meet her gaze. "He doesn't have Damian."

She blinked a couple of times. "What do you mean?"

"I'm just saying, we have the best hacker in the world on our side. Eli should be a little fucking worried right now. Not you."

A smile tugged at her lips, but she didn't look convinced. "I hope you're right."

I was right, but she didn't realize it yet. I'd unleashed my own personal hacktivist on Eli. Whatever dirt there was to be found on Eli, Damian would find it. He always did. I scooped her back into my arms. "We're gonna get through this. Together. I promise you."

She buried her face in my chest, clutching at the lapels of my jacket, nodding. "Okay. You're right. We will."

"You are mine and I am yours," I whispered into her ear. "He's not gonna take you away from me again. Him *or* your father. Do you hear me?"

She nodded again.

"Look at me and say it, Cora."

She lifted her head, her watery eyes rimmed with red. "He's not going to take me away from you." Her throat bobbed. "I just hope he doesn't ruin everything else instead."

"He won't." I claimed her mouth with my own. One kiss bled into two, and then a thousand. I kissed her until I'd erased every last drop of doubt. When she stood taller in my embrace, I raised my head.

"There we go." I swiped my thumb over her cheek. "Now are you ready for our special dinner?"

Her smile was a mile wide. "I've been ready for years."

I put two fingers in my mouth and whistled. The pilot looked over at us, gave me a thumbs up, and started the chopper. I led Cora by the hand across the cement pad. The wind from the helicopter blades lifted our hair when we got close. The helicopter pilot helped us inside, fitting us with earphones and seatbelts.

Moments later, we were cleared. The helicopter lifted slowly from the helipad, the small rush of adrenaline a welcome thrill as we picked up vertical speed. Soon, the majesty of the city stretched beneath us. This was my favorite moment. The hustle and grind of Manhattan was reduced to a prismatic blur, something contained and comprehensible. I reached for Cora's hand as we vaulted through the sky. And for that moment, everything was perfectly right in the world. Her mulberry smile at my side was all I needed. All the tangles that awaited us could only be blips if Cora was in my life.

The ride to my Hamptons home was quick. The helicopter touched down on the cement helipad at the far end of the property, tucked into the sprawling yard halfway between the house and the ocean. When the blades slowed, I hopped out first, helping Cora out next. The pilot retrieved our bags and sent me another thumbs up, which meant he'd be back for us when I called.

The smells of late evening near the water were intoxicating as we trekked toward the house. Cora heaved a sigh, pausing to slip off her heels and walk barefoot through the clipped grass, foregoing the brick path that cut through the yard.

"Watch it," I warned. "You're turning into a country girl."

"Thanks to you," she said, squeezing my hand. "You were the one who turned me on to freshly laid eggs, after all."

"But you never took to the hay baling, did you?"

Cora laughed. "I'd rather leave that part to the professionals." Her eyes sparkled as she took in the property. I'd opted for a wooded and secluded paradise and paid a pretty penny to obtain it. But I had my golden getaway whenever I needed it, with the ocean only steps away and nobody to fucking bother me unless I asked them to.

"I'm in love with this place already," she said.

"You haven't even seen the inside."

"I don't need to." She tipped her head back to look into my eye. "Just being here with you is enough. We could sleep outside for all I care."

"I have something much more comfortable than that lined up." I kissed the top of her head, my heart swelling painfully. Sometimes it felt like I could pass out from how much I still loved her and how much I wanted to take away all the suffering of the years she'd spent at Eli's side. "Though I appreciate your vote of confidence. Next time, I'll just set up a tent."

We passed the quietly burbling in-ground pool as I led her to the climbing rose-covered pergola. The pink and fuchsia rose blooms were the size of my fist, vining across the slats of the pergola, tumbling down onto the handrails leading up to the mahogany deck. The scent of the roses mixed with the nearby woods flooded my senses as we climbed the steps; earthiness mingling with the humid bite of summer. I took another look at the waves rushing against the small beach before I led Cora to the back entrance.

"Think there's any beach glass out there?" she asked.

I blinked, looking down at her. *The beach glass.* That question had cut unexpectedly deep, but the sweet smile she offered dulled the blow. I hadn't thought about the beach glass in years. How could I have forgotten? It was a constant love song we sang to each other. Combing the beach for glass in the exact shades of each other's eyes.

"I haven't looked," I told her.

"Oh, come on. These are the important property details that you're supposed to know."

"Oh, you want to hear property details?" I curled my arm around her waist, bringing her in step with me as I pushed open the door. My chef was already here, preparing the dinner I'd requested, so the scent of garlic was the first thing to hit our noses. We stepped into the big living room, with its vaulted ceiling and exposed beams, the hardwood oak floors gleaming. This was different than my home in Manhattan, but it was home all the same.

"The residence offers six bedrooms," I said in my best, fakest realtor voice, "five full and one half baths, with a delightful open floor plan..."

She laughed, swatting my chest. "That's not how I sounded on the building tour, right?"

"No. You sounded much more anxious than that." I dipped down for a quick kiss.

"Being within arm's reach of you again, after so long?" A humorless laugh escaped her. "Yeah, anxious barely covers it."

"Well, it was really Eli who made the whole thing a warm and cozy party," I mused, leading her deeper inside. I drank in all my favorite features of the house—the oversized windows, the wainscoting, the coastal sunlight filling the space. I'd worked with an interior designer to select furniture that reflected the best blend of coastal comfort and modern, moody designs. It had been a fun passion project, and the result filled me up whenever I came to visit.

"This place is incredible," Cora mused, pausing at the built-in bookcases beyond the fireplace. She looked back at me. "It's so homey."

"That's what I was going for." I tipped my head in the direction of the sizzling sounds wafting from the kitchen. "Let's go meet Renault."

She cocked a grin. "Where's Butch?"

"He's our Manhattan chef. Renault is Hamptons only. He doesn't like to come into the city, and he's too good to not obey his demands. He makes a circuit between my house and a few others."

"A chef-share," she quipped.

"Exactly." We stepped into the kitchen. Renault's back was toward us. The kitchen was in full production mode—gleaming mixing bowls on the thick granite countertops, pans sizzling, asparagus chopped and waiting on a cutting board. "Wow, Renault. This looks amazing!"

Renault turned toward us, his face flushed as it often was in the kitchen. He held out his hands. "Axel! Finally I get to feed you again!"

I stepped forward for a quick bro hug with Renault and then gestured to Cora. "I'd like you to meet Cora. She's the guest of honor today."

Cora stepped up, offering him a hand. But instead of shaking it, he brought it to his lips.

"It's a pleasure," he said, glancing meaningfully my way. "Any lady Axel would honor by hiring me to cook for her is truly a special person."

I laughed, tongue in cheek. "Renault, you're good at complimenting others *and* yourself at the same time."

He winked. "Learned it in chef school."

The three of us chatted for a bit, until Renault needed to return to his preparations. I led us to an alcove in the dining room, where a small refrigerator and drinks cabinet were set into the wall. I pulled out a chilled bottle of chardonnay and showed it to her. "Can I interest you in a beverage?"

"Always." She watched as I readied two white wine glasses, which were hanging from a rack in the alcove. I poured two generous glasses, then we clinked the rims together.

"To the Hamptons," I said, before tasting the wine.

"It's always been our place, hasn't it?" She grinned before she tipped some into her mouth.

"For better or for worse."

"That sounds an awful lot like the wedding vows we never exchanged," she said wryly.

"Ooh. Are we at the broken engagement level of joking now?" I snaked my arm around the dip of her waist, jerking her body closer until she was flush against me.

"I have to joke about it or else it'll destroy me."

I set my wine glass down so I could cup her face in my hands. "Destruction is not an option. So joke away. You know my morbid ass likes it."

She pushed onto her tiptoes, silencing me with a kiss. The faint whisper of wine on her breath mingled with the clementine scent of her perfume, which had my heart thumping. I wanted her—again and again. I'd never stop wanting her.

We kissed like adolescents for what felt like forever, until Renault cleared his throat loudly several times and broke us from our dreamy make-out session. He summoned us to the table, where our first course awaited: leek and potato soup. Renault had some particularly harrowing stories of other Hamptonite homes pretending the help didn't exist, so I made a point to insist he join us for each course. For the main course, grilled yellowtail came accompanied with caper aioli and baby root vegetables. Renault had created a strawberry and peppercorn sorbet to transition to dessert, which was a chocolate torte with espresso foam.

Cora and I oohed and aahed our way through dinner. If I could have orgasmed from food alone, Renault would be the man to push me over the edge. Hell, I liked to pretend that he *had* given me the big O from his flavors alone. He was a wry guy, and I could tell he liked that I wasn't as uptight as most of his Hamptons clients.

Once the last bit of espresso foam had been licked clean, I dragged Cora back onto the mahogany deck with a freshly uncorked bottle of red wine for us to share on the beach. This time, we both ran through the grass barefoot, laughing as we tripped our way toward the shoreline, wine sloshing out of the bottle. The sunset settled over the horizon in the most glittering way possible, golden hues draped over us like shawls.

Our laughter was overshadowed only by the rush of the ocean waves. We paused at the gazebo by the shoreline, setting down the bottle of wine. Cora stripped out of her dress while I grabbed beach towels from a small cabinet I kept stocked for just such occasions. Once her long, creamy legs were on full display, my cock was already half-mast. I shucked my button-up, my eyes fastened to her svelte form as she turned to me in her bra and panties.

"You planned on going for a dip, right?"

"I planned on whatever you were planning on." I wet my bottom lips, pushing my pants down over my hips. My boxer briefs were tented, which only became more obvious as her gaze dropped between my legs.

Cora reached behind her back. A moment later, her silky bra loosened, and the straps fell down her shoulders. She tossed it aside, her breasts heavy and on display, nipples hardening to dusty-rose points.

"Oh, so *that's* what you're planning."

"Mm-hmm." She stepped out of her panties next, never breaking my gaze. "Planning on *you.*"

Her words might as well have been a gunshot to start the race. I tore my boxer briefs off and crossed the space between us in two powerful steps. I gathered her warm body against mine, our skin gliding like silk. I hooked my hands behind her thighs, and a moment later she was hoisted against me, the sweet heat between her legs throbbing against the tip of my cock.

"That was fast," she purred.

"You make it hard to go slow."

"Can we go on the beach and make love in the sunset?" Her innocent question cracked my heart open further. How many moments like this had Allan stolen from us? How many thousands of conversations and kisses and sweet embraces would never be ours because of what that man had forced her to choose? I'd always hated her father, but now my hatred had fermented into something new altogether. I'd started acquiring shares and planning a hostile takeover as a way to prove to him I could do what he never believed I could.

But now? I wanted to take from him what he'd taken from me.

"Do you ever think about how many times we would have been able to do that by now?" I swallowed hard. "If it weren't for Allan."

"Every day," she whispered.

"We would have been married by now." I dragged my lips over her cheek. "We'd have two kids."

She shook her head, looking up at me with unshed tears shimmering in her eyes. "Axel, I've tortured myself with these thoughts since the day we broke up."

"I have too."

"I can't think about it anymore. Can't we just pause this right now? So we can stay here forever?" A sad smile lifted her lips. "When everything feels right for once."

I squeezed her ass cheeks, the heat of her against me bringing me back to earth. "Truth. And this is about to feel *extra* right."

She giggled, tightening her arms around my neck as I stepped out of the gazebo and headed for the sandy shore. The sun hung low and bloated in the sky, partially obscured by the treeline, almost touching the horizon. Sailboats dotted the water, but none were close enough for us to care about. Warm sand squished beneath my toes. Once my feet found the ocean foam, I let her slide to standing. I gripped her chin between thumb and forefinger, snagging a deep kiss.

And then I led her by the hand into the water, finding the perfect shallow incline to settle into. The water rushed around us, warm and inviting, as she settled on top of me. Her thighs encircled my waist, creating the most delicious vice. A satisfied sigh escaped her.

"You sure know how to wine and dine a woman," she said.

"I only dined you—we barely touched the wine."

She laughed throatily, rocking her hips in a slow circle on top of me. My cock strained toward her, eager for more than just the occasional brush of her slick heat. "You don't think Renault is watching us right now, do you?"

"Not unless he brought binoculars." I grabbed big handfuls of her ass, jiggling her silky skin on top of me. My abs were tight from how hard I was clenching. Waiting for her to sink down and swallow me whole.

"Too bad he won't see how I make your whole cock disappear," she murmured into my ear. The water receded around us, pulling back like a sheet, until it rushed forward again.

"Jesus, Cora." I gripped her hips, thrusting upward. I needed to be inside her. *Now.* "How you gonna talk like that and not fuck me?"

"Oh, I will." She licked my earlobe, then took a bite at it. "Give me time."

"Come on, babe." I wrapped a hand around my shaft, searching out her swollen folds with the crown of my cock. Something about the trifecta of the moment had me fucking dying for it—the orange sky ablaze behind her, the shallow, ocean water rushing and then receding, the warm silk of her body draped over me. "I'm so ready."

"Oh, I can see how ready you are." She chuckled throatily.

"Is this payback for when I fucked you with my fingers in the back hallway of La Fève ?"

Arousal flashed in her eyes. "You'll be paying for that for a long time."

I took a bite of her neck. *Hard*. "Good. I've been a bad boy."

"You are so fucking naughty, Axel." She made slow, wide circle on top of me, my cockhead slipping inside her for the briefest of seconds before she rocked her pelvis away from me. "You edge me. You flaunt your little girlfriends in front of me."

I squeezed her waist, my fingertips digging into her flesh. "Guilty."

"Not only that," she added, "you make me fall in love with you so hard I can't even hope to get over you."

Her fingernails dug into the ridge of my shoulder as she rocked in a slow circle again. But this time, when the water rushed around us, it stole the stability from beneath her knees in the sand. *Thank you, Ocean.* She sank on top of me, sucking in a sharp breath as the ocean pushed me into her.

"Ohhh, fuck." My eyes closed and everything went hot and loud for a second. "Fuck."

"Why do you feel so good?" She caught my lips in a kiss as she sank on top of me, finally making my cock disappear. And I didn't fucking care if Renault was watching, or anyone else. All I needed was Cora.

I moaned into the space between her breasts, cinching her tighter against me.

"Axel," she begged.

"Do you realize how wet you are?" My mind grew muddy from the drugging sensation of her pussy wrapped around me.

"For you."

I tugged at the tip of her ponytail, exposing the creamy arc of her neck. I sank my teeth into her pulse again. "Only for me, huh?"

"Forever for you."

Her words echoed inside me as I filled her. I was so swollen and hard, I felt like I could pop off at any second. I started with short thrusts, one hand splayed across her lower back to make sure we didn't lose an inch of connection, the other one sliding behind her neck and staying there. Her breasts were smashed against the hard plane of my chest, small grunts escaping her as I drilled up, over and over again.

I groaned, our mouths connecting in a greedy dance. Cora rocked with wild abandon on top of me, her pussy clenching like a vice around me.

"I can feel you getting close," I whispered hotly into her ear.

"Axel," she begged.

"Come for me," I commanded, looking into her face. Everything that had been pushed aside for the evening—her confession about the birth control, the ongoing anxieties over Eli, the sheer amount of repressed desire and love that had been stacked up over the years—swirled through me, seeping into my bloodstream, desperate for an outlet.

The water whooshed around us again, droplets spraying us, and Cora bucked on top of me, her eyes pinching shut as she rode me as if this was the last chance we'd ever have. She cried out, stuttering and breathy, the sunset glinting off the curve of her cheek as she arched away from me. But I gathered her into my big arms, holding her closer while she thrashed and moved through the body-wracking orgasm.

The raw pleasure on her face pushed me over the edge. Pleasure coiled and uncorked deep inside me, spreading through my limbs with an urgent fire. My whole body went tense as the orgasm roiled through me, something guttural and animal floating past my lips. The heat of my release coated her insides, spilling out, washing away with the ocean.

Cora's chest heaved as she collapsed into my arms. I held her, pressing lazy kisses to her forehead, as we basked in the aftermath. My dick pulsed softly inside her, and the rush of the waves tickled us.

"Thank you," she finally said, tipping her head up to look me in the eye. She wiped at a spilled tear.

"For what?"

She nestled against my chest, making a home there as she always had. "For reminding me there's a whole life worth living."

Her words landed like the saddest spear. I kissed the top of her head. "You can still have the life you've always wanted, Cora. Are you willing to fight for it?"

"I've always thought I had no right to fight for it," she said softly. "Not when I've had everything a person could ever dream of."

"That's not true," I told her. "You've had everything except the most important part. Freedom."

She nodded, her gaze drifting to the horizon. "I want that. I want it so bad."

"I'll do everything I can to make sure you get it."

She blinked, another tear sliding silently down her cheek. "You will?"

I nodded.

"You'd do anything, even if it took me away from you?"

I didn't like the question, not even a little bit. I'd spent too many years being away from her. I didn't want to consider more years of the same. But I sensed she was asking it as a test. To see where my priorities lay. And they would always be aligned with her best interests. Nothing less.

"Your freedom is number one. The rest will sort itself out afterward."

We sat like that for so long, lost in the rhythmic rush and return of the waves, kept warm from the heat of the other, saltwater lapping at our thighs. After a while, she started dragging her hand through the thick, dark sand. And then she sat up, holding a glinting piece of glass between her fingers.

"There's beach glass," she said, showing off the sky-blue nugget. "But it's not quite the right shade of Axel Fairchild blue."

I drew a deep breath. "Do you still have yours?"

"They're hidden at the condo. What about you?"

My gaze dropped to her shoulder. I hated to admit it, but the beach glass remnants in the exact shade of Cora Margulis green eyes had been a burden too great to bear at the time. "I threw them away. Years ago."

She nodded, looking a little disappointed. "I would have done the same in your position."

I nuzzled her neck. "I'm sorry."

"Don't be."

"Heartbroken is an understatement of how I lived for...years," I admitted in a rush. "I tossed the glass into a dumpster in Chinatown one drunken night, and I always regretted it."

Her smile started out sad, but then it glinted with mischief. "I guess this just finally proves that I've always been a little bit more devoted than you, huh?"

I laughed, covering her mouth with a kiss.

I'd let her win this one. *For now.*

When devotion was on the line, she had no idea just how I intended to win this battle.

CHAPTER TWENTY

CORA

Our getaway to the Hamptons became the benchmark of happiness against which I'd measure everything that came after. On this new scale, my previous life could no longer exist.

If I'd started the tides of change, Axel was helping them continue to rise. For every step forward, my anxiety tried to tug me two steps backward. But Axel was there to hug the anxiety away. To smooth my hair, call me *cowgirl*, and remind me that I could fucking do this. The birth control delivery had been a warning shot. More was coming—I just didn't know what. Or when. I was up against a ticking timebomb.

I laid low. I used Axel's penthouse as my safe space, and only went out to work or the Hamptons house with Axel. He understood my need for privacy. I didn't want even one random photo to circulate; I could have no public outings with Axel. I planned to execute a controlled demolition of my life, and any disturbances from outside forces—like the media—threatened to cause an avalanche.

I barely saw my father in the week or two after our confrontation in his office. If he was content to ignore me and look away, then so was I. I worked remotely as often as possible. I needed more time to get my ducks in a row. Information from different legal offices had started to come in. Axel and I pored over the options together, treating it almost like a fun project as opposed to the single most important factor to my future freedom. Anything to stave off the encroaching sense of doom was welcome, even if it meant Axel and I creating catchy jingles out of the lawyers' last names.

Two Fridays after the Hamptons getaway, I was set up in Axel's breakfast nook—my new favorite spot to work—with Axel at the other end of the table. We'd become a power couple in no time, opting to work side-by-side from the penthouse when we could, pausing for grilled cheese sandwiches that Axel prepared himself, lingering over cups of steaming coffee when our inboxes got too overwhelming.

How could I be living a fantasy life alongside the worst and most tumultuous chapter yet? It didn't make sense. All I could do was continue forward.

"You ready for more coffee, sweet cheeks?" Axel lifted a brow as he rose from his laptop at the other end of the table.

"Always." I sent him a cool smile, ignoring the three new messages popping up from my assistant.

TATIANA: Eli just stopped into the office and was asking for you.

TATIANA: He says you guys had a meeting, but I'm not seeing it on the calendar. He seems impatient.

TATIANA: Where should I send him?

I waited until Axel had returned with two freshly filled mugs of hazelnut coffee—our personal favorite—and mulled over my response. I was hours, if not minutes, away from sending an initial payment over to a new divorce lawyer. This cat would be clawing its way out of the bag soon enough. Maybe I could loosen the drawstrings with Tatiana. Just to see how it felt.

CORA: Please don't send him anywhere. I'm not speaking to him currently.

I stared at my message so long the letters began to run together.

CORA: Please keep this quiet. I haven't announced yet but I'm seeking a divorce.

Air whooshed out of me. She needed to know, so we could avoid future conversations like these. Axel looked up from his computer.

"You okay?"

"Yeah. I just told my assistant I'm filing for divorce."

Tenderness flooded Axel's face, and he rose from his end of the table again and came over to me, wrapping me in his big, safe embrace. There was no other place I wanted to be, other than smashed up against his chest, inhaling his manly scent. In his arms, everything felt right.

When he pulled away, I said, "Thank you for that. You always know when I need a hug."

"I'm always ready to give them." He tugged at my earlobe before heading back to his computer.

We worked in companionable silence for a while. In midafternoon, stirrings at the front door told us that Damian and Trace had arrived. They showed up in the kitchen a moment later, their clean-as-a-whistle business presentation a stark contrast to Axel's and my work-from-home loungewear.

"What's new, guys?" Axel headed for his brothers, holding up his hand for a high five from each. Trace couldn't even muster a smile as he offered up his palm.

"There's some news," Damian said with a sigh, setting his briefcase on the big island before he slid off his suit coat.

"I don't like what I'm seeing right here," Axel said, gesturing toward Trace's face. "What the fuck is it? Before I have a heart attack."

Trace shook his head, his gaze stuck on the floor. His jaw flexed repeatedly as he rested his hands on his hips. "I just don't fucking understand."

"Understand what?" Axel demanded.

Trace studied Axel's face for a moment before he spoke, his eyes holding something unreadable. "We lost our biggest client today."

Axel didn't move, didn't breathe, didn't even react for what felt like a full minute. Then he finally blinked. "What?"

"They dipped. They're going elsewhere. After five fucking years making more money for them than anyone else could offer." Trace raked a hand through his hair, leaving it mussed. "I don't fucking get it."

"Wait, are you talking the Goodwyn account?" Fear lined the edges of Axel's voice, but it was so faint I barely caught it. "They couldn't have left."

"It's the Goodwyn account," Damian confirmed softly.

"How did this happen?" Axel spat. "Why didn't you guys tell me?"

Trace cleared his throat, and something else swelled in the air between them. Like the conversation had suddenly taken a swerve, but I'd been thrown from the car.

"It happened when we were at lunch," Damian said. He'd always been the one to reel Axel in when he started careening. And Axel had started to careen. "We ran into Rob himself, which was weird timing because just before lunch they'd informed the office of their intent to withdraw from our services."

"Except we hadn't gotten the memo yet," Trace clarified. "So we were chatting him up like a couple of fools."

Damian sent Trace a weary look. "It was awkward as fuck."

"We didn't know," Trace added with a groan. "And so he *told* us to our faces. And then we spent the next hour backpedaling and trying to get more information out of him."

"Did you hijack his lunch?" Axel demanded. "I would have fucking hijacked his lunch."

"Oh, we hijacked it. Emergency negotiations were held. We pored over numbers while he ate his fucking soup, man." Trace shook his head, looking more defeated than I'd ever seen him. "They're gone."

Axel sputtered. "What reason did he give?"

Damian drew a deep breath, studying something on the ceiling. "Our practices are not aligned with their vision."

A strange silence snaked through the kitchen. The brothers spoke volumes in the serious looks they traded.

"What could they possibly know about that is questionable?" Axel asked in a low, threatening voice.

Finally, Trace glanced my way. "I don't know. Maybe we should go over this later. I need to change."

Some of the urgency cracked and shattered around them. Axel heaved a sigh, shaking his head. "I'm going to call him."

"Don't," Damian warned him. "We beat that horse already. All we can do is exit gracefully."

"But—" Axel started.

"He's right," Trace said. "We did all we could do. They're gone. Now we just need to pick ourselves up and hunt the next big client."

The brothers went their separate ways, leaving Axel pacing the kitchen with his hands on his hips.

"I'm sorry, Axel," I said softly. "You guys will recover, though. I have faith."

Axel tutted, focusing on something invisible on the floor. "They were a quarter billion of our yearly revenue."

I winced. This wasn't chump change. And it wasn't easy to replace a client like that. Even though we were in different industries, I felt the sting of this loss just as hard. "Fuck."

His gaze moved around the kitchen, but he focused on nothing, as if he were studying something in a different dimension altogether. "I just don't understand what they could find questionable. It doesn't make sense to me."

"Client turnover at this level is common," I started.

"We have the highest retention rate in the industry," Axel said, chewing on the inside of his cheek. When he finally looked at me, a thunderstorm brewed in his eyes. "I've got to figure this out."

"And you will. I know you will."

Axel roamed the kitchen for a while longer as I sank bank into my seat, tension in the air. Damian reappeared in the kitchen, dressed in basketball shorts and an NYU T-shirt. If it weren't for the longer hair and the small lines at his eyes that betrayed the stress he lived with, I'd have mistaken him for the college version of himself.

"Cora, I completely forgot about this. I'm sorry." He held a file folder, which he waved in the air. "I have some information I think you'll want to see."

"Okay..." My brows drew together as he brought me the folder. He handed it to me but didn't let go right away.

"Let me warn you—it's not going to be easy to see this." He glanced at Axel. "You told her I was doing this, right?"

Axel paused, looking my way guiltily. "I didn't."

I widened my eyes. "Uh, guys? What is in here?"

Damian cleared his throat, easing into the chair beside me. We set the folder on the table between us. "I did some investigating."

"That's code for hacking," Axel piped up.

Damian shrugged. "Call it what you want. There's no trace of it anyway. I just did some digging into Eli at Axel's request. I combed through the files that I could find."

"Which were probably all of them," Axel added.

Damian twisted to look at him, then looked back at me. "He makes it sound like I don't do anything but absorb illicit information."

Axel laughed. "I'm just giving her background information."

Damian rolled his eyes before he continued. "Listen. There's some difficult stuff in here. I brought out the most important information though. What you do with it is completely your call, of course. But I think it'll help you in your next steps." He squeezed my wrist before standing. "And now, I need to go work out some stress. I'll be in the gym if you guys need me."

Damian saluted his brother before heading into the recesses of the penthouse. When it was just Axel and I, we shared a heavy look.

"So you don't know what's in here?" I asked.

"I don't. I didn't even realize he'd done it already." He came over to the table, occupying the seat Damian had used. "I completely forgot to tell you I'd asked him to do some digging. But I did tell you Eli didn't have my hacktivist."

"You did." I licked dry lips. "I'm just a little nervous to open this."

"Do you want me to look first?" he offered.

I nodded, swallowing a knot in my throat. I had approximately one hundred bad ideas of what might await me in that folder. I just hoped that some of it might make my pending divorce case even slightly easier.

Axel took the folder from me gently. I tried to gauge his expressions as he read silently, but he remained staunchly neutral. He'd only give the occasional "Hm" as he read.

"What's in there?" I finally asked, when the thumping of my heart had grown almost painful.

Axel didn't respond right away. But when he finally dragged his gaze up to meet mine, I saw the reactions he'd been hiding from me. Sadness spilled out of him. He was hurting for me. And that made my stomach plummet all over again.

"Do you want the bad or the worst news first?" His words came out on the edge of a whisper.

"Worst."

"He's been cheating on you since before you got married."

I pinched my eyes shut, relief warring with disgust. I had no right to feel wronged—I'd been technically cheating on him for the past few weeks, even though our separation had started months ago. But when we'd been living under the pretense of a happy couple, I'd never have imagined sleeping with anyone else.

And I'd stupidly thought that might have applied to him, as well.

"The woman he's texted the most over the past year is someone named Jazz," Axel murmured.

A gasp rocketed out of me. "Jazz? Are you fucking serious?"

Axel looked up at me. "Do you know her?"

"She's my fucking Pilates instructor." Pieces began clicking together. I remembered the last time I'd seen them in the same room, the oddly intimate undertones to their conversation that had struck me as odd, but I'd brushed off. "I thought she was cool. I really liked her."

"Fuck Jazz," Axel confirmed. "I'll find you a cooler Pilates instructor."

My shoulders sagged. "I shouldn't feel so duped. But...I do."

Axel set the folder down, scooping my hands into his. He pressed small kisses to my knuckles. "Babe, you have every right to feel duped. He duped you bad. That shit sucks."

I swallowed hard. "What else is there?"

"Are you sure you want me to go on?"

"Please. I want to hear it all."

Axel opened the folder again, keeping the contents hidden from me. He cleared his throat. "He's also seen prostitutes regularly. There's a lot of mentions of payments here. He's paid off someone before..." Axel trailed off, his brows drawing together. "I'm not sure what for, though. That might be something we can circle back to. And then it looks like..." He flipped a page, letting out a low hum. "His pornography preference is primarily one in which women rub up against latex balloons."

I blinked. "Really?"

"Really. And apparently, the correct term is a looner." He checked something on a different page, and then nodded. "Yeah. He's particularly opposed to the popping of the balloons, which makes him a non-popper."

I expelled a breath of air. "This is news to me."

"He's been to a balloon fetish convention," Axel added.

"Great. I'll be sure to ask him how it was."

Axel laughed, rubbing the back of his neck. "At least it's a more innocuous kink. Something I would rather not know about him, honestly. Can I please give him shit about this if we're ever in the same room again?"

"Oh, absolutely."

"I might have a little nameplate engraved for him," Axel said. "It'll say 'Non-Popper Rossberg.'"

A laugh escaped me, even though my head was spinning. "It somehow works."

Axel squeezed the top of my thigh, searching out my gaze. "Are you okay?"

I nodded, drawing a fortifying breath. The truth was, I had a lot of conflicting emotions. I'd need to process the unexpected hurt of these revelations, even though I'd entered the marriage in love with someone else. Neither Eli nor I ever had any illusions about being madly in love. It had been a business partnership, bolstered by the fact that he was highly attracted to me, and I merely found him cute. I'd hoped that it might grow into love, but it had only veered in the opposite direction. He acted like I was the love of his life to certain people, but behind closed doors, we all knew the story was vastly different.

And this just proved how different the truth really was.

"There's more in here. But I'll let you look at it on your own. You got the worst of it. The rest will just be peanuts."

"Thank you." I surged forward, wrapping him in a hug. And though emotion pulsed through me, there were no more tears waiting in the wings.

I felt fully cried out. It was a blessed relief.

The time had come to mount my offensive. I didn't fucking care what Eli had planned anymore. I didn't care what my father thought.

This evidence marked the end of the Margulis-Rossberg chapter.

CHAPTER TWENTY-ONE

AXEL

The divorce papers were served to Eli within a week. Every moment after that felt tense as we waited for the blowback.

But none came. I was buying up more Margulis stock and ready to breathe easy, but Cora couldn't relax. She was worried Eli might be cooking something up that would demolish the protections their prenup had put in place.

By week two post–divorce papers, she still hadn't heard from him. Her own father had stonewalled her, which made me think the Margulis camp was unnerved. By week three post–divorce papers, the other side remained unnervingly silent. If anything was coming, it was a contentious divorce. And I'd be at her side every step of the way.

I dressed for the office bright and early, feeling pretty fucking good about everything. Now that Cora was back in my heart and in my life, everything felt wonderful. Next level. Top notch fan-fucking-tastic. Even amid the business setback of losing the Goodwyn account, a deeper truth prevailed.

Nothing could stop us now.

After eight years apart, we were finally able to make up for lost time *and* fulfill the destiny that had always been ours. That Allan had tried to keep from us.

The August sunshine warmed the tops of my shoulders as Zero and I stepped onto the rooftop patio to drink in some vitamin D before hitting the office. Zero did his business in the corner pee pad while I stared out at the mess of Manhattan, my chest on constant swell mode as I relished the rightness of life.

I'd vowed never to reconcile with Cora, but I'd only had half the story. The reality was that reconciliation led to more strength. A healthier me, a stronger business, a brighter future.

And who the fuck wouldn't want that?

Once Zero was done, we headed through the penthouse and to our private elevator. I was early today, because Cora and I had started getting up early to exercise together, as if we'd been together for years instead of weeks.

Couldn't say I minded.

As soon as the elevator doors pulled back, I stepped into a strange tension. The air felt gelatinous in its strangeness. Like a very questionable uncovered Jell-o found in your grandma's fridge. Eyes flickered my way then darted away. A few underlings seemed downright skittish as I passed.

Were those whispers I heard?

This shit wasn't flying in my own business. I spotted Francis in the lounge area, facing big windows overlooking the city. I pulled him aside.

"What's going on?"

"Well good morning to you!" He removed his arm from my grip and looked me up and down. "You came in extra feisty this morning. I take it you saw the news?"

His words sank like a freighter in my gut. "What news?"

Francis's dark brows drew together. "Oh, shit."

"Francis."

"Axel, I'm not supposed to be the one to break this to you." Nervousness creased his features, and he looked around, as if plotting his escape. "Where's Trace? He can tell you."

"*Francis.*" I gripped his arms, making him face me. "What. The fuck. Is going. On?"

His nostrils flared as he drew a fortifying breath, his brown eyes searing through me. "There was an article published in *Big Apple Mag*. About you. About the Fairchilds."

I blinked once, then again. "About *what*?"

Francis shook his head, waving it off. "It's just a rag-mag anyway. This will blow over. I promise. I've already contacted the PR firm—"

Anxiety stalked me, a silent predator. "Just tell me or I'm going to fire you."

Francis studied the ground for a moment before answering. "It's an expose about a sex trafficking ring you three are apparently involved in."

"A—a *what*?" The words didn't even make sense to me. *Sex trafficking* and *Fairchilds* only existed on the same continuum as opposite ends.

Especially after what had happened to Kaylee.

"There's a copy floating around here somewhere. Sit down. I'll go find it." He pointed at me sternly and I crumpled into the nearest armchair and tried to persuade myself that this was an elaborate joke somehow. But the whispers of my own employees told me something was seriously amiss.

What in the fuck is going on?

Francis returned a moment later and handed me the glossy *Big Apple Mag*. It wasn't purely rag-mag material—he'd just been saying that to make me feel better—but it did dance the line between journalism and gossip.

On the cover was an artistic silhouette of my brothers and me. Big typeface letters spelled out: *The Unfairchilds and Their Secret Lives.*

My fingers were jelly as I thumbed through the magazine. I could barely read the words on the page. A two-page spread highlighted the information obtained by an investigative journalist, linking my brothers—*me*—to a known trafficking ring.

The further I read, the more the mystery clarified, shadows pulling back to reveal something murky but identifiable. The reporter had linked the sex trafficking allegations with the reputation of Strata, the business we'd acquired last year.

And he wasn't wrong. Strata *had* been linked to sex trafficking, specifically via its former CEO, Yagel. But he didn't have the story straight. We'd forced that CEO out; we'd bought the company to *stop* its functioning as a trafficking conduit.

Which meant this was a fucking emergency.

I tucked the magazine under my arm and bolted for Trace's office. I burst inside, finding a quiet, empty office. I sat in his chair and called him, knee bouncing wildly as the phone rang.

"Axel, is this—" Trace began.

"Did you see the article?" I swiveled manically in his chair.

"Yes." His voice came out a hiss. It wasn't often that Trace lost his shit, but this situation had the potential to push all of us over the edge. "Fucking *fuck*. Who could be the source?"

"Probably Yagel himself." I dragged a hand down the front of my face. Unscrupulous was one of the kinder words I could have used for Yagel. He made millions off peddling underage girls, so I didn't give a fuck about playing nice with him. I'd considered physically castrating that asshole myself, but that shit was harder than it sounded in this day and age. His exile to Australia was small consolation. He lived with every move tracked, hacked, and monitored. He knew it. And maybe he was tired of it.

"I'll be at the office in five." His breaths came out labored. The swell of honks around him told me he was probably sprinting down Wall Street to get here, which meant he'd probably spent the night at a lover's house somewhere.

The call clicked off, and I tossed the phone on his desk. The doorknob turned a moment later and Damian barged in.

"You got the memo too, I take it?" I asked.

Damian's lips were turned downward in a glower. He propped his hands on his hips as he paced the office.

"We need damage control."

"Francis said he's getting PR up to speed," I said. "But I don't think that's going to be enough."

"We need legal too," Damian said, snapping his fingers.

I nodded, picking up my phone again, this time to summon Francis. "Let's get Francis in here to take notes." I tapped out my message—*NEED U IN TRACE'S OFFICE*—and then looked at Damian wearily.

"Who the fuck is behind this?"

Damian stopped pacing, looking more distraught than I'd ever seen him. "How many enemies do you think we have right now?"

I blinked. "Not that many."

"You sure about that?"

Frustration burbled inside of me. "I can think of a hundred idiots who might have beef with us for whatever reason. But that doesn't mean they'd go digging around in ancient history like a fucking paleontologist looking for the bones of our past."

Damian watched me, his jaw working. He wanted to say something but didn't. The door opened a moment later, and Trace strode in.

"Welcome to the shit storm," I deadpanned.

Trace dropped his briefcase in a chair, covering his face with his hands. Then he let out a gruff "*FUCK!*" He followed that up with an impressive string of curse words, ending with *prickstain*.

I almost never saw Trace lose his cool. Not about anything. But this was different.

Francis showed up a moment later, his brows drawn together in concern. "Did I just hear enough foul language to wake the dead?"

"You did." Trace sighed, pinching the bridge of his nose. He leaned against the far wall, squeezing his eyes shut. "Can somebody please tell me we have a way out of this?"

"We have a way out of this," I said, more because I felt like he needed to hear it. Not because I believed it.

"Axel told me you called PR, but what about legal?" Damian asked. "This magazine is read by millions. There's no way this allegation is going to be swept under the rug."

"What are they saying out there?" I asked Francis. "Does everyone really believe this bullshit?"

Francis looked between the three of us, grimacing. "We're all confused. This is just...Wow. A surprise. You know?"

"The company we bought used to traffic underage girls." My voice sounded strained. Almost insane. Like I'd snap if he didn't believe me. "We took it over so that we could *stop* it from happening. It's as simple as that."

"We never should have done it," Damian mumbled into his closed fist. "The risk was too great."

"This is confidential information," Trace said, searing Francis with a look. "Heard?"

"Heard." Francis had dropped all pretenses of joking or joviality. This was the stone-cold sober reality now. And it wasn't pretty.

"If we hadn't put a stop to it," I told Francis, "it would have gone unchecked. And we have deeply personal reasons for working toward the complete obliteration of sex trafficking rings."

A knot hit my throat, and I pulled out my phone again, eager to divert my attention before I completely fucking unraveled in front of Francis. He knew us—but he didn't *know* know us. There was a limit to how deep the average person could pry. And right now, the list of people who'd made it that deep was pretty short.

I scrolled through the news outlets while Damian and Francis talked about the next steps with the lawyers. I needed to know what was being said out there. What people thought. How much of the truth might be circulating.

Whether we still had a shot at salvaging our reputation.

I scanned the trending headlines. We weren't there. *Yet.* But when I moved to other social media outlets, the forecast was dire.

How the fuck did this happen? And why now?

I didn't know the answers, and I might not ever. Unless I could personally corner the journalist and find some answers...

"Axel? Are you listening?" Trace's voice held none of the usual patience.

"Sorry. I was checking headlines." I guiltily stored my phone, but not before seeing the most damning comment of them all. Comparing us to Jeffrey Epstein. My stomach pitched to my feet. Sickening.

"Best we can get is a retraction," Francis said, for what sounded like possibly the second time. "But they won't publish it front and center. After all, they're only obligated to *publish*—it doesn't say *where*."

"So the damage is done," I concluded.

Damian raked a hand through his longish tresses. A low, terse sigh escaped him. "This is so fucked."

"Beyond fucked," Trace agreed.

"One wrong detail, and they publish an entire smear campaign." I sat back in the chair, working my jaw back and forth. "I never got a call from anyone at Big Apple before they published this article. Did you guys?"

Damian and Trace shook their heads.

"So they publish this bullshit without even asking for a comment from us," I spat, "much less an interview. We have no chance at a rebuttal. We just have to lie down and take this? This is ridiculous. We're suing their asses."

"Agreed. We have to stamp this out," Damian said. "That's the priority here. We're not letting our name go under because of a twisted half-truth."

"Let's get this reporter on the phone," I blurted. "We need to find out who his source was."

"Do you have any idea who it could be?" Francis asked.

An uncomfortable silence spread through the room like a noxious fog.

"It could have just cropped up organically," I said. "Maybe Yagel got busted for something again. Or maybe someone ratted on him, and he was trying to save himself by throwing *us* under the bus. Or maybe..."

Damian's gaze met mine, and it felt like a slap.

"Or maybe it's Eli." Damian's words floated uncomfortably through the room.

I let a few extra seconds pass before I answered. "It can't be."

"Why not?" Damian challenged. "His wife is living with you. He's got to be pissed."

I worked my jaw back and forth. I took issue with his use of the word *wife*. "Because there's a more likely explanation. Eli has no idea about this and has no way of knowing. But Yagel has both knowledge and motive. He's probably resenting us hardcore by now, seeing how much money we're raking in on his brand."

Damian relented, heaving a sigh as he nodded. "Yeah. You're probably right."

But not knowing was killing me. Something unfamiliar crept through me, stalking low and hot. Tendrils of desperation wove through my cells. I hadn't felt this in a long time. In eight years, to be exact. Not since Cora told me she wanted to break up with me and I'd sold off stocks to be able to afford the flight out to see her. I'd begged. It hadn't made a difference.

There was no begging with the world. Once bad news hit the cycle, it spread like wildfire.

If the Jeffrey Epstein links were already here, who knew what else awaited us?

The reputation my brothers and I had scraped and scrambled for—vanished in a fucking instant.

We'd always been the outsiders of Wall Street. The bad boys who didn't do things the conventional way.

But now we were something worse. Something much more damning.

And I planned to find out who was responsible and make them pay.

CHAPTER TWENTY-TWO

CORA

My father turned stony silence into a sport.

He lobbed it around like a football. Not like he actually played physical sports, or even watched them. The only reason he was ever caught at sporting events was en route to the luxury box as part of a networking event. No, the only true sport he played was manipulating other people's emotions.

Specifically, mine.

And his three-week silence said it all.

He'd stopped responding to my emails unless the matter directly pertained to life-or-death business matters. But since the news about Axel and his brothers had spread across the nation like wildfire a few days ago, whenever my father needed something from me, he sent a courier. Even if he was in the office down the hall.

My relationship with Axel wasn't common knowledge, and already I was suffering the consequences. Apparently the divorce papers I'd served Eli with also applied to Allan—especially now that Axel was under scrutiny. My father showed me how it would feel to go all the way with Axel. He'd already weaponized my own actions against me without even saying a word, and it was only the tip of the iceberg.

My kneejerk reaction was fear. I had an urge to cower, contemplate my actions, and chart a course back to what he wanted from me.

I was sick of cowering, contemplating, and charting the course that wasn't even mine.

I was ready to charge ahead into the unknown. I just hadn't planned on how deeply uncomfortable things could become in this new space.

Three weeks after serving the divorce papers, Eli acted as though nothing had happened. This didn't feel like merely bad news; this felt like a hurricane when I'd been preparing for a snowstorm.

So when a board meeting brought me to the office that Friday, I had no idea what to expect.

But it certainly wasn't what actually showed up.

Eli waltzed into the hallway outside the board room, intercepting me casually with an air of *Oh I didn't expect to find you here.* His blond hair was in a Ken doll wave, not a hair out of place, his broad shoulders straining at the medium blue suit he wore. The perfect example of affable douche.

My stomach twisted into a Windsor knot.

"Cora. Looking beautiful as always." He stuffed his hands into his pockets. A whiff of his cologne reached me, a complex mixture of yacht clubs and expensive aftershave.

"Good to see you, Eli." I lied. It wasn't. "Have you thought about the papers I sent over?"

"Oh, those. Yeah. Right." He cleared his throat, looking down the hallway over my shoulder. "Put me on your schedule? Let's set a date, and we can finish that up."

My heart pounded as though I'd just run up a flight of stairs. "Seriously? My lawyer should probably come too, then."

"This is a white flag," he said in a low voice, stepping closer. "Let's just get this over with. You and me. Come on."

My mouth went dry, and I almost forgot how to speak. I hadn't expected compliance. Not like this. Not so *soon*. There was a high possibility I was dreaming. Perhaps I was feverish. Maybe this was a vision from within a coma. "Okay. Sure. How about lunch today?"

"Name the place."

"Suttons," I forced out. Suttons was a neutral lunch spot, classy enough for an intimate lunch meeting, but public enough that I would be in no danger.

He shrugged. "Fine."

This response was the last—and I could not stress this enough, the *absolute last*—response I'd expected from him.

But maybe he was done fighting for a marriage that had never worked. Just like I was done fighting to convince myself this arrangement could continue. Maybe Eli had seen the light.

We moved into the board room, where my father, Robert, and Frank already waited. My father didn't greet us. Robert and Frank grunted their hellos. I could barely concentrate. Between Eli's white flag of surrender and Axel's ongoing media fallout, I couldn't do anything beyond hold my breath and hope.

And wait. And hope some more.

The meeting passed intolerably slowly. It was complete business as usual despite how much the foundation of this world was actively crumbling. Even while pursuing a divorce and being on the receiving end of my father's vitriol, we could still be here and pretend nothing was different.

I just wasn't sure if that was a blessing or a curse.

Our meeting broke up just as noon rolled around. My father had treated everyone with the same level of distant disdain, so I couldn't gauge what his standing with Eli was, either. I knew better than to try to speak to him to find out. I'd only face stoniness, or worse. We all filed through the doorway, but Eli stopped me in the hallway once the others had walked ahead.

"Let's ride together."

"No. I'll take my own car."

His nice guy façade cracked, a dark shadow twisting his features for the briefest of moments. "Only using the Fairchild vehicles now, huh?"

Something awful churned in my gut, as if I were seconds away from emptying the contents of my stomach after a bad takeout experience.

"It doesn't matter." I straightened my back. "I don't want to ride with you, so I won't."

He ran his tongue across the inside of his bottom lip. "See you there."

Once Eli disappeared down the hallway, I allowed myself to crumple. Whatever awaited me, it was calculated. This wasn't an expression of goodwill. This was strategized. I just couldn't see the end game. If he wanted *me*, it wasn't because he was getting anything meaningful out of it. The best I could guess was that he felt pressured to uphold the elite pairing that Wall Street loved, the type of power marriage that would go down in the history books.

I didn't want to go down in history with the sadness on my face that every trapped and abused woman would recognize. I couldn't stand to look at pictures of us in the media, either. All I could see was my own misery, written into the shadows of my face.

If nothing else, I wanted to look at a picture of myself and know that I had tried to be happy. I wanted to fucking try.

I repeated this to myself as I prepared for the lunch meeting and braved crosstown traffic in one of the Fairchild vehicles, as Eli had correctly guessed. Axel hadn't texted much since our goodbye kiss that morning. Just one text had come in during the board meeting.

AXEL: Tell me how the board meeting goes. Stay strong, cowgirl.

CORA: Survived. Surprisingly. I'm meeting Eli for lunch now to go over the papers. Wish me luck.

AXEL: Do you need reinforcements? I can come lurk in the lobby of wherever you go.

I laughed, my throat tightening suddenly from emotion. He was willing to drop what he was doing to come support me, even in the middle of his own shitstorm. Axel had extended more support and tenderness to me in a matter of weeks than Eli had shown in years.

CORA: Personally, I want that. But practically, we shouldn't. I'll text you after. Promise.

I entered Suttons with my game face on. I'd brought my briefcase full of legal documents and leaked emails courtesy of Damian, just in case Eli needed to cross-reference something. I'd made the divorce as palatable as possible, ceding him all the gains jointly acquired throughout the marriage. Our prenup protected what I'd walked in with, which meant he was getting all the houses and helicopters. Fair enough. When it came down to it, I wanted nothing anyway.

I was doing this for the freedom.

The restaurant was packed and clamorous, excited conversations echoing through the high-ceilinged room. Enormous antique portraits dotted the walls, while servers skittered around wearing frilly black aprons and high buns. I spotted Eli across the restaurant, smiling at the server in a way that made my gut constrict. I knew that smile. It was the same smile he'd sent to Jazz all those times he'd shown up during my sessions with her. He was probably fucking the server. He'd probably been fucking her for months. I swallowed back a wave of nausea.

You can do this.

Axel thought I could do it too. That was just as important.

Keep moving forward.

Eli waved when he spotted me. I offered him a fleeting smile as I took my seat at the table. Ice water awaited me, as well as a glass of chardonnay.

"I went ahead and ordered for you," he said. "Since your cab ride was significantly slower than mine."

"Thank you." I took a sip of water, ignoring the comment on my transportation. "Thanks for meeting with me."

"Of course." He leaned back in his chair, crossing his arms over his chest. "My pleasure."

I cleared my throat, popping open my sleek briefcase to bring out the documents. When the first folder hit the table, Eli leaned forward, waving it away.

"No, no. Just wait."

I glanced around the table. He had brought nothing. No counter-documents. No folders. Not even a pen. "What?"

"Listen, I've been thinking. We need to reconfigure this approach altogether."

I blinked a few times, schooling my face to not crumple or betray any ounce of the trepidation snaking through my veins. "What are you envisioning?"

He sighed, scooting forward so that he could lean on the table, elbows propped on the white tablecloth. "Cora...we're both guilty here."

I didn't like where this was headed. Not one bit. "How so?"

"We've both committed sins in the eyes of our families. I mean, look at you." He gestured at me, disgust licking at his features. "You're living with your ex-boyfriend, and you think that's okay. I mean, you're lucky I even agreed to entertain you today."

I rolled my lips inward. There was so much to unpack every time he opened his mouth. And I was tired of the heavy lifting. He just barreled right along, adding more weight.

"Listen, I know I get too drunk sometimes. But it's not like I don't have a good reason. I mean, what do you honestly expect?" He seared me with an imploring look. "You've been lying to me for the entire duration of our marriage. Leading me on. Making me think you wanted a family when really you've been taking birth control behind my back."

I swallowed hard, looking around the restaurant to avoid his gaze. For how intolerable he was, he had a point. One that didn't just cut into me, it hit an artery. I'd probably always carry guilt over this, because I *had* lied to him for the duration of our marriage. I'd always blame myself for buying into the idea that I'd be happy in a business-first marriage. For turning away true love when I had it, to follow the demands and responsibilities that somebody else required me to maintain.

"Don't you have anything to say about that, Cora?"

I clenched my teeth, forcing myself to look at him. "I didn't want to bring kids into an unhappy marriage. Kids deserve parents who at least like each other. Besides, you really think you're ready for kids?"

"I've been ready since the beginning. And I think things might have turned out a little fucking better if you'd bucked up and done what you were supposed to do from the start."

His words crashed over me, adding a fun extra layer of misogyny to the shit pile. The worst part was that he sounded genuinely upset about it. Maybe I *had* deprived him of something he genuinely wanted.

But I shouldn't have to give him a child just because he wanted one. I needed to want a baby too.

"Not only have you been lying to me, keeping my unborn children from me, you've also been living with another man." He threw his hands up into the air. "I have a lot of excellent reasons to make this divorce as messy as I possibly can. Any judge would agree with me."

"There's no need to make it messy unless you're being a masochist," I told him through gritted teeth. "I've given you everything. I don't want anything. I just want your last name, and everything about you, as far away from me as possible."

An evil smile glinted on his lips. "Honey, that's not possible. Not anymore. In fact, that ship sailed the second I joined the Margulis board. You're not getting rid of me for the rest of your life. So why don't you just face the facts? It's easier to stay married. There's more in it for you that way, too."

The server returned, and we clamped our mouths shut. She set down a plate of stuffed mushrooms, white cheese melted in a fancy zig-zag across the plate.

Once she'd offered to refill our drinks and drifted away to another table, Eli steepled his fingers.

"What could there possibly be for me if I stay in this marriage?" My voice came out a hiss. "You've already proven I can't trust you. I'm not safe around you. You want what I don't want to give you. Let's just part ways and quit pretending."

He dropped his chin, his gaze hardening. "You need to act right. If you aren't careful, you're going to become an embarrassment. Look at this scandal with the Scarechilds. Have we not always told you those sleazes need to be avoided? They're disgusting, and they're pulling you into their trap. Whatever you think you have with that prick, you're wrong. It's going to be short-lived. They live in a fantasy world, and your real-life reputation will tank because of them. It's not a question of if, but when."

"And how are they so much worse than a family like mine?" I challenged him, leaning so far over the table the steam from the mushrooms hit my chin. "I've got a father who won't speak to me unless I do things his way. I've got a husband who thinks raping me is part of a healthy marriage. At least with the Fairchilds, I can fucking breathe. I just want to be free, Eli. Why can't you give me that?"

An unamused smile flicked at his lips. "Free. That's so quaint. Don't you realize you *are* free? You're living the dream. How can you not see that? If you don't want the life you have, then nothing will make you happy. It's as simple as that."

"You're wrong." I fought a swell of emotion. It was risky to have such a heated conversation in public, but it was the only way I'd feel safe around him. The clanking of silverware and the rush of voices around us drowned out our discussion. "And even if I'm the wrong one, I want to find out for myself. Who cares if I'm unhappy in something else? It doesn't affect you. Let me be the unhappy one."

"You already are the unhappy one," he spat. "And the selfish one, for thinking you need even more."

"Not more." My heart hammered in my chest as the words I'd been repeating to myself tumbled out of my mouth. "Just something else."

He shook his head, as though this were solely his decision. "No. Listen, I'm willing to give this another shot with you. And I think we can both agree that is *excessively* generous of me. But you need to keep your head down. We can be insanely powerful together. Don't you get that? We can make history, Cora. But only if we work together."

The final pieces of the puzzle clicked into place. He'd never agree to the divorce. He'd never give me the freedom I wanted, because he saw me as his ticket to immortality. Through me and the Margulis empire, he thought he'd secure his position in history. The Margulis-Rossberg collaboration that would change the face of the aerospace and realty industries. He couldn't do that with Jazz or with the server at Suttons or with any woman he'd encounter at his latex balloon conferences.

Which reminded me...

"Why aren't *you* happy with what you have then?" I sniffed, rummaging for my briefcase. I clicked it open and removed a different folder. "Why do *you* need more?"

"I *am* happy with what I have." The *duh* tone in his voice made me want to slap him.

"Are you?" I placed the black folder on the table, using my fingertips to slide it across the white linen tablecloth, past the untouched mushrooms. "Peruse at your leisure. They're copies, so I don't need them back."

Eli snatched it off the table, searing me with a look before he examined the contents. Papers rustled as he looked at the evidence of his cheating. Copies of emails. Receipts that Damian had dug up. Declarations of love with women all across the globe.

"Where did you find this?" His voice was a threatening rumble.

"It doesn't matter. All that matters is that I don't plan on backing down from my demands any time soon. I caught you. So let's quit pretending. Sign the damn papers, Eli."

His nostrils flared, and he leaned across the table, practically hissing his words. "Tell me where you got this."

"Looks like it touched a nerve."

"Was it the Sleazechilds?"

I blinked demurely, sipping my water. The ice paired nicely with the sense of refreshment I felt from serving Eli with the truth. "It really doesn't matter."

"This is fabricated," he spat, tossing the folder on the table. "A complete lie. And character assassination, on top of that."

"Whatever you want to call it."

"My lawyer will be handling this," Eli said, jabbing his index finger at me. "To the fullest extent possible. So whoever has created this shit, passing it off as truth, is going to pay."

"It can't all be false," I said, lifting my brow. "After all, you and my Pilates instructor exchanged a *lot* of texts. I verified that on the phone plan. Makes sense, now, why you never wanted me to have anything to do with handling that account."

He dipped his head, dark clouds filling his gaze. "What do you want from me?"

"Sign the papers."

"Fucking dream on."

I pushed my chair back and stood, smoothing down the front of my dark slacks. "I think it's time for me to go."

Eli shot to standing after I took a step away. "Wait."

I turned to him, shocked he'd actually try to stop me. Especially with an audience around us. Maybe now the negotiations would be turning in my favor. "What?"

"It's a shame things have gotten so bad with your little lover boy." He watched me intently, as if gauging my every micro-reaction. "Don't you want all that drama to stop?"

I stepped closer to him. "What are you insinuating?"

"Come back to me, and I'll make sure it all goes away," he said in a low voice, his gaze darting back and forth across my face. He was so close I could taste the tang of alcohol on his breath. "He's only going to drag you down. And something tells me it's about to get a lot worse."

Something tells me. He probably had plenty to do with that *something.* The mere thought sent a shiver of fear whispering through me. How much worse could it get for Axel? Did I even want to find out? Maybe I should stop trying for the divorce, if it meant I could keep the waters calm.

Going after what I wanted might bring down others in the process. But no. No no no.

Something tells me be damned. I wasn't falling into the same trap again. The same cycle. The same tired situation of being manipulated by men who wanted what I didn't want to give. I'd lived this once before, and I didn't want to be the same scared twenty-two-year-old. For God's sake, I wanted to believe that I had learned something. That I had grown a spine. That I could make a choice that benefited *me*, and things would be okay.

My nostrils flared. I stepped so close I could have kissed him. But there would never be any of that anymore. "Fuck. You."

I turned on my heel before I could think better of it, snatched up my briefcase and stormed out of the restaurant. I didn't care that I left a wake so angry I could have capsized a ship. I didn't care that I'd turned down Eli in front of curious eyes.

All I cared about was trying. Moving forward.

Grasping for *something else.*

CHAPTER TWENTY-THREE

"Good morning." I tapped the small black microphone attached to the podium I stood in front of. A sea of eyes looked up at me, bright stage lights making me squint. We'd called for an emergency press conference in the huge conference space of a nearby hotel—neutral ground. My voice floated magnified through the room. "We're ready to begin."

My brothers stood solemnly on either side of me. This was our first public reaction to the allegations that had surfaced in *Big Apple Mag*, three days after the story had hit. We'd needed every second of those three days to investigate, contact lawyers, and craft our response.

And here we were. Ready, if not a little fucking terrified.

"Go ahead," Damian urged me, nodding in the direction of the microphone.

I cleared my throat, trying to pick out any familiar faces in the crowd. The press conference marked the official start to the legal proceedings to convince *Big Apple Mag* to retract their story.

"Thank you all for coming. The three of us never expected to have to set something like this up, to address such serious and mind-boggling allegations. So forgive me if I sound...confused. Or maybe just exhausted. Because the past three days have been a whirlwind for us. One that I hope never to repeat."

I drew a fortifying breath. Public speaking had always been easy for me. But it hit different when I was defending my reputation in front of a world that wanted to find a new villain at the top of every news cycle. It didn't feel as lighthearted or easy when my brothers and I were clinging to the edge of the cliff of our reputation, and the journalists were the ones lifting the heels of their boots, ready to stomp.

I knew it didn't matter what I said or did—I couldn't reach everyone who had already made up their mind from what they'd initially read. But we also couldn't let this go unaddressed. We'd already lost one of our most important clients, and every hour with this misinformation out there felt like a threat. Would others follow in Goodwyn's wake now? We still didn't have a clear reason why they'd left. We didn't want to give others any hint of a reason to follow suit.

"As you all know, *Big Apple Mag* published a very concerning article that directly affects our reputation. We're here to clear up the rumors and to set the record straight. *Big Apple Mag* did *not* do their due diligence. They didn't even reach out to us for an interview, much less a comment, and we are responding appropriately with our legal team. But the crimes they incorrectly linked to *us* did in fact exist in the history of the business that we recently acquired."

Cameras flashed as I spoke, and the heat from the extra lighting we'd set up beat down on me. Sweat prickled at my temples, though I wasn't sure if it was from the lighting or the heightened intensity. Trace shifted beside me as I reviewed the notes in front of me.

"We acquired the tech company Strata a year ago. Unbeknownst to us"—This was where I chose to fib. It was best not to admit what we had known about the CEO prior to purchase, nor what we'd ensured happened to him as a result—"the CEO of that company was actively involved in overseeing a sex trafficking ring. He used his business for a cover. When we integrated Strata into our operations, we completely restructured it, keeping only the brand name. Everything was reworked into our existing operations framework, which meant the illegal activities came to a screeching halt.

"As far as we know, the author based his reporting solely on rumor and innuendo. The facts of the matter are that we have never been involved in any trafficking operations. Not then. Not now. And not ever. In fact—"

I swallowed, my vision blurring slightly as I toyed with the idea of going off script. I wanted everyone to understand just how ridiculous this notion was.

"Axel," Damian whispered, as if he knew what I was struggling with. Because he always knew.

I ignored him. "I'd like to share something with you all, just so you understand where I'm coming from." I gripped the sides of the podium, surveying the sea of reporters.

"You don't have to do this," Damian said in a low voice, which I ignored again.

He was wrong. I did have to do this. We'd been on a rampage—barely eating. Practically living at the office. I saw Cora only to sleep and kiss her goodbye in the morning. We just wanted this to be in the rear-view mirror. And the only way to do that was to bare our truth.

"Our younger sister was a victim of human trafficking," I said quietly, studying the wood grain of the podium. A murmur rippled through the room. "Her name was Kaylee, and she died when she was sixteen. She's the main reason my brothers and I fight to ensure that stories like hers don't keep happening. Why we dump millions of dollars a year into anti-trafficking coalitions. We have the receipts. But this journalist didn't care to do his job. He couldn't have made a grosser error. We'll take questions now."

Reporters sprang out of their seats, the volume of the room flipping from reverent to chaotic in an instant. Arms waved in the air as journalists vied for our attention.

"Mr. Fairchild! Right here please!" A reporter from CNN got my attention first. I pointed at her to speak, and the room quieted.

"There's no record of any Kaylee Fairchild in the public information available for your family. Only you, Damian, Trace, and two parents—Gary and Deb—are listed. Can you explain?"

"Kaylee wasn't a Fairchild," I said into the microphone. "Damian and I were adopted by Trace's family when we were eleven and twelve, respectively. We took our adoptive family's last name. Kaylee was a Haynes."

More arms shot up, a swell of voices. I pointed at the *Forbes* reporter.

"Are you concerned that the Securities and Exchange Commission might take interest in your company?" he asked.

My brows drew together. "Why would they take interest in my company?"

"Don't interview them," Trace said under his breath.

"They might take interest because of your high-profile activities," the reporter stammered. "Your company has one of the highest return rates of all the wealth management companies out there, and..."

I looked over at Trace then back at the reporter. Anxiety spiked inside me. "We have no reason to be concerned about an investigation. Next."

It went like that for almost fifteen minutes. Answering every question and its mutant offspring. By the time we wrapped the press conference, my limbs were shaky and I needed a nap. Or a hamburger. At the very least, I needed Cora.

"You did good out there," Trace said as we stepped behind the curtained sidelines. They attempted smiles, but both of my brothers wore their worry etched deep into their faces.

"Thank God you're good at that stuff, because I couldn't handle it," Damian said, pushing his fingertips into the front of his hair.

"No problem, brothers. Anytime." I clapped them both on the back as we headed for the back exit. I was more than ready to shake of the stress of the day and start hoping for a better tomorrow. "But where the fuck did that question about the SEC come from?"

It still gnawed at me. Damian sent me a dark look.

"I don't even want to say those words in a sentence."

"You think we have something to worry about?" I asked quietly, looking between them. The Securities and Exchange Commission was the highest authority in our line of work. Plenty of businesses got investigated for wrongdoing. And while we weren't exactly breaking laws, we'd started our business treading water in the moat that surrounds the Castle of Wrongdoing.

The waters were murky.

Made murkier when we purchased Strata and forced Yagel into obsolescence.

"We're fine," Trace said. "Let's just focus on suing the magazine and moving on from this."

I followed my brothers, letting them lead the way into the back hallway of the hotel. Moving on from this felt like a fantasy at this point. But I knew something that would help take the edge off for a little bit at least.

I needed to visit Kentucky. Immediately.

And I needed Cora there with me.

CHAPTER TWENTY-FOUR

CORA

After a three-day getaway, Axel and I were back in Manhattan, refreshed and ready for the next shitstorm to hit.

Axel had whisked me away on a no-questions-asked trip to the outskirts of Louisville. He had a house on a horse farm out there, only a mile from the house he and his brothers had built for his parents. We'd eaten dinner one night with Mr. and Mrs. Fairchild. Even after I caused Axel to spiral and nearly ruin his life from heartbreak, they still had the grace to welcome me into their home.

Miracles were real.

Nobody could tell me otherwise.

But back in Manhattan, something felt different as soon as I stepped off the private jet. The air sagged with humidity, as it always did in mid-August. But Kentucky had been just the same. Maybe the weight of everything I'd tried to escape for a blessed weekend was causing atmospheric imbalances.

Trace was the first to text. Axel showed me the message as we settled into the car: *You guys ready for the real world yet? There's a new round of headlines. This time, you two are in the spotlight.*

My stomach twisted into impossible knots. We spent the car ride catching up on the news that had broken during our getaway. Whatever was responsible for rending the clouds and unbalancing the atmosphere, this was probably it.

"Jesus fuck," Axel muttered as he scrolled through his phone. I hesitated to follow along, but it was impossible not to.

MARGULIS MARITAL MESS: The Princess of Manhattan Heads for a New Prince

MARGULIS-ROSSBERG POWER COUPLE SPLITS

FROM ROSSBERG TO FAIRCHILD

MARGULIS HEIRESS SEEKS NEW INDUSTRY PAIRING

Each new headline tightened the knots in my stomach, until I was gasping for breath. Axel rubbed my back, murmuring calming things to me.

But there was no calming down from this. Somehow, the news had broken through. We'd been careful to not go out in public together, to never be seen. Inside private spaces, like arriving via private jet or using our personal vehicles, we didn't have to worry about paparazzi. But even with all the precautions, there was never an ironclad assurance that somebody wouldn't sell information for money.

Even the tightest NDA couldn't prevent someone taking the risk and making a quick buck off our private lives.

"I have to go into the office today," I finally forced out, barely able to draw air. "My father is going to kill me."

"Do you want me to come with you?" Axel offered.

I laughed in spite of the tension. "God, that would make the situation worse."

"I'm willing to do it if you need me there. If you need help getting through the day." Axel gathered my hair to one side and kissed my cheek. "I'm here. Zero could come too."

I sank against him, drawing support from his warmth as the car would through morning traffic. I'd get dropped off first, then Axel would head into his office with our luggage. Every block closer to

Margulis headquarters ratcheted my tension tighter. By the time we reached the building, I could hardly force myself to stand. Axel stilled me before I stepped out of the car.

"You sure you don't need me?" he asked, the sky-blue storm in his eyes rooting me to my spot. As always, he was the grounding force. The one who could bring me back to earth.

"I've got this," I assured him.

"Allan's gonna raise hell."

"There's no way through but forward," I said, pressing a kiss to his lips. Every cell of my body vibrated with dreadful anticipation. This was the outcome I'd been avoiding for eight years. But things were different now. My father couldn't prevent Axel from succeeding. He and his brothers had already climbed their way to the top. No amount of raging or shit-talking could prevent them from finding their clients. In a way, I'd been smart without realizing it, even though it had come at a high personal sacrifice.

Now was the time to claim my life. My future. My love.

I drew a deep breath, climbed out of the car and was greeted by the lenses of several cameras. Paparazzi. They'd been staked out and waiting. Cameras flashed as I stared up at the glossy black walls of Margulis Realty, schooling the annoyance off my face. They already had more than enough fodder, spotting me exiting a Fairchild vehicle. Which meant this was just the beginning of a whole new chapter. *Game on.*

I walked on autopilot through the lobby and into the elevator, barely noticing anyone around me. Up on the executive floor, people murmured quietly as I passed. I headed straight for my father's office, knowing that there was no time like the present to completely light everything on fire.

The media was the gasoline...and I was the burning match.

I knocked once on my father's door before pushing it open. He sat glowering at his desk, facing someone tucked into the chair before him. It took me a moment to realize who was here.

"Mother?" I asked, the knot of my gut executing a freefall.

If my mother was here, this was a four-alarm emergency. She rarely came into the office, preferring instead the utmost separation between my father's work and her private life.

She twisted to look at me, not even bothering to feign a smile. Both of my parents embodied the opposite of happy to see me. A roar erupted between my ears, and that dull throb returned behind my rib. If my parents didn't murder me in this office, then the Eli-inspired cancer would surely finish me before much longer.

"Cora Margulis-Rossberg." My mother's voice shook. I'd never heard her say my name like that before. Ice spread through my veins.

"What's going on?" I forced out, immediately cursing myself for acting ignorant to the headlines. I squeezed my eyes shut. "I mean—I'm here to talk. I saw the headlines."

"I am beyond words right now," she said, her voice thick with more emotion than I'd ever heard in my life. Possibly not even after Chris died. "You need to fix this. And it needs to happen immediately."

My father remained silent at his desk; he looked profoundly unwell.

"I don't know how this happened," I said, holding my position near the door in case I needed to bolt at a moment's notice.

"How can you not know?" she screamed. "Have you been living under a rock? When did you become so careless?"

I drew a shaky breath. I could barely see straight. "Mother—"

"After all that your father and I have done for you," she went on in low, shaky voice, "this is how you repay us. With a disgusting scandal. Your father is so sick over it he can barely function. Look at him." His normally dour face was twisted in rage. He looked moments away from passing out. "This will send him to the hospital, Cora. And if he dies from it, his death will be on *you*."

I pressed a palm to my forehead, my mind spinning like a tornado. I could always count on my family to make a bad situation worse.

"Listen—"

"There's nothing to listen to. You have completely ruined everything," my mother spat.

Silence advanced on the office like a steamroller. I stared at the ground, trying to figure out the best angle. Anxiety slithered through my veins. Dizziness threatened to topple me.

Axel had been right to offer his support. I needed someone to help prop me up. I pressed a palm against the wall. If I fell and cracked my head open, I didn't trust either of my parents to pick me back up. They'd probably see me unconscious and figure my eventual death was the easiest solution to this mess.

"Axel and his brothers are being unfairly disparaged in the news," I said slowly, methodically. "That article was a hatchet job. It's incomplete information. There's no way they can be linked to sex trafficking. Not when their own sister was a victim to it."

My mother's eyes fluttered shut, and she pressed her fingers to the side of her face. "How can you even associate with people who live adjacent to such filth?"

"They are not filth," I said slowly.

"But they're so close you can hardly tell the difference," she said, rising to standing. She started a slow, lethal walk toward me. Her matte black Manolo Blahniks might double as a weapon shortly. "When you smell like trash, people assume you *are* trash. You know what our priority is here, Cora. No drama."

"Even at the expense of my physical and emotional health," I bit out. "Got it."

Her lips formed a thin line despite the fillers I knew she regularly got. "We keep a seal on the drama. At all costs. Got *that*?"

"This isn't my fault," I said, though I regretted it the second I said it. This news had gotten out somehow. And it wouldn't have, if I'd just done what they wanted me to do. If I'd done what they wanted, the news wouldn't even exist.

A bitter laugh rolled past my mother's lips. "Of course it is. You welcomed it in the second you opened the trash can to take a peek."

This would be my fault forever.

I swallowed the protests bubbling to the surface. "What do you want me to do that doesn't involve continuing my marriage to Eli?"

My father ejected a disgusted grunt and tapped a closed fist against his forehead. I wasn't sure if he was going to faint or explode. Either seemed equally likely.

When they didn't say anything immediately, I added, "I'm not going back to him." My voice wavered as I spoke. My mother crossed her arms slowly, looking back at my father.

"It appears she's ready for negotiation."

Every inch of my heart that had been bolstered by my return to Axel wilted. Nothing felt good right now. Nothing in this office, at least.

My father cleared his throat, acting like it required a Herculean effort. Without looking at me, he said, "Stop living with the filth. It's a PR nightmare. Paparazzi are following all of us now."

I squeezed my eyes shut. The timing couldn't have been worse. Maybe, just maybe, if this had broken any other time, it wouldn't have been such an explosive story. But on the heels of the misinformation posing as an exposé of Fairchild Enterprises, of course the whole world wanted to tune in and see what happened next.

Tabloids lapped up any chance to bring in the *Princess of Manhattan* too. The whole thing was a mess, and my father wasn't wrong to be stewing in discontent.

"You helped create this salacious story," my mother added. "The only way to make it stop is to not give them what they want. You need to keep your nose clean."

I balled and relaxed my fists a few times, working over the possibilities. Axel's home was the only place I wanted to be. No, scratch that—at Axel's side, wherever *he* was, was the place I wanted to be. And I fully planned to reside there as long as humanly possible.

"I'll consider it," I said. "But I am not moving back in with Eli."

"You need to be seen entering and exiting property you own," my father said, still not looking at me. "There's no further consideration required."

I straightened my back. For how fucked up this all was, there was an important silver lining. I could continue with Axel. I could play the game for them a bit longer until I figured out what made sense. I didn't have to move in with Eli. I didn't need to pretend I wasn't getting a divorce.

In the Margulis world, this was a major win.

"I'm still proceeding with the divorce," I stated.

My mother wilted. "You haven't even *tried*, Cora."

My father made another disgusted grunting noise, flicking his hand toward me like trying to get something gross off the tips of his fingers. "You should think hard about how important this tryst is to you," he spat. And then he turned his head, his gaze searing through me, all the rage and disappointment swirling there in a vicious vortex. I took a step backward.

"Because there are limits," he said in low voice. "Our company is perilously close to being dragged into the filth along with you. If things don't take a turn for the better soon, I'll be forced to take matters into my own hands."

His words landed like a hammer, and I blinked a few times, nodding. My mother berating me first had been a blessing. I might not have survived a verbal dressing down by Allan Margulis if he'd started and ended this session.

"Now leave," he finished.

I looked between them, bewildered. So many hurtful things had been lobbed at me today. My entire childhood had been a back and forth between loving kindness with Chris and distant manipulation and molding from our parents. After Chris's death, I'd finally learned to armor up before meeting with either of them. And though I'd entered this office today with every bit of my invisible emotional guards in place, it wasn't enough to fully protect me.

It could never be enough. The words they used wedged themselves into my heart like spears, always reminding me that I was the constant, unrelenting disappointment. I could never do the right thing—not even when I followed their guidance to a tee.

So why bother following their wishes anymore?

I turned on my heel and let myself out of the office. Emotions stormed my head, unused comebacks biting through me. There were so many things I'd overlooked in the spirit of negotiation, but they'd all return to haunt me for the remainder of the day.

When I checked my phone, I had one missed text.

ELI: Enjoy.

What the fuck was that supposed to mean? I could only assume it was a mistake message, and right now, I had more important things to stew over. I didn't need to add Eli's cryptic one-word texts to the Monday pile.

I barely made it back to my office before Axel was calling. Relief warred with anxiety as I saw his name on the screen. I had so much I wanted to tell him, but the sheer emotional effort of recounting what had just transpired made me want to sink into a heap and never collect myself.

I shut my office door and answered the phone. "Hey, Axel."

"Cora." He sounded winded, like he'd just finished a run. But that was impossible. He'd gone straight to the office. "Can you talk? There's an emergency."

CHAPTER TWENTY-FIVE

AXEL

My hands shook as I held the letter. Cora was on speakerphone as I scanned the text for what felt like the billionth time this morning.

This letter had shown up in the morning mail. Postmarked, stamped and sealed by the Securities and Exchange Commission.

"I have received an official subpoena," I said slowly, every quake in my voice begging me to crack altogether, "from the United States Securities and Exchange Commission."

Cora's silence said it all. Finally, she sighed. "Axel, I'm so sorry."

"We're being investigated for fraud," I added, the words sounding tinny and false. I couldn't even believe I was saying them. I dropped the letter onto my desk and dragged my hands down my face. My heart beat so fast I thought it might race right out of my body. Maybe it could go find a new human to live inside. One that wasn't being constantly wracked with devastating news. "I think I'm going to die, Cora."

"Axel," she hissed. "Don't even say that."

"I can't handle this," I told her, gripping the arms of my chair. "This is the worst possible timing. Like somebody planned this for the exact moment I felt at my lowest point. And they said, 'Guess what, bitch.

It's gonna get worse. We're gonna take the whole fucking thing from you now.'"

"I'm coming over," she said. "You're not going anywhere, right?"

"Only to an early grave," I muttered glumly.

"Stop it. Where are your brothers?"

"Slowly perishing from humiliation and failure," I told her. We'd spent a couple hours that morning poring over the details of what this investigation meant. In conclusion: we were fucked. We certainly hadn't committed fraud, but the gray areas of our approach might not look so above board to a committee designed to sniff out malpractice. The whole thing made me want to crawl underneath my desk, fall asleep, and never wake up.

Everything we'd worked for: down the drain.

"I'm on my way," she said. "Don't do anything rash. Stay where you are. I'll be there in twenty."

Once the line went dead, I stared at the wood grain of my desk, completely unable to move. To think. I wasn't even sure I was breathing. A knock sounded on my door, seconds or minutes or hours later.

"Who is it?" I could barely raise my voice enough to be heard.

"Damian." He pushed open the door, poking his head in. "Can I?"

"Why are you even asking?" I slumped back into my seat.

"I didn't want to interrupt...whatever." He shut the door behind him, raking his hand through his chestnut and dirty blond tresses.

"Oh, you mean my slow and inevitable decline into depression? Don't worry. I'm already there."

He didn't even react to my words. Instead, he paced the far wall, deep in thought. "So, let's think. Let's do the thought experiment. What's the worst that can happen here?"

"The entire business goes under," I told him. I didn't even have to think about the worst possible outcomes, since they lived rent-free in my head since the letter had arrived. "We have to let go almost one hundred dedicated and loyal employees. Our reputations tank and we can never do business in the wealth management world again. We get convicted of fraud and go to fucking prison."

He stopped pacing, finally meeting my gaze. "Right. That's the part that concerns me."

"Yeah. Me too." I let my forehead drop to my desk. "How confident are you and Trace in the extra-vestments?"

"Not confident at all, when it comes to the SEC." He resumed pacing.

"Great." I slammed my fist against the top of my desk, making the pen cup jump. "This is great."

"Trace is on the phone with one of our lawyers who specializes in these investigations," Damian said. "We'll have more info soon."

"Cannot wait."

"Axel, if anyone goes to prison, the max sentence is twenty years but there's a high chance it will be much less," Damian said, his words coming out rushed. "If we prepare for the worst, then anything less will come as a huge relief."

"Prison was not in my five-year plan, bro. Nor was losing our entire business."

He stopped pacing again. "We can make this work. Whatever happens, we can make it work."

"Says the man who invented the algorithm the SEC is taking a keen interest in."

"I thought you'd be a little more positive about this," Damian snapped. "You spend your life talking shit about anyone who dares to rain on your parade, but you get one letter from the SEC and you crumble like this? Come on."

I glared at him over the tops of my forearms, where I'd buried my head on my desk. "Fuck off. I need a day."

He expelled an irritated burst of air and headed for the door. "I'll keep you updated."

"I love you," I called out as he opened the door.

"I love you too," he muttered, then slammed the door behind him.

Silence consumed my office, and that's when the nausea began to creep in. I swiveled my chair so I could line up with my trash can if need be. This was the mother of all Mondays. I wasn't sure I'd make it through alive. Even the promise of Cora's arrival didn't help. In fact, it barely registered. Nothing registered, except the all-encompassing doom that covered my life like a storm cloud.

Who the fuck reported us to the SEC? And with what information?

Did it have anything to do with losing the Goodwyn account?

And what the fuck with that reporter asking about the SEC during the press conference?

I buried my head in my arms again, groaning exaggeratedly. It didn't help. Nothing did.

A soft knock barely made me stir. "Come in, I guess," I shouted, since I couldn't lift my head to project toward the door.

The door opened and closed. And then a moment later, arms were around me. The soft scents of clementines and Tahitian vanilla invaded my senses. Cora.

"Axel, I'm so sorry." She sounded like she'd been crying.

I forced myself to look up at her. She clasped my face in her cool hands and pressed soft kisses to my lips, my cheeks, my forehead.

"Me too." I didn't even have the energy to kiss her back. "Can this be over now? Oh wait. It won't be over for a long time. And then, it might only end when they throw me into prison."

She covered her mouth with a hand, pinning me with her watery gaze.

"Whatever headway we made with our press conference last week is completely demolished," I said. "Our reputations are tanked. I won't be surprised when our clients start lining up to say adios."

"Axel," she murmured, squeezing my arm. "There's a way out of this. I know there is." She sniffed, and that's when I noticed her eyes were rimmed with red. She *had* been crying.

"Why are you crying? Is it because I'm going to prison?"

"Axel, this is all my fault."

"I don't follow."

She ran an index finger below each of her eyelids, mopping up tears. "Eli threatened to make things worse for you. I thought he was bluffing."

I blinked slowly, struggling to fit her words into the mess of neurons and despair I called my brain. "What?"

"I met him for lunch after the most recent board meeting. He acted like he wanted to discuss the divorce papers, but of course he didn't agree to anything. He made a comment about how things were going to get worse for you."

"Why didn't you tell me this then?"

"It was right after the sex trafficking article hit. It didn't seem like the time." She wrung her hands together, looking at me with concern etched into her face. "I never imagined he'd do *this*." She swallowed. "He said if I went back to him, he'd make all the drama with you go away."

My head sank into my hands. Her words inspired a very distinct type of misery. Because not only was someone actively invested in my demise, the woman I loved was attached to him.

"Why didn't you tell me this then?" I repeated, feeling the first zip of anger. At least I could still feel something beyond despair.

"I told you," she said, scooping up one of my hands in hers. "You were devastated. It got lost in the swirl. I thought he was bluffing, because I showed him the evidence that Damian dug up."

I didn't say anything. I didn't know what to say anymore. I was just so tired. I needed to sleep for a year. And even then, I'd probably need a nap afterward.

"Please, Axel," she said, maneuvering so that she stood in front of me, between the chair and the desk. She grasped my face again, forcing me to look up at her. "Say something."

I closed my eyes in response. I didn't have it in me. I'd never felt this low. Not in my adult life, at least.

"Everything is going to be fine," she insisted.

"Maybe for you," I said with a bitter laugh. "No matter what, you'll have all your savings and investments. The SEC won't leave us shit. You ever thought about how you'd lay off a hundred loyal employees from behind bars?"

"That time is not now," she said, searching out my gaze. "You do not get to flagellate yourself with the worst-case scenarios. Do you hear me?"

"I'll remember your advice when I'm in prison," I muttered.

She covered her face with her hands. "You're not going to prison."

"You don't know that. But you did know someone was coming after me. Thanks for the heads up, by the way."

Cora crossed her arms, lips pursed as she studied me. "Don't be like that."

"How else should I fucking be, Cora?" I hissed. "My entire world is falling apart. Right now. Everything is crumbling, and you want to sit here and tell me to not be like that."

"I'm trying to help," she said, placing her hands on my shoulders. I shrugged them off, pushing to standing.

"Well, it's not fucking working," I snapped, heading to the windows. Everything swirled inside me, a painful, nauseous jumble. I knew snapping at her like this wasn't the answer, but hell if I could control anything right now. "Maybe you should go."

Cora was silent for a moment, but I didn't turn to look at her. Instead, I tried to focus on the details of my view from the window. The glint of sunlight off a neighboring skyscraper. The sparkle of the East River. But any attempts at focusing were drowned out by the insistent cadence of my misery. Nothing could overpower it. Not now.

"Should I not come back to the penthouse, either?" she asked quietly.

"I guess that's up to you," I said.

"Noted." She sniffed. "I'll give you your space. You won't have to worry about me coming around."

Tension prickled through me. Every inch of my body wanted to fight. To take this out on someone. To bring the whole damn building down with my frustration and despair. "That's not what I fucking said. Unless you're just looking for an easy out."

"There's nothing easy about this."

I twisted to look at her. "So you do want out. Not surprised. The whole ship is burning and sinking."

She wilted. "Please don't do this. I know you're upset—"

"That doesn't even begin to cover what I am right now," I spat. "Don't act like you know."

"Fine. I'm just going to stop." She held up her palms like surrendering. "Whatever I say is wrong, so I'll just stop saying anything."

"Yes, definitely make this about you," I muttered, re-focusing on the glittering skyline out my window. *East river. Skyscraper windows. Consuming heartbreak.*

"I'm not. I'm just trying to give you what you want. Whatever it is that will help. I'll stop talking. I'll disappear. I'll move out. Whatever you need."

"Ahhh, there we go." I stuffed my hands in my pockets and turned back toward the desk. "You disappearing is always the solution, isn't it?"

"Sometimes I feel like maybe you would have been better off if I had just stayed away," she blurted. The sheen of tears in her eyes told me she wasn't joking. "Now that we started something again, look what happened. What if that's the reason it's all falling apart?"

My heart thumped with an angry passion. I wanted to kick her out of the office as much as I wanted to pin her to the desk and fuck the pain away. Thoughts formed a logjam inside me. Pain spawned more pain, and I was adrift. Fucking drowning in the awful sensations flooding my entire being.

"I guess you know best, Cora Margulis," I bit out. "If you need an excuse to disappear, then take it." Her offer rang like defeat to my ears, and I hated that her loyalty could crumple at the slightest provocation. Not that this provocation wasn't intense. No, it was a pretty fucking big provocation. But here we were, less than ten minutes in, and she was ready to bolt.

"I'm not trying to disappear—" she started, emotions choking her voice.

"Then what are you doing?" We stood ten feet apart, but it could have been a mile. *Tell me you'll stay. Tell me you'll fucking stay.* I didn't know how to come back to earth. I couldn't stop goading her. The drumbeat of my anxiety was going to burn every bridge in my life, and I didn't know how to stop it. "I need people who are on my team. Because if you're not on my team, you're working against me. If you're working against me, then just get the fuck out of here."

Cora pressed a hand to her mouth, a strange noise escaping her, like she'd swallowed a sob. She stood shakily.

"Exactly. There we go. Go on." I made a shooing motion with my hands.

"You're being unreasonable," she said in a low voice. "But I'll give you what you want. You want someone to blame this on, so go for it. I'm all yours. You got lucky—I'm used to being a punching bag."

She snatched up her purse and headed for the door. I watched her go, knowing this was all wrong. This wasn't the answer. It wasn't the solution. But I couldn't stop or alter it.

The only thing that made sense was to rage until I felt better.

Cora had taken the bait. She'd let me goad her into making things worse.

And once the door clicked shut behind her, I realized I'd gotten what I wanted.

If I had been low before, this was rock bottom.

CHAPTER TWENTY-SIX

CORA

Axel wanted space?

He'd fucking get it. But not for long.

It wasn't hard to move out of Axel's penthouse and back to the condo. The past few months had prepared me for a life of vagabonding. I had unlimited resources at my disposal, but I required very few of them. Multiple walk-in closets? Unnecessary, now that I'd gotten use to using one corner of someone else's dresser. Shoe racks for days? I'd adjusted to switching between three pairs of footwear. Endless designer clothing options? I switched the tops and bottoms of four different outfits and had eight days of fashion programming to be used on repeat.

I could start my own billionaire-on-a-shoestring-budget reality TV show.

Hell, if I lost my job at Margulis Realty and Axel really ended things, I could contact a TV producer to pitch the idea.

The only hard part about moving out of his house was the sense of failure. I'd failed the most important man in my life for a second time. And this time, it had happened while I was actively trying to not fail him ever again.

Damned if you do. Damned if you don't.

There wasn't a truer idiom. I planned to tattoo it somewhere on my body, once I truly hit rock bottom.

A knock on the condo door made me jump. For the past few days, I'd pretended that I was working from home, but really, I was plotting. Scheming. Arranging the pieces of a puzzle I'd spent too long avoiding putting together. The work accomplished for Margulis Realty was negligible. Instead, I had a whole cockamamie scheme brewing.

I didn't want more. I wanted something else. And I was preparing to fucking grab it.

At eleven a.m. on a weekday morning, I should have been presentable, but I wasn't. I wore my lone T-shirt, stolen from Axel's closet with no intention of ever returning it, paired with exercise shorts that I'd used for Jazz's private Pilates classes, once upon a time. Those classes felt like another lifetime. But however scant my wardrobe, this outfit was intentional. No, I wasn't just lounging. The shirt was a reminder as much as the shorts were.

I had places to go. Things to leave behind. Fires to fucking stoke.

I approached the door silently, peering through the peephole lest I needed to pretend to be gone. A deliveryman waited outside. I pulled the door open just enough to peer at him like any seasoned New Yorker would—half crazed, fully suspicious.

"Yes?" I asked.

"Delivery for Cora Margulis." He presented an obscenely large bouquet of flowers. Pink lilies and white roses spilled out of the round glass vase. I received them, thanked him quickly, and shut myself back into the condo.

The note stuck into the flowers was simple, in a clean handwriting that I could only imagine some floral shop attendant wrote out while wondering who the fuck these crazies were: *Are you ready to cooperate?*

It didn't need a signature to tell me who *that* sweet nothing came from. The best part about it was that the bouquet design was titled *Smells Like Forever*, according to the delivery slip.

Smelled more like a lifetime of regret.

I set the vase on the kitchen island, frowning at the white roses. I wondered if Eli had any inkling by now how much I detested them. They reminded me of too many decades strung together by anxiety and foreboding. And maybe his goal had always been to remind me of my thorough training in *bending over* and *letting it happen*. But I was done with that.

Done with white roses. Done with the submission. Done with *him*.

I huffed, starting a slow prowl around the kitchen island.

"What a fucking bastard you are," I told the roses. Yes, rock bottom couldn't be far away. Part of me hoped these roses were mic'd. Maybe Eli had bugged the condo. I hoped he could fucking *see* me right now.

"A disgusting, pitiful, condescending, idiotic douchebag," I shouted at the roses. God, this felt good. It was therapeutic in a way I couldn't quite articulate. Wearing Axel's clothes, parading around in shorts that I'd bought for Pilates classes taught by a woman my husband had been fucking for at least eight months, according to the text history. Yes, this was what cracking open felt like. For the first time in years, the energy of the unknown buzzed through me.

"I don't even like white roses!" I screamed at the vase. "I don't even fucking like *you*!"

I picked up the gorgeous arrangement by the neck of the vase, and I hurled it at the slate-and-white feature wall in the kitchen. Glass shattered, sending shards everywhere. The water splashed and sloshed against the wall; lilies and roses and baby's breath scattered across the wet floor. My chest heaved, though I hadn't really exerted myself.

I wanted to do it again. I looked around for more arrangements to destroy. More beauty to disassemble. For more cooperation to shred. But there was none.

I was locked inside my cooperative palace.

One inch from rock bottom.

I'd done exactly what my parents wanted: moved my few items and my small life back to the condo near Central Park. And now that I was here, living outside Axel's orbit, my insides rioted. This didn't feel right. I wanted to slither out of my own skin with how badly I wanted to resume the direction I'd been going at Axel's side. That, at least, felt like forward motion.

But now? Here? This felt like putting on soiled clothes. Reusing underwear that was long past needing washed. Every part of me felt icky.

What are you fucking doing, Cora?

No matter how stilted it seemed, I knew what I was doing. I was charting new territory.

My cell phone vibrated with an incoming call. Laughter popped out of me. "Eli, is that you?" I sauntered toward my phone in the living room. "Are you watching me, lover boy? Or can you just feel how much I *detest you*?"

My own voice came out snarled and strange. Who the fuck was this person? I was in the privacy of my own home, sure, but even in this space I didn't just open up like this. I didn't saunter. I didn't snarl.

I had never sauntered or snarled.

Ever.

A New York-based number stared back at me. I answered it right before it switched to voicemail. "Hello?"

"Ms. Margulis-Rossberg. This is Harris from Liddon & Wenchell Law."

I pressed a hand to my chest. I'd been waiting for this call. "Oh my God. Thank you so much for calling me back." I'd been so busy smashing vases and talking back to an invisible Eli that I forgot about the very outcomes I awaited from all my plotting and scheming.

Harris wasn't my divorce lawyer. No, he was in a different specialty altogether. He was helping me craft my escape route.

I was ready to do more that saunter and snarl. I wanted to jump ship. I wanted the fuck out.

"I'd love to hear more about your particular circumstances," Harris said, his no-nonsense voice a strange balm to my wild and free feelings.

"Well, how can I put this?" I laughed as I tipped my head back to look at the ceiling. "I'm getting ready to do something very contentious. I'm getting ready to burn every bridge I ever walked across." I sucked in a breath. "I want to violate an NDA I signed when I was eighteen years old."

Harris hummed. "And who was the NDA with?"

"My parents."

"Pertaining to...?"

I swallowed a knot in my throat. Tears had arrived, despite my attempts to keep them at bay. "My brother. His death, specifically. They deny the facts around his departure, let's say. I agreed to remain silent and signed the contract. But I'm done. I can't." I shook my head, swiping away the tears that had fallen. "I need to violate this NDA, and I want to share the truth of his death with the world. I need to, for my own sanity and to honor his memory."

Harris cleared his throat. "Yeah. Well, the good news is—you have options. But you'll need to prepare to pay for them. Depending on the terms of the NDA, breaking it could cost you dearly."

"I'm prepared to pay any amount necessary," I said. "My brother committed suicide, and I'm ready to tell the world."

The truth was simple.

Shit happened. To everyone.

What mattered was how you alchemized it. How you twisted, reshaped, and turned the outcome into something that served you, as opposed to sucked you dry.

That's what I was working on. Alchemy, pure and simple. I prowled the halls of the condo, shedding the skin of my old, compliant self. I was hellbent on finding a different future. For a different self. A Cora that had always been inside of me, just waiting for her chance to emerge.

I watched the headlines, keeping tabs on the Fairchilds, Eli, my parents. We were the hottest news item in the tabloids, so it was easy to catch any cough or smirk whenever they stepped into public. The world was fascinated by the Fairchilds' meteoric rise and flaming descent.

But the world didn't know what was coming. The Fairchilds weren't the final spectacle.

I worked, worked, worked in a way I never had before. I knew all the steps ahead of me. The calculated risks. How much money it would cost. The exact nature of my subversion.

I was done being a white rose in an unhappy bouquet. My family had done nothing but sabotage my attempts at happiness and normalcy. They'd forced me to fit their mold from the beginning. When I was seven, I'd shown an interest in drawing. My mother had reviewed one of the drawings I'd brought home, tutted, and thrown it out.

"Making art doesn't make you money, my dear," she'd told me, patting my head. "It's a commodity to be enjoyed, to make money from. Your father will explain more."

Maybe that was where this had all begun. The thumping behind my ribs. The complacency. The cooperation. Chris and I grew up with a desperate need to fit in. For our parents' approval. It was the one thing they wouldn't give us.

Not even after three decades of giving them what they wanted.

I prepared myself to return to my main home on the Upper West Side. The actual home I'd once shared with Eli. My *legal residence.* I wasn't going to call a truce or cooperate. No, I had a laundry list of tasks that needed completed. This was merely step ten of fifty.

I'd started using ride share apps to get around the city. I refused to use any Margulis Realty driver, and asking Harry or any Fairchild driver to cart me around seemed tone deaf since I hadn't seen Axel after our argument a week and a half ago. Actually, it seemed wrong to use *anybody's* luxury services while I was in the process of burning everything to ground. If etiquette existed around detonating one's own life, I didn't know it. I just knew I needed to start from the ground up.

On the way to Eli's and my brownstone, I called my assistant. I hadn't been to the office much recently, and Tatiana sounded surprised to hear from me.

"Cora! Are you coming in today?"

"No, no, unfortunately. Still feeling under the weather." I cleared my throat, as though this would bolster my story. But then I thought better of it. "Listen, you should know what's about to happen. I won't be coming back into the office."

"Oh. You won't? Why not?" Nervousness wrung out her voice. I could practically see her nibbling on her bottom lip like she always did.

"I need you to help me with a few tasks. I'm preparing to leave Margulis Realty. For good."

She stammered for a moment. "But...you're about to become CEO."

"I know." I looked out the window as the Upper West Side flitted by. "I never wanted to be CEO, though."

She expelled a breath. "Oh. Well...why not?"

My eyes fluttered shut. "It's a long story, and I don't have that much time. I need you to work on a few things for me, though." I rattled off a long list of tasks: get the condo appraised for current market value. Review my resignation documents for errors. Research a new lawyer who could help me be declared legally single, since Eli refused to budge on the divorce. "And last but not least: figure out if you want to take a leap with me."

"Y-you mean...like...quit with you?" she asked.

"Yes. I won't be offended if you choose to stay. But I'm giving you the option. I don't have a golden parachute to offer. But I can offer you something else. Something different than what you've been doing."

The car eased to a stop in front of the steps leading up to my brownstone. I hadn't been in this house for months. Seeing it again sent a spasm of nostalgia through me. It was a six bedroom, nine bathroom monstrosity that included bay windows, a cellar, and six stories of renovated townhouse glamour. For all the crap Eli and I had lived through, I loved this place because I'd thrown so much of my passion and energy into making it perfect.

But no amount of energy would ever make anything perfect; especially not in my family. And nostalgia was no longer a valid excuse for continued misery. That's all my nostalgia had gotten me. I'd clung to the wisps of happiness from my childhood for too long. I'd honored my parents so much, I'd dishonored myself.

"Oh, and last thing, Tatiana," I said, reaching for the car handle. "Can you tell me if Eli is there right now?"

"I saw him come in about twenty minutes ago for the board meeting," she said.

"Good." I smiled up at the front door of my former home, certainty pumping through me. "Once that board meeting is done, keep him there as long as you can. I have a few matters to resolve, and I want to make sure I have as much time as possible."

I ended the call, humming to myself.

Eli's absence would make this part of the plan much easier.

All those Margulis stocks in our joint portfolio? They'd be mine shortly. Damian had shown me exactly what to do on Eli's computer.

Eli wouldn't miss them. They were only a small part of his portfolio, and losing them would barely be a blip on his bottom line.

But neither he nor my father would like what I planned to do with them.

CHAPTER TWENTY-SEVEN

AXEL

If anyone wondered what the definition of misery was, it involved an official subpoena from the United States government and three scowling Fairchild brothers.

My brothers and I spent thousands of dollars per hour to figure out how to proceed. Life turned into an anxious whirlwind. Practically every day brought some new headline or a new shade of gray to the tabloid circuit.

I had to stop listening after a while. Because after about a week, the tabloids said that Cora and Eli had gotten back together. The mere words strung together caused a painful jumble in my gut that seemed destined for ulcer status. I couldn't believe it was true; deep down, I *knew* it had to be gossip. But whether or not she'd truly gotten back with Eli, I'd sent her away and let her show me how much I meant to her. Apparently not much, if she could she just drift away like that.

It hurt worse the second time around. Cora had fooled me into thinking she was serious about us. That she and I might have actually had a future together. But it turned out, I was the same chump as always.

I fell head over heels for the girl who played in a different league and was never even half as serious about me as I was about her. I fought with myself every day not to call her, not to show up at her doorstep and demand she return to the penthouse. Nothing felt right without her at my side, which was a fact I needed to come to terms with, once and for all.

I just didn't know how I could make my bones believe it. My body and heart knew something my mind didn't want to believe. There was nobody for me but Cora.

But how could I reconcile having Cora in my life when she still allowed Eli and her father to be there too?

The only way my brothers and I could distract ourselves from the drama cycle was work. Restoring our reputation was a full-time job. We had a solid PR team, and we could counteract some of the negative press, but we couldn't avoid losing some clients. Trace, Damian, and I worked overtime to make sure we replaced departing clients with new blood. Eli wasn't going to ruin us. He could make me stumble, but he wouldn't get the satisfaction of watching me fall.

At least not yet.

"Axel." Damian's baritone broke through my midday Manhattan contemplation. I stared out the window of my office so fucking much. But I drew energy from the gorgeous fury below. It singlehandedly fueled, healed, and held me. It was no wonder I couldn't get out of New York City permanently.

"What's up?" I turned to look at him. We'd all been sullen recently, but Damian took it the hardest. I was the CEO, but as the CTO, he was the brains behind the algorithms responsible for both our success and our potential downfall. And as the architect behind our mad scientist success, he was particularly worried.

He held up a newspaper. "New headline you gotta see."

I shook my head, turning back to the gorgeous mess of life outside my window. "I'm taking a sabbatical from the news. I thought you knew."

He cleared his throat, striding forward undeterred. "This one's an exception."

"What if I told you I don't care?" I muttered, already knowing that I wouldn't win this one.

"Come here."

The no-nonsense tone prompted a big sigh from me. I turned to him. "I'm not interested in learning how our lives have gotten a little bit worse. I'm ready to be done with rock bottom, okay?"

He tossed the newspaper on the surface of my desk and pointed at it. "Whether you're done or not, now you've got company."

I couldn't lie—he'd piqued my curiosity. I drifted toward the desk, spotting the headline.

A VERY PRINCESS MELTDOWN: Real Estate's Golden Girl Jumps Ship

Cora's photo took up a full eighth the front page. I stormed toward the desk and snatched up the newspaper.

"Thought you'd want to see it," Damian said.

I gobbled up as much of the text as I could, but I was so eager to learn more that I had to read everything twice to absorb it. My heart pounded. The more I read, the further my jaw dropped. By the end of the article, it was hard to pick my favorite part, but these were a few top contenders. Cora Margulis stepping down as CEO-in-waiting of Margulis Realty was a big one, but so was the fact that she'd not only filed for divorce from her womanizing husband but also asked a judge to declare her legally single on top of that. I also particularly liked how she'd written a damning tell-all letter that was scheduled to be released in *Big Apple Mag*. It was rumored to air family secrets that had been festering for decades. But the cherry on top? Her declaration of support for the Fairchild brothers in the midst of their scandal, imploring anyone who doubted us or our ethics to take a hard look at themselves.

"Holy shit," I murmured as I went for round three on the article. "She did it."

"Go, Cora. She just blew up her entire life," Damian said with a little smile. "Been a long time coming, huh?"

"Way overdue." My voice came out in an awed whisper. "I almost can't believe this."

"I want to read this tell-all," Damian said, shoving his hands into his pockets.

"Me too." Though I already knew what it would contain. The biggest festering truth in her family was the facts of Chris's death. "I just can't believe she's willing to break the NDA. Alan is gonna go nuclear. He'll sue the living fuck out of her."

"She must be prepared. She found a judge to declare her legally single, after all. Cora is getting creative."

I smiled down at her picture in the newspaper, my chest tightening. It was her classic business head shot, dark hair pulled into a low bun, her mulberry lips curved into a polite smile. But there was a shark swimming behind those eyes. A shark Allan had helped create. But Cora Margulis was done playing his games.

She was no longer the Princess of Manhattan. Now, she was the outcast.

Just like us.

I dragged my hands down the front of my face, my heart still pounding.

"You okay, bro?" Damian asked.

"Yeah. I'm okay. Just got sucker punched by how much I fucking love this woman." I picked up the newspaper, coming to my feet. "I need to go find her."

Damian nodded, clapping my shoulder. "Thought so."

I tucked the spread under my arm and bolted from the office. My surroundings receded into an uninteresting blur as I called Cora and headed for the ground floor.

She answered on the second ring, like she'd been expecting the call. "Hello?"

"Cora Margulis. I need to see you."

"Hmmm. Why's that?"

"No reason." My legs felt like jelly, all the jitters returning to me, as if this was our first date all over again. "Just read something interesting about how you're single suddenly. Thought maybe we could change that."

A laugh rocketed out of her, drifting on in pure delight. My own smile stretched ear to ear.

"I'd like to enjoy the single girl status for at least a full day, once I'm finally granted it," she said. "But we can see about what comes after that."

"Where are you? Can you meet?"

"I'll go wherever you want, Axel." She sounded dreamy, like she was floating in outer space.

"Meet me at the building." I wet my bottom lip, knowing I hadn't said it quite right. "*Our* building."

I arranged for cars to collect us at our respective locations. A half hour later, we were both stepping out of Fairchild SUVs on Tenth Ave, late-August sun warming me down to my bones through my light gray suit.

Cora's sun kissed calves caught my attention. She wore a breezy green romper, her bare, toned arms spreading for a hug as she approached me. At eleven a.m. on a weekday, I'd never seen her so dressed down. I bridged the distance between us in two powerful steps and then she was in my arms, hands clasped behind my neck.

"I'm so sorry, Axel," she said, her gaze bouncing all over my face as if we'd been apart for years instead of days.

"I'm the one who owes you an apology," I said, nuzzling her neck. I could sense the attention of passersby sizzling over us. Phones were out, photos being captured. We needed to give the people what they wanted. I covered her mouth with my own and coaxed a long, sloppy kiss from her. For the tabloids, sure. But also for our health.

She giggled when we broke for air. I pressed my forehead against hers.

"I'm so sorry, Cora. For doubting you. For pushing you away."

"I don't blame you for doubting me," she whispered. "But I needed to go. I had to get everything in order."

"I know you did." I tightened my grip around her, my cock pricking to life. "Let's go inside before we make a scene and we're in the paper for a different reason altogether."

"I'm ready to make the headlines for every single possible reason," she said. "Quitting my job. Divorcing my husband. Seducing the Fairchild CEO. Airing my family's dirty laundry. Filling Eli's office with inflated balloons."

"Don't forget public indecency," I said, slipping a hand beneath the hem of her romper. "Which of course will lead to conceiving our first child right here on the sidewalk. Did you really fill that looner's office with balloons?""

She laughed into my shoulder. "I did. Two hundred of them."

Something in her bare face was so refreshing, so freeing, that just looking at her cracked me wide open. I led her by the hand toward the building. *Our* building. Inside the lobby, our footsteps echoed through the cool, musty air.

"You're glowing," I told her, bringing her knuckles to my lips.

"That's what jumping off a metaphorical cliff will do to you, I suppose," she said with a cheesy grin. She looked like she'd just gotten back from a monthlong getaway in Mexico. Sunkissed. Brimming with life. *Free.* "Better than any facial."

"You're tanner than before."

"I've been testing out the rooftop patio on a new place I'm having renovated." She sent me a cryptic smile. "Maybe you've seen it before. I can personally attest it has room for a helipad and everything."

"One that Eli doesn't know about, I assume?"

Her face fell, but only briefly. She traced invisible patterns over the lapel of my suit coat as she spoke. "I'm sorry for Eli. I'm sorry for choosing him, for marrying him. I'm sorry that he brought all of this to your doorstep."

"Babe. It's not your fault." I brushed my lips against her forehead. "You thought you were doing the right thing all those years ago. Nobody can fault you for that. And when it comes to you, I'm glad to battle the evil, level-ten boss because it'll feel all that much better when he finally gets defeated."

She smoothed her palms over the flat planes of my chest. "We both have to battle some evil bosses, huh?"

"What's life without a little bit of crippling drama?" I wrapped my arm around her as we drifted toward the elevator. "So where is this new place? Might it have a nineties office floor in desperate need of modern decorations?"

She laughed and smiled up at me. "I've been throwing myself into the planning for the community theater floor. I can't stay away. And I know I'm not an engineer, but I think the rooftop patio *will* work for a helipad. So we can just do a straight commute between the Hamptons and here, basking in how good it feels to re-purpose my father's building for all these scandalous initiatives."

"I like your definition of revenge," I told her.

"It comes at a steep price." Her expression turned sober. The elevator doors opened, and we boarded, standing just inches from each other as the elevator lurched upward. "But it's one I'm willing to pay."

"I'll up the ante." I captured her chin between my thumb and forefinger. "Whatever price you're willing to pay, I'll pay it too."

"We've been paying it for years," she said with a sigh. The doors opened on the top floor, and we stepped into the abandoned office space. "I want this to be done."

"You're so close to being done," I told her. "You've left Eli. You've left Margulis Realty. What's left?"

She smiled at me cryptically, something mysterious churning behind her gaze. "I can think of one last thing."

"You have an evil glint in your eye, Cora, which I'll have you know is a major turn-on. So you better spill it, or we're going to have to fuck right here."

She laughed, wrapping her arms around my neck once more. With her pressed up against me, her soft warmth against the front of my suit, everything felt right with the world. Even amid the wild destruction of both our lives. With her in my arms, filling the empty spaces of my heart and life, none of that mattered.

"I want out of Margulis Realty," she said, something serious edging her tone. "Completely. I'm divesting myself of my share of Margulis stock." She pushed up onto her tiptoes so that our lips brushed as she spoke the next words. "I want you to have them."

The meaning of her words washed over me in undulating waves. First confusion, then shock, then evil glee.

"You can't be serious."

"Deadly," she said, then captured my lips in an intense kiss that sucked the air from my lungs.

When we broke, my mind was racing, both from the lack of oxygen and the trump card she'd handed me. Once upon a time, I'd thought convincing Margulis Realty to use my business for their wealth management services could be an acceptable revenge. But this opportunity was a whole new level of happily-ever-after.

"Cora," I said, nearly panting. "I've been buying Margulis stocks. If you give me your shares, I'll have enough for a hostile takeover."

The grin on her face was the stuff of legends. Gorgeous, furious, and all the best types of conniving.

"I don't think there's a better way to get back at my father than if you become the majority shareholder," she said, batting her eyelashes. "Welcome to the board, Axel. Do with it what you will. It's your company now."

CHAPTER TWENTY-EIGHT

CORA

"Babe? You still out here?" Axel's voice drifted toward me from inside the house, floating on the warm, early-September breeze. This was my favorite time of year in the Hamptons, when the ocean air swelled in the heat but was tempered by the tang of autumn lingering on the sidelines.

I turned to look back toward the house. Zero lifted his head non-committally from his spot at my feet. We'd been spending almost all our time at Axel's Hamptons house, riding out the negative press. I was treating it like a vacation of sorts, if vacations normally included fielding near-constant requests for interviews, frequent calls with my legal team, and the occasional irate message from people I used to call family.

My tell-all letter was being hailed as the media event of the year. Women had started pouring out of the woodwork, coming forward with their own stories about Eli's transgressions. Maybe it was the sheer number of allegations, but yesterday Eli finally signed the damned divorce papers, which meant the judge I'd painstakingly tracked down to declare me legally single was no longer required.

Everybody and their brother was tuned into this drama. But now that the truth was out, I was done.

I needed to lay low and recuperate.

"I'm here. I finished my call and now I'm working on my project." I called into the Suicide Hotline daily now that I had the time. When I wasn't pouring my pain into helping other people resolve their own, I crafted. I had a craft area set up on the back picnic table, so I could soak up the late-summer sunlight while working on the first project I'd consciously put together in...decades. The type of project that was explicitly for me. No, for both of us. Not designed to make money or become an investment opportunity. Just art for the sake the of art. All the beach glass I'd ever collected in the shade of Axel's blue eyes lay on a small glass tray. Other trays contained additional treasures: interesting beads, pieces of fluff, all manner of twine and cords.

"How's it coming?" He came out onto the deck, lowering his designer sunglasses as he headed my way. The man grinned ear-to-ear almost all the time now. There was no denying it: hiding out together, tucked away in our own Hamptons paradise, was not a hardship for either of us. Axel left via helicopter several times a week to head into the office or take meetings. Otherwise, it was just the two of us—and Zero, of course.

Exactly as we wanted.

"I found a few more pieces today," I said pointing out the new additions. He sat on the bench next to me, taking in the scene. I'd started off trying to hide this project from him, since it was ultimately going to be a gift. But it was too hard to stay away from him for extended periods of time. No, scratch that—I didn't *want* to stay away from him for as long as this project would require. So I outed it early on, and now he followed along like the doting, curious, attentive boyfriend he was.

He rested his chin on my shoulder, then pointed to the far tray. "Is that the ornament?"

I lifted the ornament in question. I was *that* girlfriend now, making ornaments for my love out of beach glass in the shade of his eyes. "Looks good, doesn't it?"

"It'll look amazing on our tree." He kissed my cheek, squeezing his arms around my waist. "Is it wrong that I'm excited for Christmas already? It's only September."

"We can start hanging decorations now, if you'd like." I kissed the tip of his nose. "But I'll need some more time to finish your present, so how about we wait?"

"Fine. But we should have two trees." He twisted back toward the house, gesturing to toward the huge window near the back door. "One to fill that window, and then one for the front hall."

"Agreed. I'll make the appropriate number of ornaments." I kissed the tip of his nose again. "Now *I'm* excited for Christmas."

We laughed, getting lost in each other's eyes. For how messy the world beyond our Hamptons paradise was, everything sure felt just right. Today and every day.

With Axel at my side, none of the rest mattered.

Chris would have died from excitement knowing I was dating the bad boy of Wall Street. And I suspected he wouldn't have any issue with the fact that I'd let down his wish for me, which he'd set down in a letter just before he died. My parents had shown it to me during my last year of grad school. I still wondered if they'd saved it all those years just as a bargaining chip. A tool to bring out when they sensed I wasn't heading down their prescribed path. Chris had asked me in the letter to give our father what he wanted, since Chris couldn't—a Margulis offspring at the helm of the beloved family business.

And though part of me still felt guilty to have technically not followed my brother's parting wishes, I knew he'd written that letter in his darkest moments, trying to be someone he could never be. Sometimes, in the late evening breezes by the water, I could hear Chris chatting with me from Heaven, asking me why I hadn't rebelled earlier, telling me he couldn't wait to see the new theater with his name on it. Asking what Axel and I planned to name our kids, once we finally had some.

I knew I was making Chris proud. And more than that, I was making myself proud. That was all that mattered anymore.

Axel's phone vibrated from inside his pocket, making the bench buzz. He fished it out, lifting his sunglasses to view the message.

"Oh. That's my alarm. I need to go get ready."

I sighed, looking up at him. "Do you have to?"

He captured my chin between his thumb and forefinger, looking at me so tenderly I thought I'd split in two. "Babe, you know it. Today's the big day!"

I gasped. "You're right! Oh my God...I can't believe I forgot." Time had a strange way of dissolving completely now that I was out of the corporate world. Everything I'd been doing was uncharted territory. My schedule, my interests, my desires. All mine. All decided by me.

It was fan-fucking-tastic.

"I need to go get changed," Axel said, coming to his feet. "What shade of suit should I wear for a hostile takeover? Black? This is the demise of Allan's dreams, so..."

"Definitely black," I said, grinning up at him.

"Actually, scratch that. I know exactly what I'll wear." The smile on his lips stretched to mischievous lengths. "My old leather jacket."

"I couldn't love that more. And hey—tell Allan to fuck off for me, will ya?" I hadn't spoken to my parents since my letter was published. All communication with them occurred through our lawyers, who conveyed to me the full extent of my parents' disappointment, ire, and dismay.

Not like anybody had to tell me. I could feel their disappointment and dismay from here. It was woven into the fabric of my being. I just chose not to let it affect me anymore. I would have disappointed them and dismayed them no matter what I did. So why not live my best life while doing it?

Eli still liked to send the occasionally nasty-gram. And when he spewed his hate-spawned rampages via email, he usually let it slip what my parents were up to as well.

"Of course. Though you and Zero might be able to hear his reaction from here." Axel dipped down to snag a messy kiss from my lips. I clutched at the back of his head, coaxing another kiss, and then another.

"Damn girl." His voice came out edged with grit. "You down to celebrate the hostile takeover tonight? We can have a sexy takeover of your body."

I cackled. "Great one. And you know it."

He swiped his thumb over my bottom lip before loping back toward the house. I watched until he disappeared inside, then I took a deep breath of the perfect late morning air.

This was real. All of this beauty around me. The churn of the ocean, the gorgeous home I shared with my boyfriend, the unchecked future before us. The beauty was real because we'd cracked open the ugliness. We'd tripped over jagged shards of discomfort and wove our way between harmful obligations until we emerged on the other side, on a sweet whisper of possibility.

The beauty was real because the ugliness was too. Finding happiness didn't make the bad stuff go away. It just made it easier to tolerate. And finding my happiness meant having a lot of doors slammed shut to me.

But that was okay. No, it was more than okay. Because whatever doors had shut on me were never meant for me anyway. And I had a whole lifetime to open new doors that I chose myself.

EPILOGUE

AXEL

TWO MONTHS LATER

"Hey man. Can somebody send for coffee?" Damian squinted as he entered the conference room. It was nine a.m., which was not early for us, but he looked like he'd been freshly ejected from bed.

"Wow. What happened to you?" Trace smirked as he sized up Damian, setting his laptop on the glass-topped table.

"Let me guess. Up all night hacking the SEC to find out the dirt they've got on us," I added, settling into my favorite oversized leather seat. Damian simply scowled at us in return.

Francis stepped into the room, looking over at Damian. "Should I have Jessa join us?"

"No," Damian snapped. "She doesn't need to know everything."

"Well, she needs to know some things," I said. She'd come on board recently to help offload some of the tasks that Francis accumulated between the three of us.

"Francis, can you send for coffee? I need the blackest shit you can find," Damian said.

"Of course. Espresso?"

"Mmm." Trace laced his fingers together. "I'd probably work better if I had espresso."

"Guys, why don't we have this shit waiting for us when we get here?" I asked. "We've owned this business for how many years? And we still spend the first ten minutes figuring out what drinks we want. Can we get with the program?"

"Francis, make a note—espresso every day," Trace said, lifting a finger.

"Got it. I'll be back ASAP." He grimaced in the direction of Damian and rushed out of the conference room. When it was just the three of us, Damian sighed again, letting his head drop into his hands.

"Is this a hangover or a code-over?" I asked.

"Hangover." Damian squeezed his eyes shut. "And honestly, I don't wanna talk about it."

"Okay." I held my palms up defensively. "Just trying to help get to the bottom of your drunken rampage. After all, you two spent a lot of time worrying about my hangovers back in the day. It's only fair I probe into yours."

Damian scowled at me.

"Anything to do with your *new confidential secretary*?" Trace asked, lifting a brow. "Who came in late this morning, I believe."

Damian's scowl deepened, which looked a lot like *yes* to me.

"Ooh, I think you might have hit the mark," I murmured to Trace. We shared a brotherly smile. The ribbing was good. It made things normal, when they were still anything but. The investigation continued, but it was impossibly slow-moving. We'd made our peace with it—as much as we could, at least, with prison sentences hanging over our heads.

But things were stressful still. Moments like these, where we just felt like brothers again—this was the shit that helped.

Living in premarital bliss with Cora in the Hamptons helped a fucking lot too.

"Listen, are we gonna talk about the agenda?" Damian snapped.

"God, I've never seen you *this* feisty," I said. "I definitely want to probe further."

Trace, ever the mediator, tapped at his laptop. "All right, brothers. Let's get down to business and save the probing for the general comments at the end."

"Finally," Damian muttered.

Trace led the meeting, as he did every Monday, about the state of our affairs. Now that I was the majority shareholder of Margulis Realty, we focused a lot on what our strategy there would look like. I hadn't done anything drastic over there yet. I merely loved attending board meetings and watching the displeasure settle across Allan and Eli's faces as I stroked Zero's head and stared at them both. Seeing those assholes so unsettled with my owning their business and reaping the profits was enough revenge for now.

But the main focus of this meeting was the future. Cora's tell-all letter had been the best damage control we could have mustered. Even though the Princess of Wall Street had fallen from grace within her royal family, the woman still held a lot of clout in her elite circles. Her confession had blunted the losses we would have incurred without her exposé.

So we were limping along. Slower than before—but still on two feet.

We'd barely gotten started on the finer points of our five-year plan regarding the charity when Francis returned with our coffees. Damian nearly leaped to receive his, immediately slurping at the dark liquid.

"You know, we have a coffee maker in the penthouse," Trace informed him. Damian just grunted in response.

"Sometimes, that's too much work with a hangover," I pointed out.

Damian grunted in my direction then.

"Anything else, boys?" Francis asked once his tray had been cleared of our beverages.

"We're good. Thank you, Francis." I sent him a cheesy smile.

Before Francis had shut the door, one of our receptionists, Kai, poked her head in. "Guys, I have a call for the three of you that you should know about."

"We're in a meeting," Trace said, using his no-nonsense tone that was very effective at getting people to shut up. He turned away from her, facing us at the table again. Francis tried to shut the door behind him, but Kai's arm shot out, blocking it.

"I think you'll want to hear this," she said, her voice firm.

I glanced between Damian and Trace before nodding her way. "What is it?"

"There's a very concerning visitor downstairs," she said.

"Do we need to call security?" I asked.

Her brows drew together, looking at each one of us in turn before she said, "He claims he's the youngest Fairchild brother."

Confusion spread through the room.

"There *is* no youngest Fairchild brother," I corrected her. "Or rather, you're looking at him. Me."

"He said there's evidence. And that the three of you would be very interested in meeting someone who is blood-related to Trace."

That got our attention. I cleared my throat, leaning against the edge of the table as I found the same spooked confusion in my brothers' eyes. This couldn't be real.

Trace was the first to react. He nodded at Kai. "Send him up."

THE END

Learn more about the ongoing investigation, the mysterious new brother, and MORE in book #3 of the Bad Boys of Wall Street, *THE PRICE OF PASSION (http://books2read.com/price-of-passion)*.

Want more Axel and Cora? Sign up for my newsletter and you'll get Axel and Cora's backstory in The Price of Passion for FREE: *http://bit.ly/EL-newsletter*

WHO NEEDS MORE BROTHERS? (Um...we all do!) Start my Bayshore series with *MAKE ME LOSE* and meet the stubborn and alpha Daly brothers. Even better? There's 5 of 'em! The Bayshore series is high-heat rom-com with guaranteed LOLs and HEAs! Find it here: *http://books2read.com/make-me-lose-el*

ACKNOWLEDGEMENTS

First and foremost, I'd like to thank Lori Powell Johannes from my reader's group (Ember's Blossoms) for coming up with the name for Axel's dog – ZERO!

This book would not have been possible without the support, insight, feedback and guidance from my incredible author and beta squad, specifically Elisabeth Nelson, Angela Howard-Seely, Whitley Cox, Kat McIntyre, and so many others who have offered an ear or a shoulder.

Big thanks to all the readers and reviewers who continue to enjoy reading what I write (!!!), this is a dream come true and my internal thirteen-year-old self still cannot believe I write kissing books for real.

Special thanks goes to my husband and children, who continue to support this crazy dream of mine despite so many reasons why I should lay it to rest. I promise you all it will be worth it.

AUTHOR'S NOTE

**Thank you so much for taking a chance on my work. It means the world to me.
I'd love to stay in touch!**

Sign up to <u>my newsletter</u>! By joining, you'll also receive information about upcoming releases, sales, and other exciting news. Score! Find it here: *http://bit.ly/EL-newsletter*

Or search for my reader group, EMBER'S BLOSSOMS on Facebook, to hang out up-close and personal! Early looks at new covers, exclusive access to ARC sign-ups, and more.

I'm active on...

FACEBOOK

INSTAGRAM

GOODREADS

BOOKBUB

http://www.emberleighromance.com/

And before you go...

Please consider leaving an honest review about this book! Even just a few words or a line mean so much to us authors.

ALSO BY EMBER LEIGH

THE BAD BOYS OF WALL STREET
The Price of Revenge
The Price of Passion
The Price of Infamy
The Price of Forever

WINTER HARBOR
(co-written with Whitley Cox)
The Bastard Heir
The Asshole Heir
The Rebel Heir
The Matchmaking Heirs

THE BAYSHORE SERIES
Make Me Lose
Make Me Fall
Make Me Yours
Make Me Choose
Make Me Hot
Make Me Smile

THE BREAKING SERIES
Breaking the Rules

Changing the Game
Breaking the Sinner
Breaking the Habit
Breaking the Fall